P9-CCY-549

HARVEY

HOW I BECAME INVISIBLE

NOV 0 7 2011

PROPERTY OF
SENECA COLLEGE
LIBRARIES
KING CAMPUS

ACKNOWLEDGMENTS

Janice Nadeau thanks the Association des vendémiaires in Saint-Mathieu de Tréviers, France.
Hervé Bouchard thanks Richard Boivin and Marie-Andrée Descôteaux for their suggestions and advice. Scott Carey is
freely inspired by The Incredible Shrinking Man, *a film made by Jack Arnold in 1957.*

Copyright © 2009 by Janice Nadeau and Hervé Bouchard
Copyright © by Les Éditions de la Pastèque
English translation copyright © 2010 by Helen Mixter
First published in French as *Harvey* by Les Éditions de la Pastèque, Montreal, Quebec
Published in English in Canada and the USA in 2010 by Groundwood Books

All rights reserved. No part of this publication may be reproduced, stored in a retrieval
system or transmitted, in any form or by any means, without the prior written consent of
the publisher or a license from The Canadian Copyright Licensing Agency (Access Copyright). For an Access Copyright license, visit www.accesscopyright.ca or call toll free
to 1-800-893-5777.

Groundwood Books / House of Anansi Press
110 Spadina Avenue, Suite 801, Toronto, Ontario M5V 2K4
or c/o Publishers Group West
1700 Fourth Street, Berkeley, CA 94710

We acknowledge for their financial support of our publishing program the Canada Council
for the Arts, the Government of Canada through the Canada Book Fund (CBF) and the
Ontario Arts Council.

Janice Nadeau thanks the Conseil des arts et des lettres du Québec for its financial support.

Library and Archives Canada Cataloguing in Publication
Bouchard, Hervé
Harvey / Hervé Bouchard, author ; Janice Nadeau,
illustrator ; Helen Mixter, translator.
Translation of: Harvey.
ISBN 978-1-55498-075-8
I. Nadeau, Janice II. Mixter, Helen III. Title.
PZ7.7.B68Ha13 2010   j741.5'971   C2010-901098-1

Illustration and design by Janice Nadeau
Text by Hervé Bouchard
Computer graphics by Stéphane Ulrich

Printed and bound in China

HERVÉ BOUCHARD AND
JANICE NADEAU
TRANSLATED BY HELEN MIXTER

HARVEY

HOW I BECAME INVISIBLE

GROUNDWOOD BOOKS / HOUSE OF ANANSI PRESS
TORONTO BERKELEY

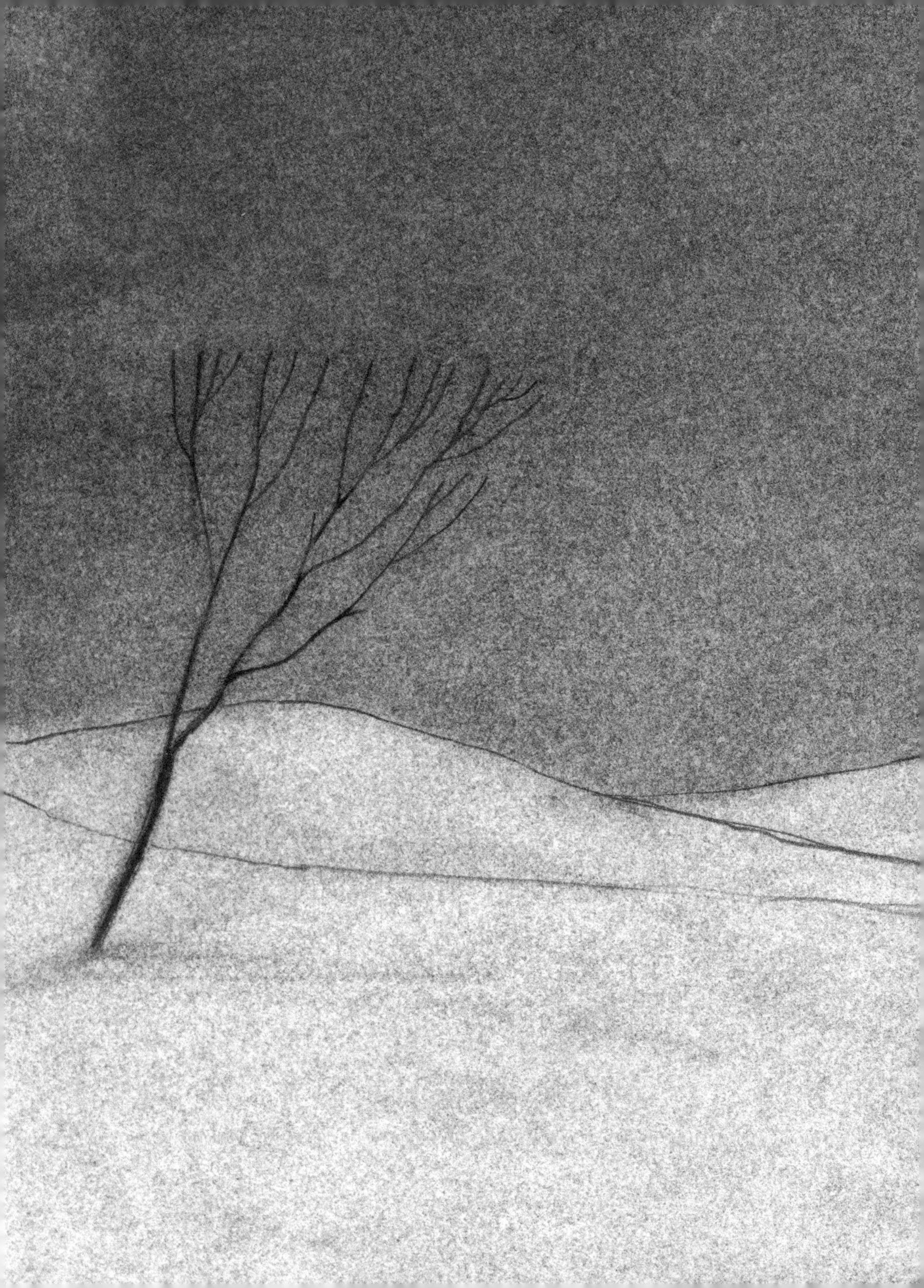

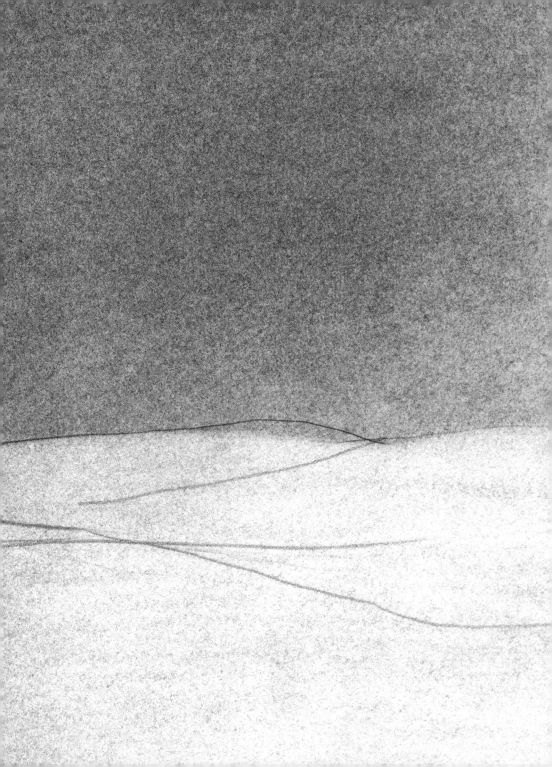

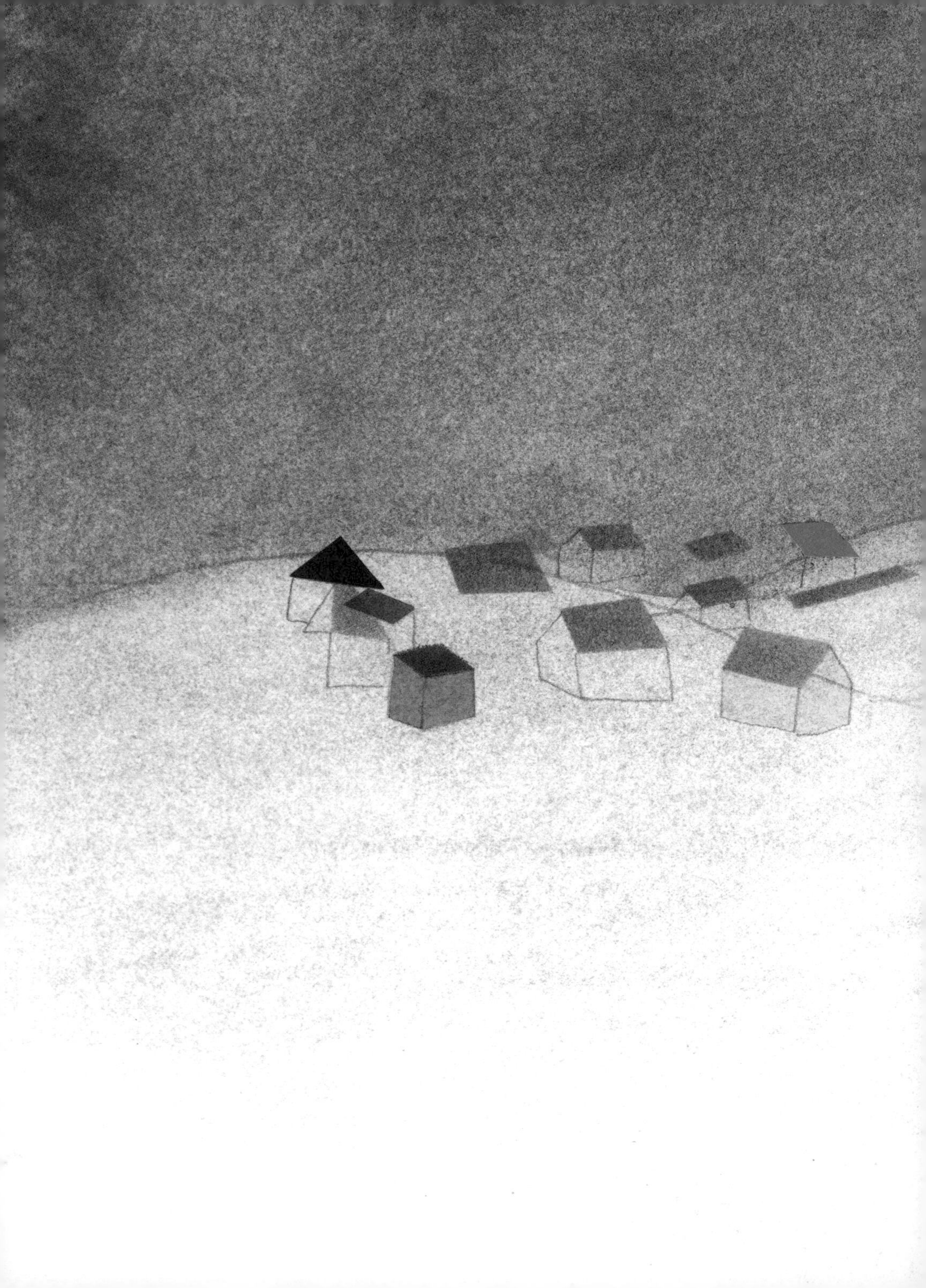

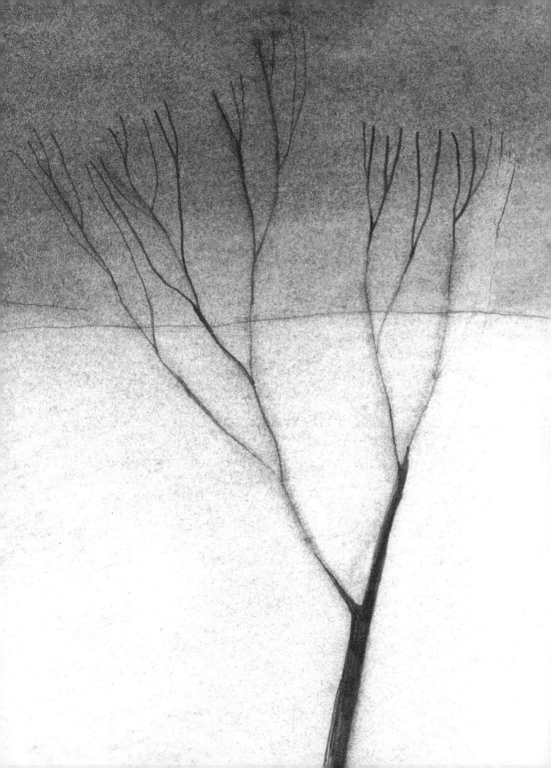

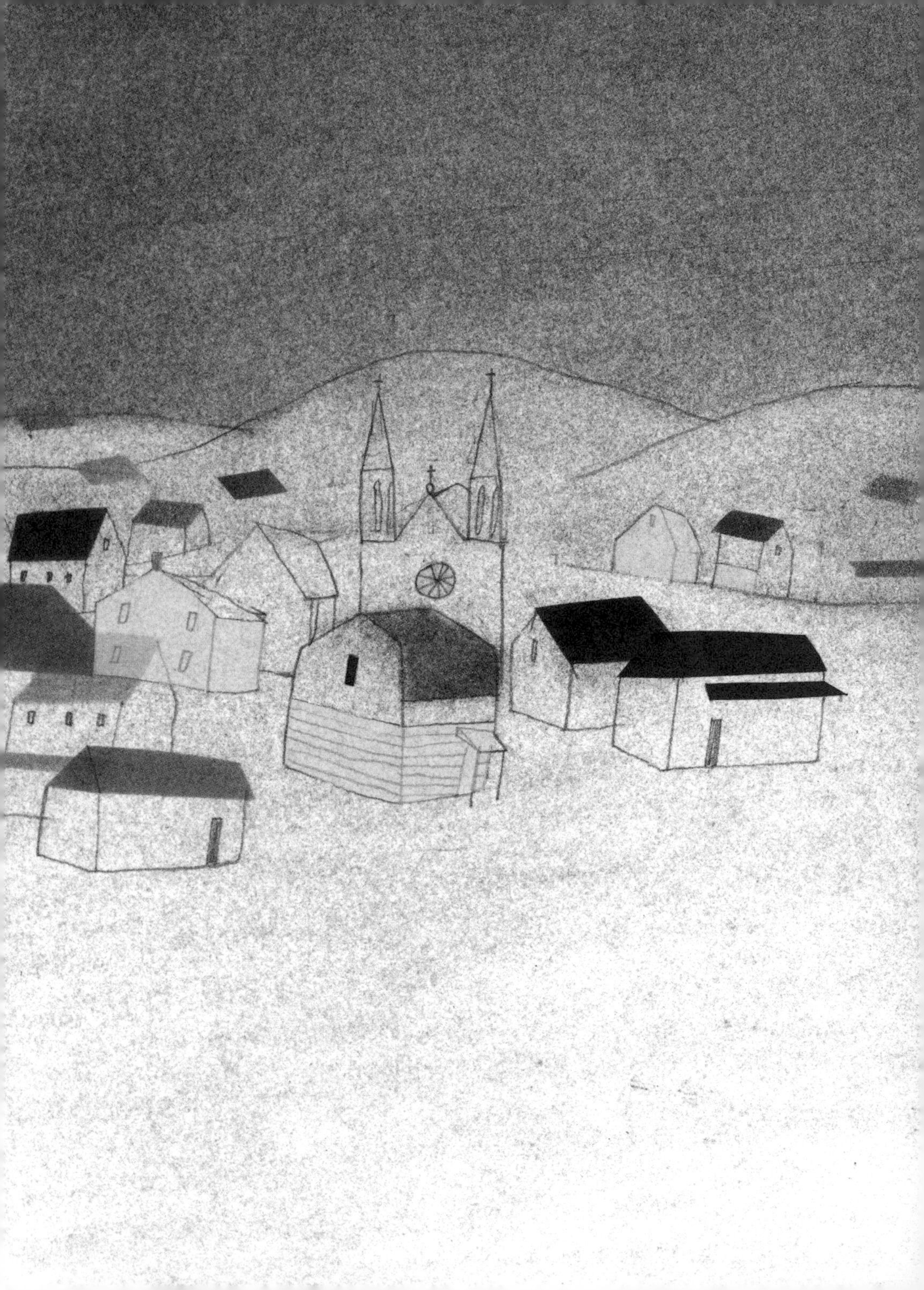

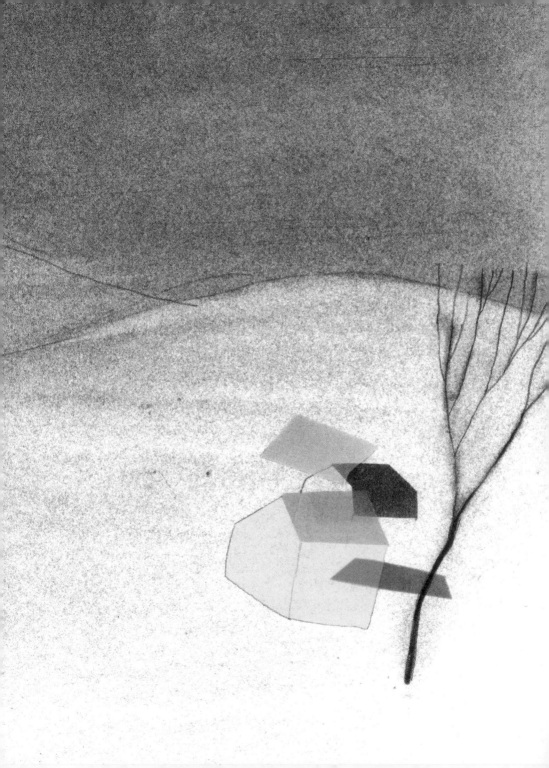

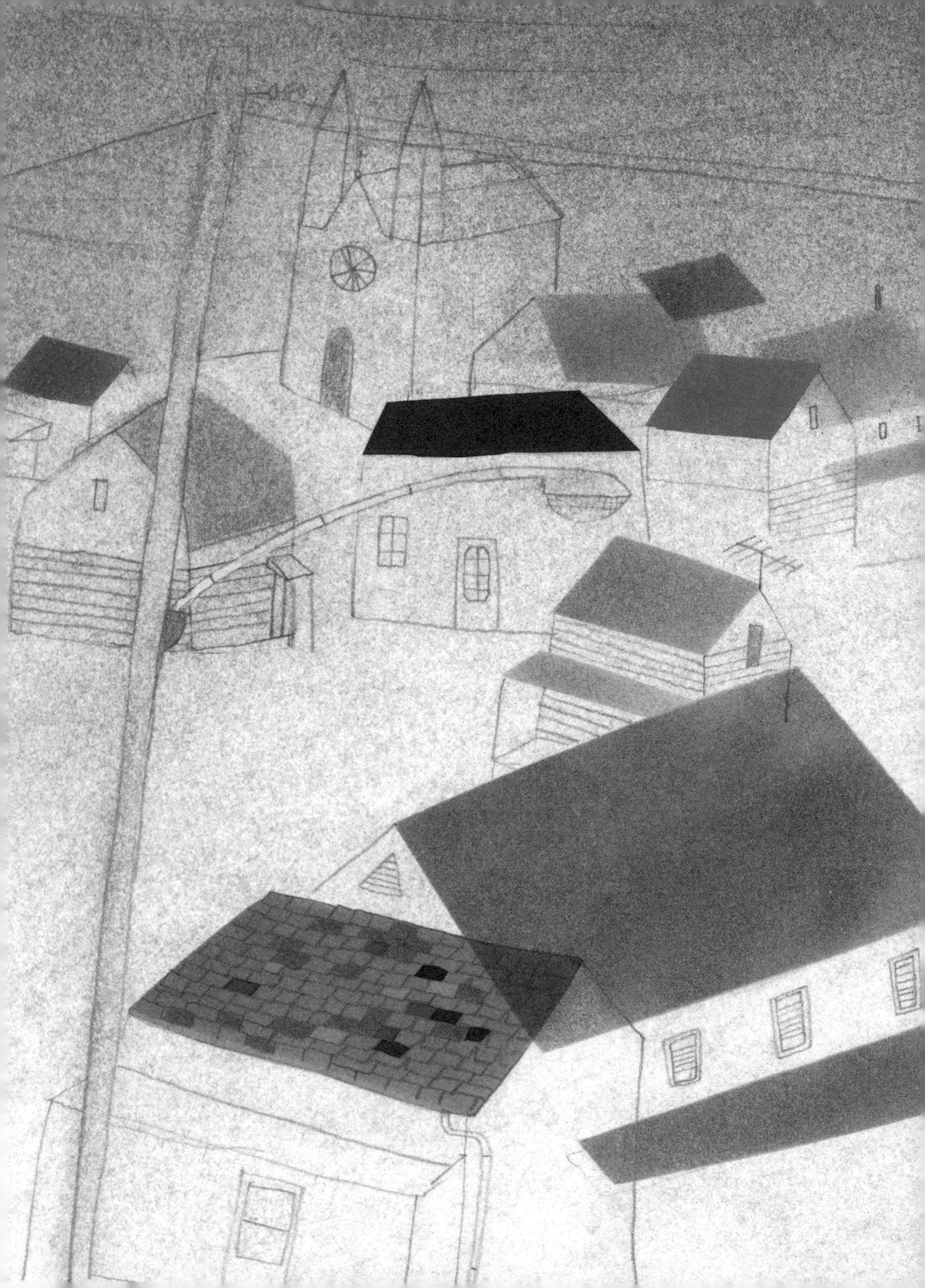

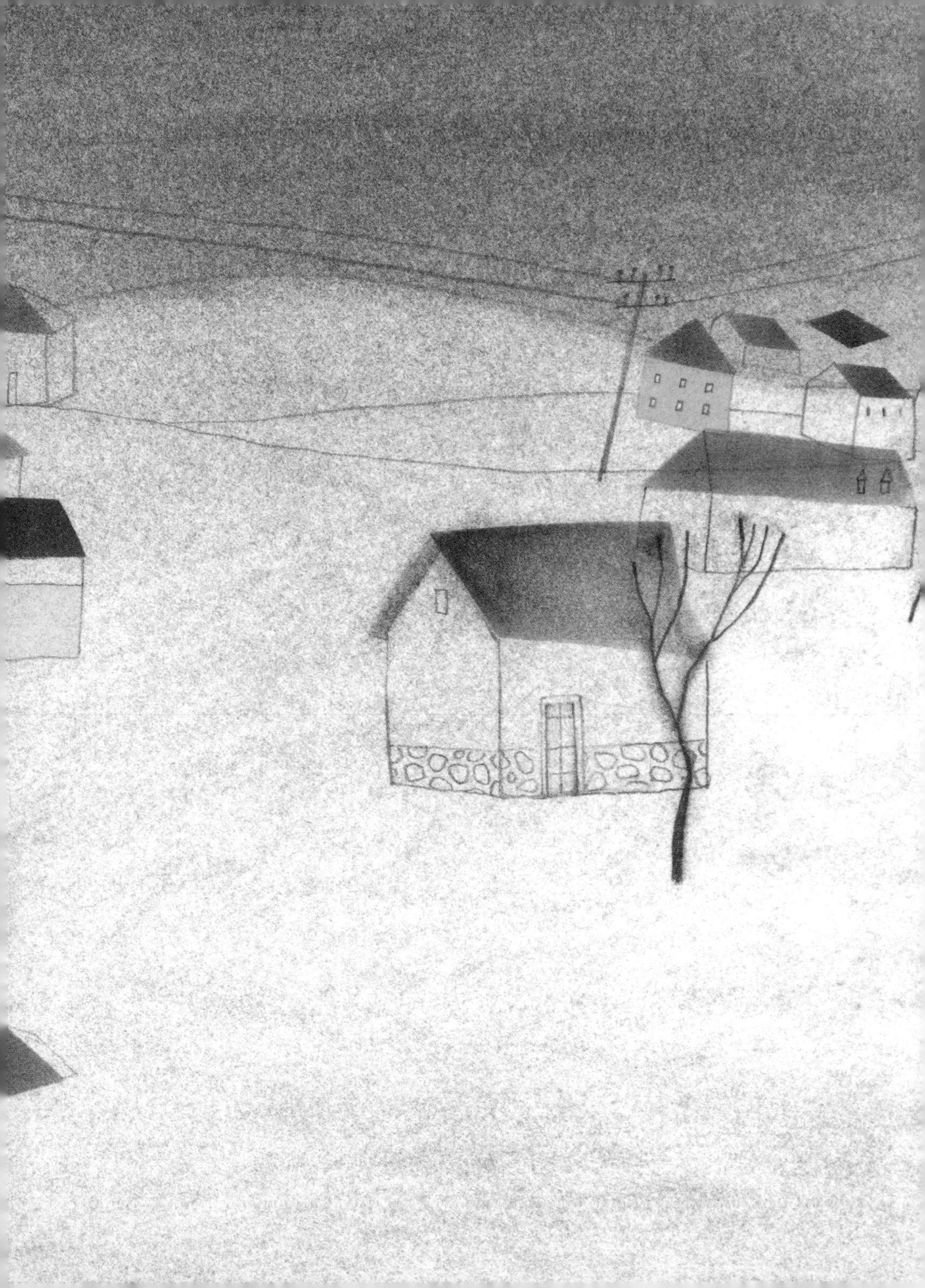

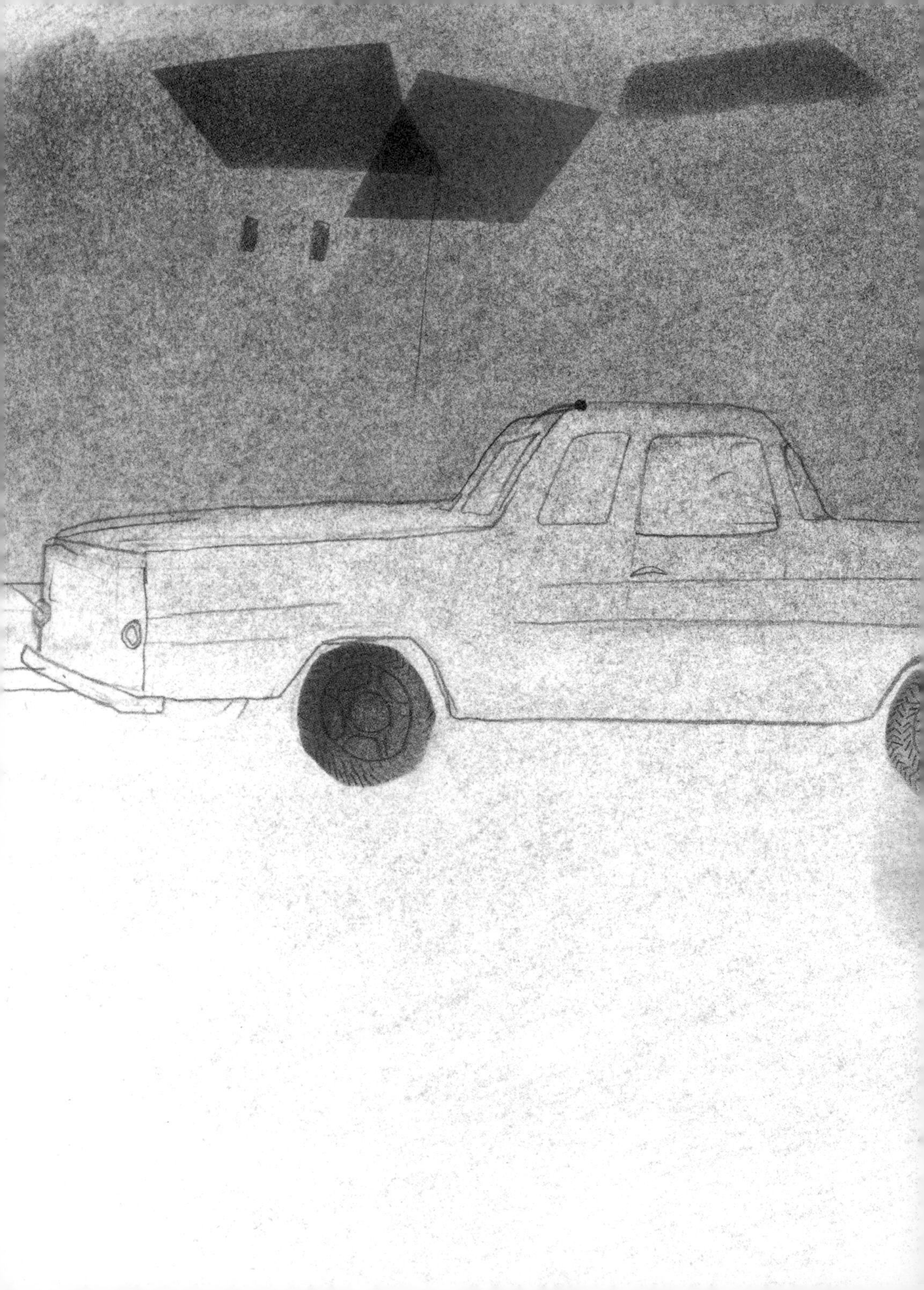

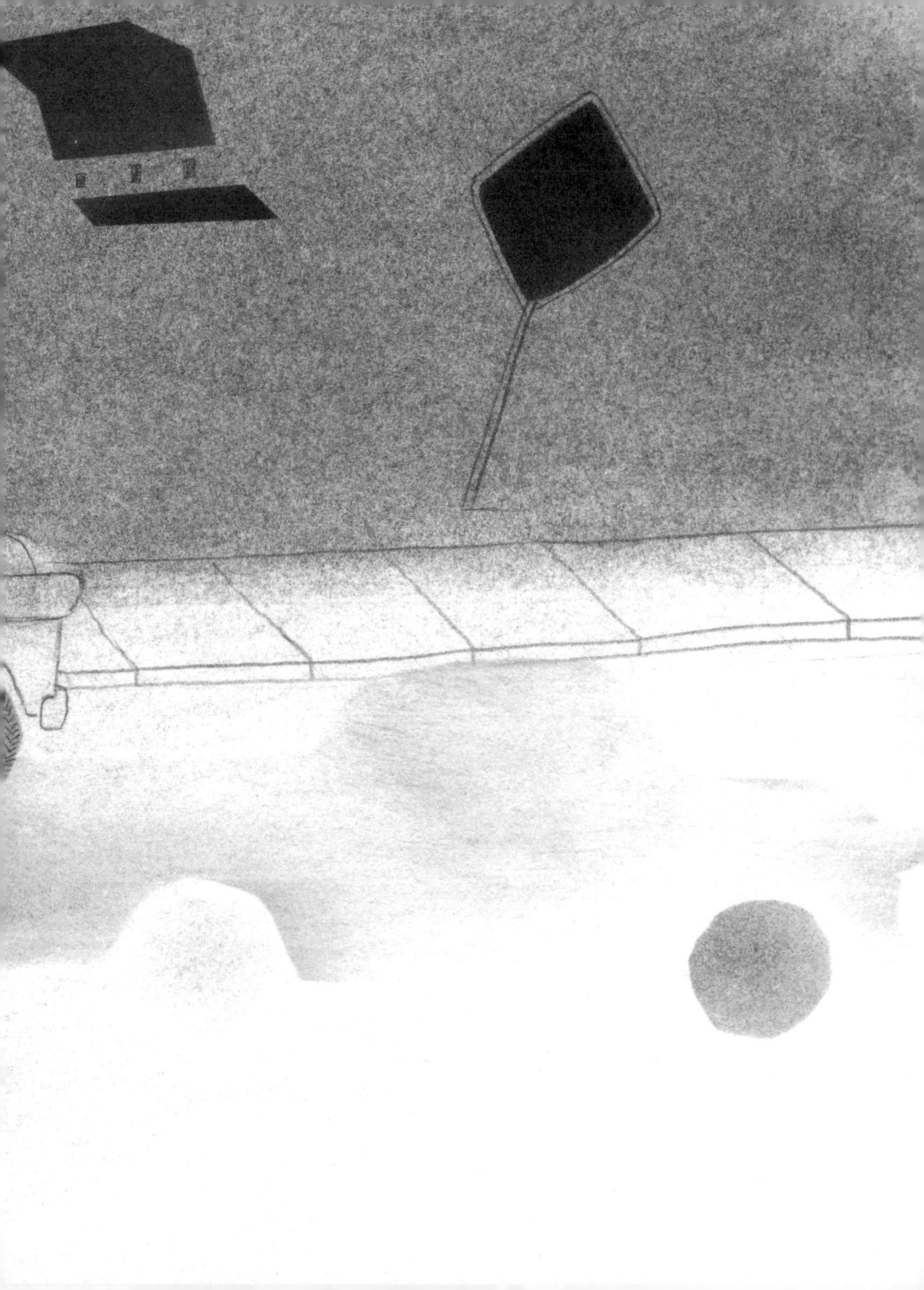

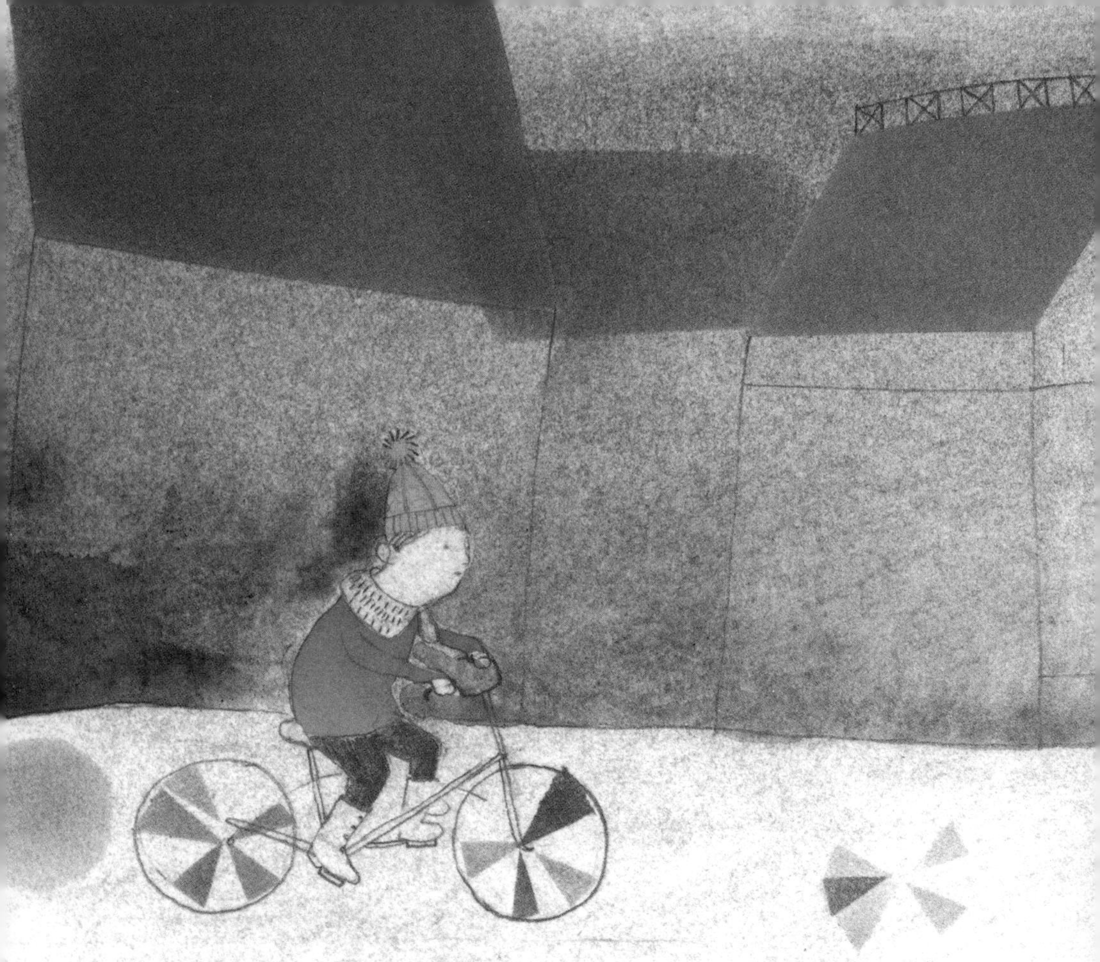

EVERYBODY CALLS ME HARVEY.

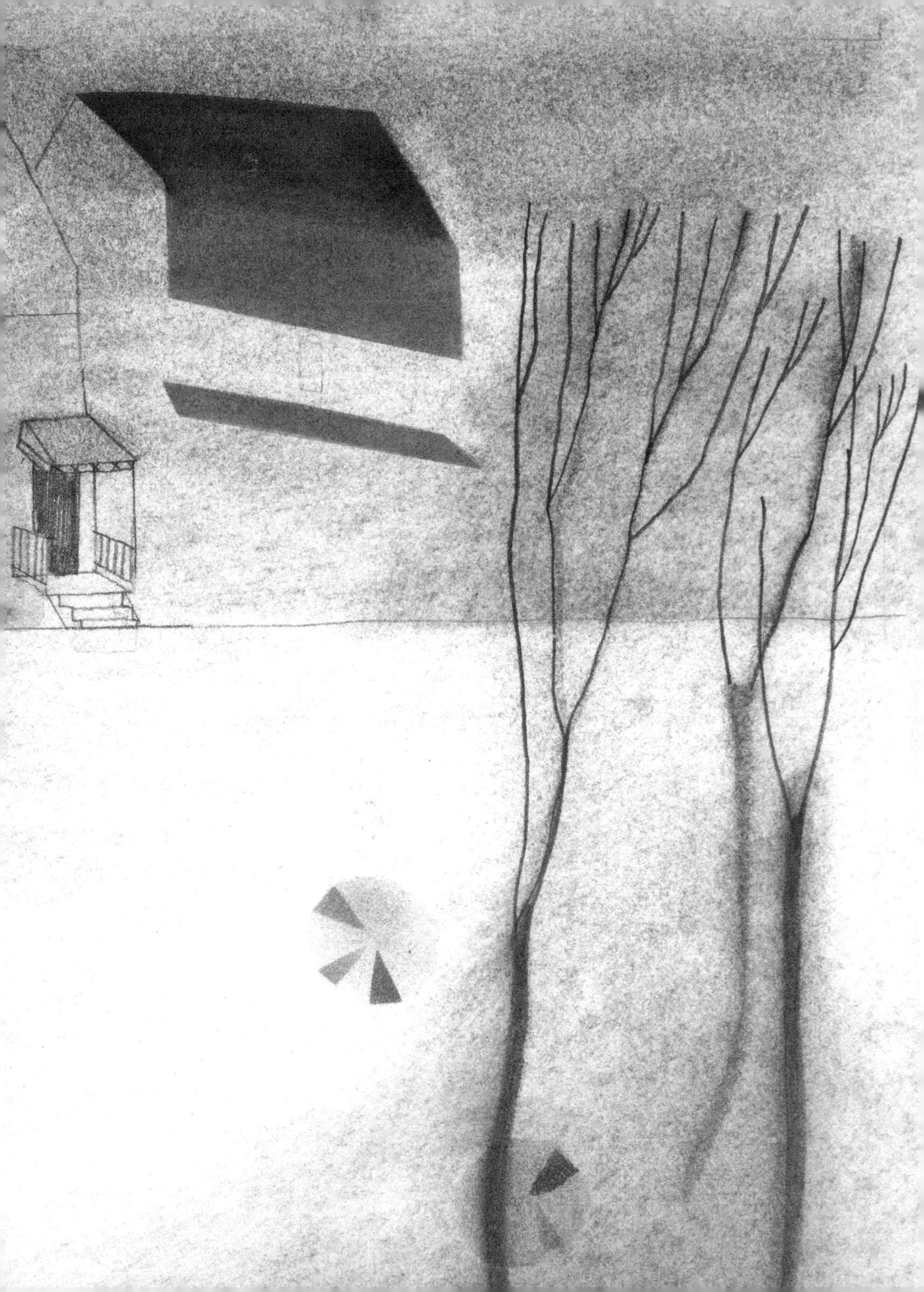

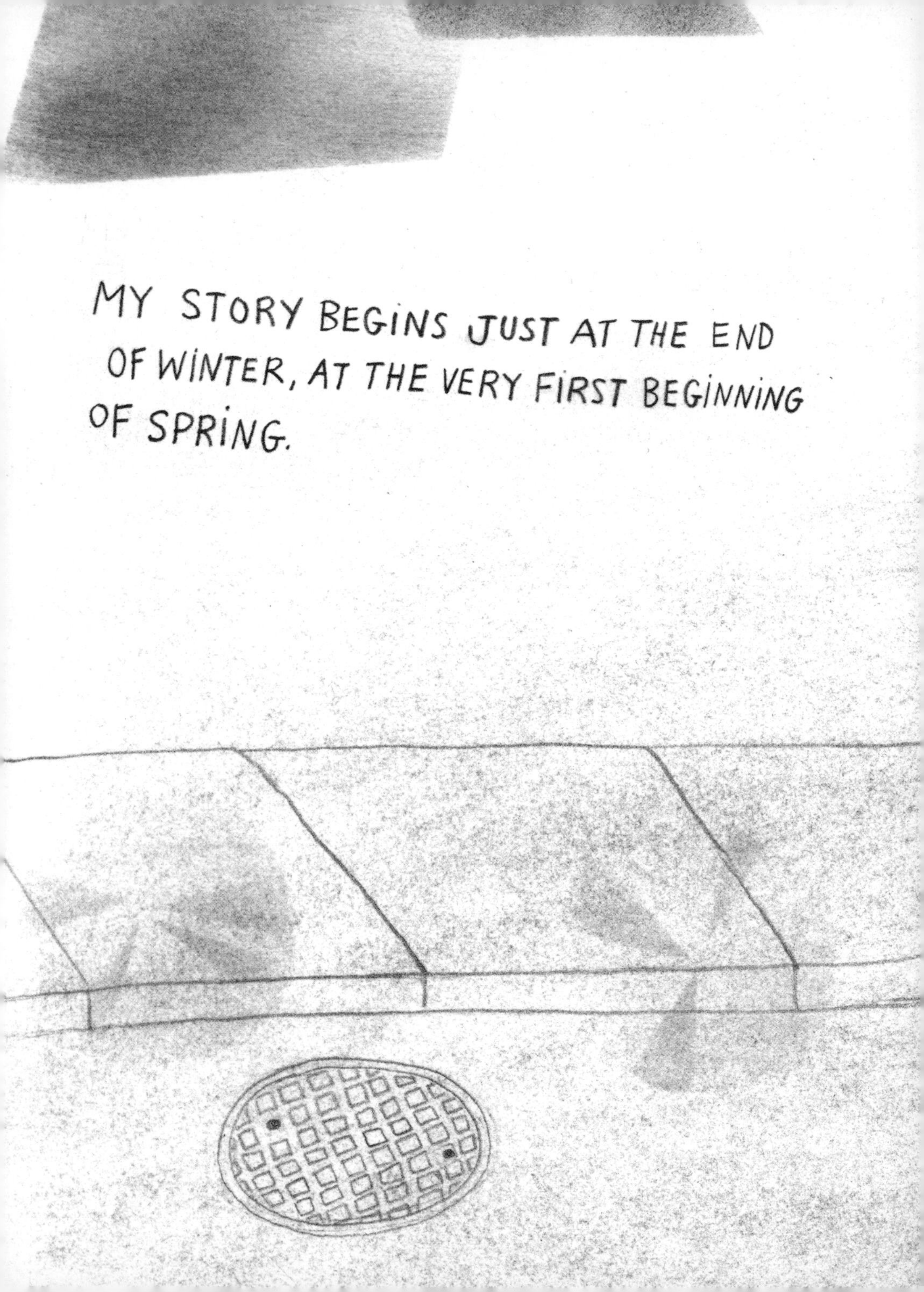
MY STORY BEGINS JUST AT THE END OF WINTER, AT THE VERY FIRST BEGINNING OF SPRING.

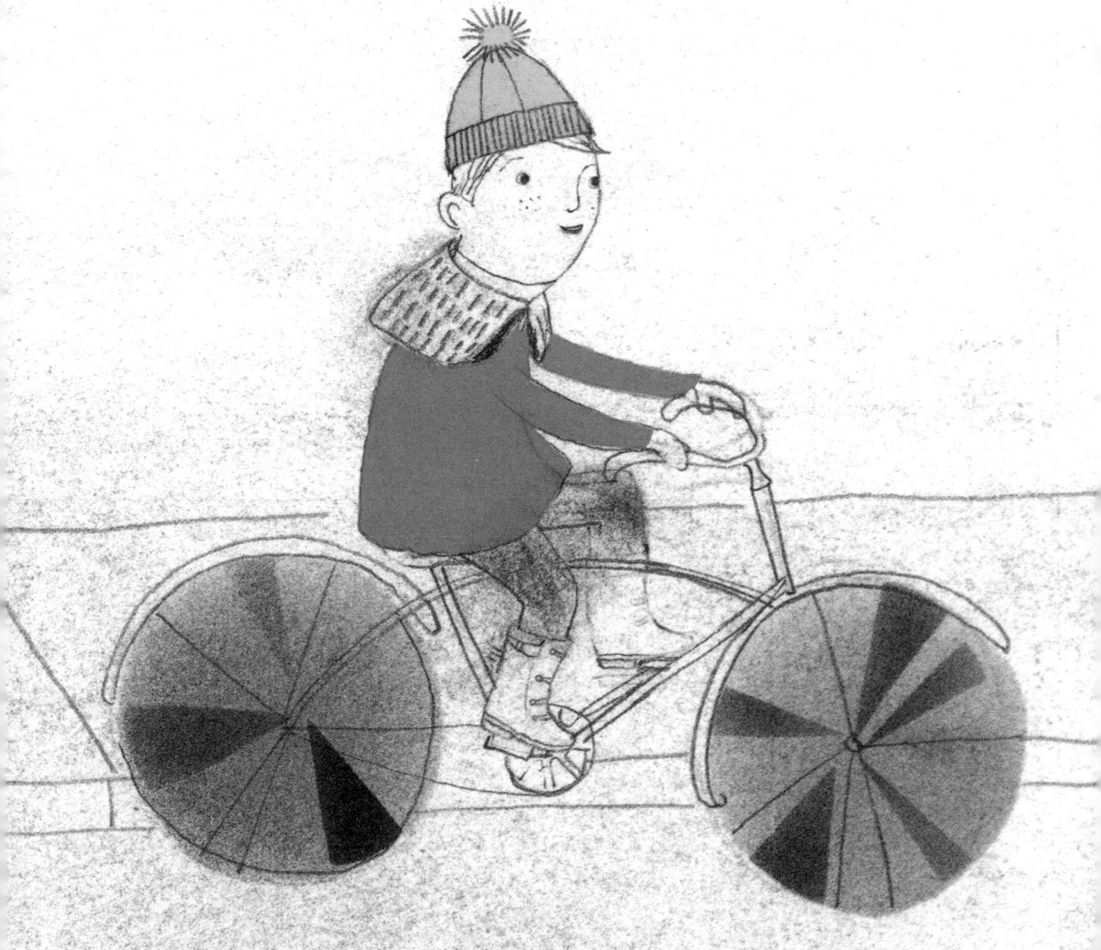

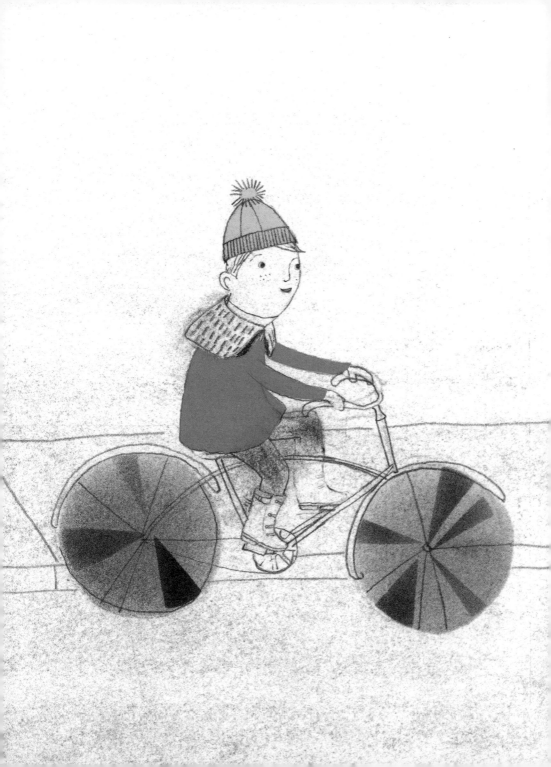

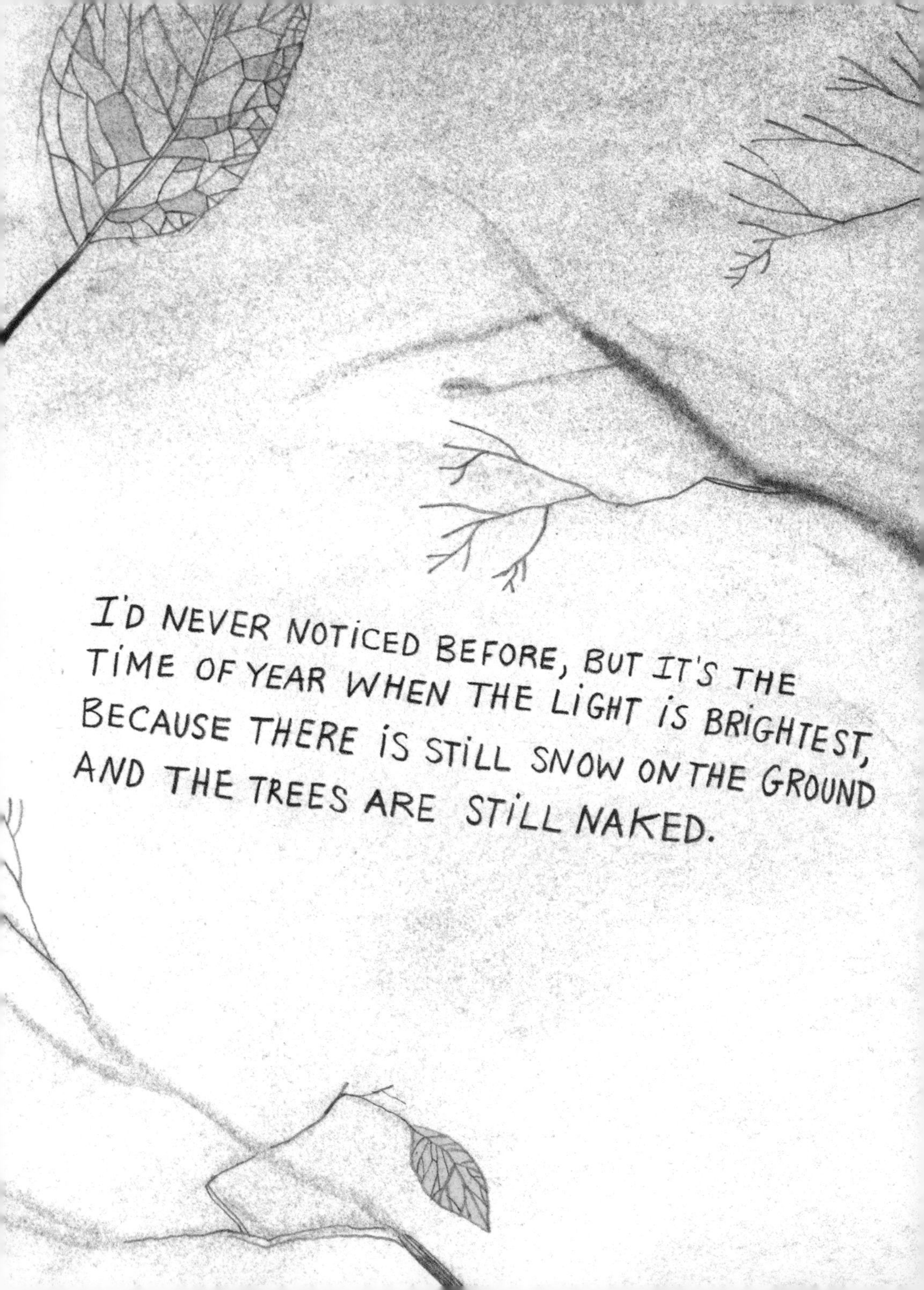
I'D NEVER NOTICED BEFORE, BUT IT'S THE TIME OF YEAR WHEN THE LIGHT IS BRIGHTEST, BECAUSE THERE IS STILL SNOW ON THE GROUND AND THE TREES ARE STILL NAKED.

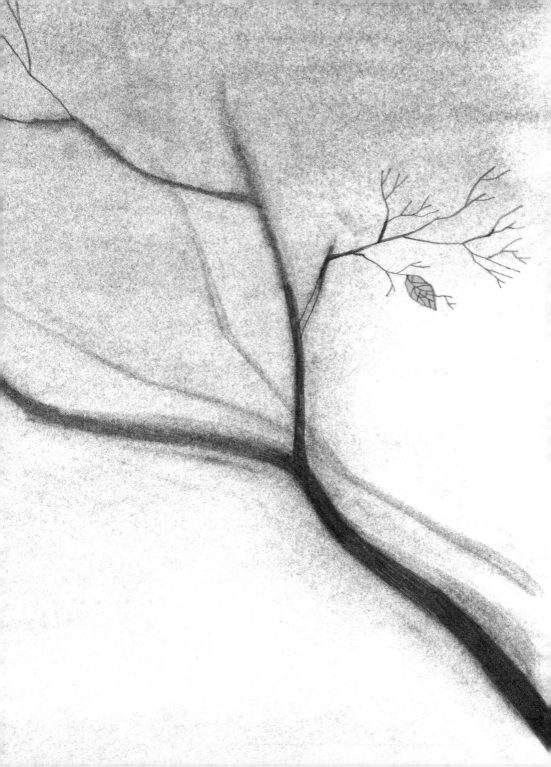

THAT'S WHAT MY FATHER BOUILLON USED TO SAY, THAT THERE ARE TWO SPRINGS: ONE THAT IS WHITE WITH LIGHT AND THEN THE NEXT THAT IS GREEN WITH GRASS AND LEAVES. FOR MY MOTHER BOUILLON THERE ARE ALSO TWO SPRINGS, BUT SHE DOESN'T SEE THEM THE SAME WAY. AND AS FOR CANTIN... FOR CANTIN, I DON'T KNOW.

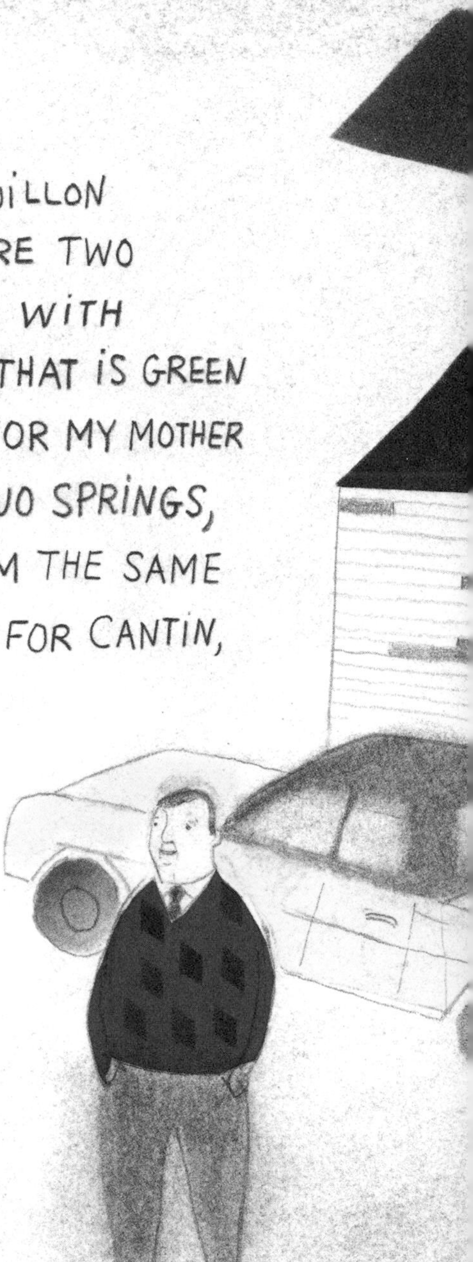

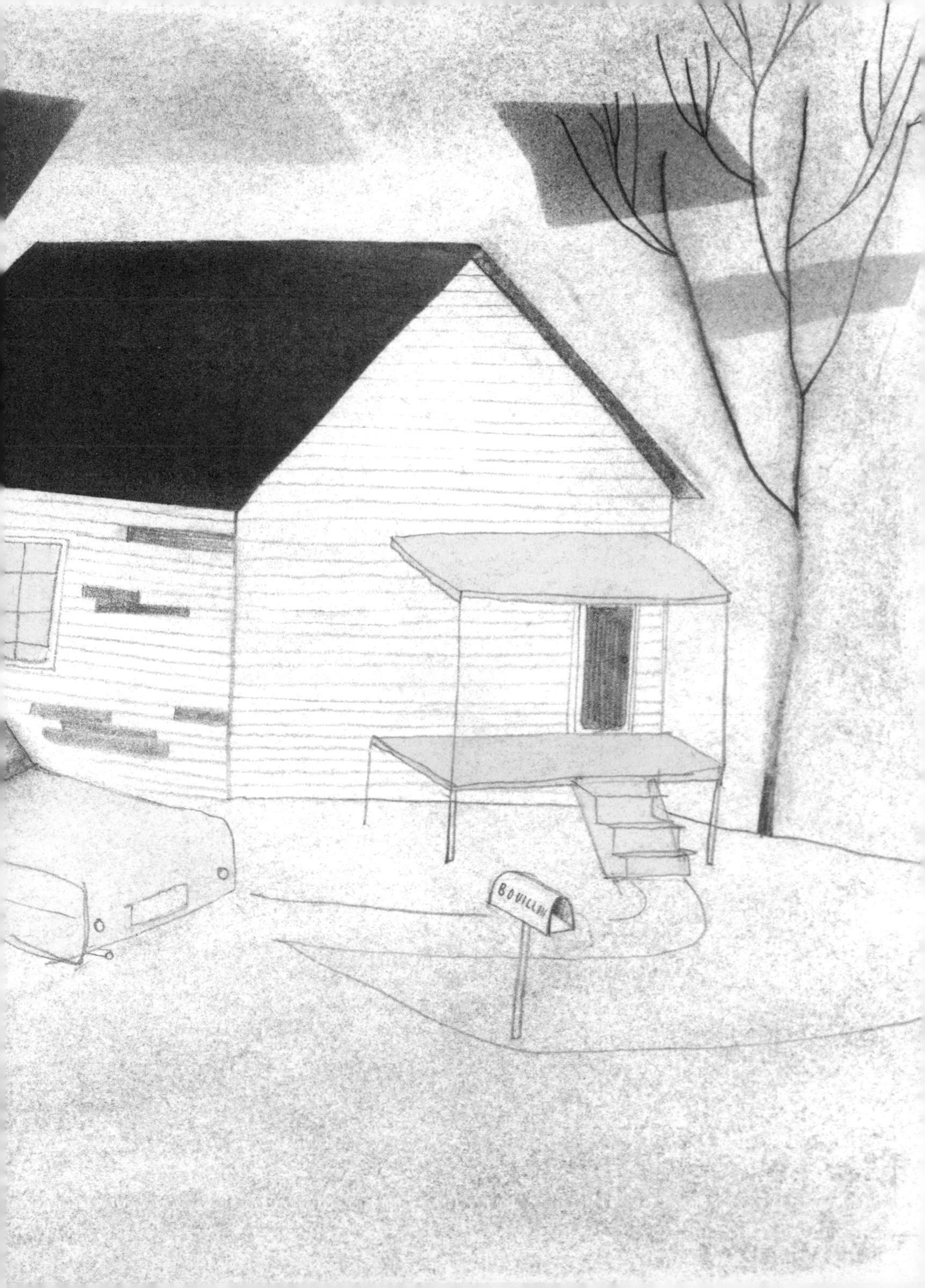
BOUILLON

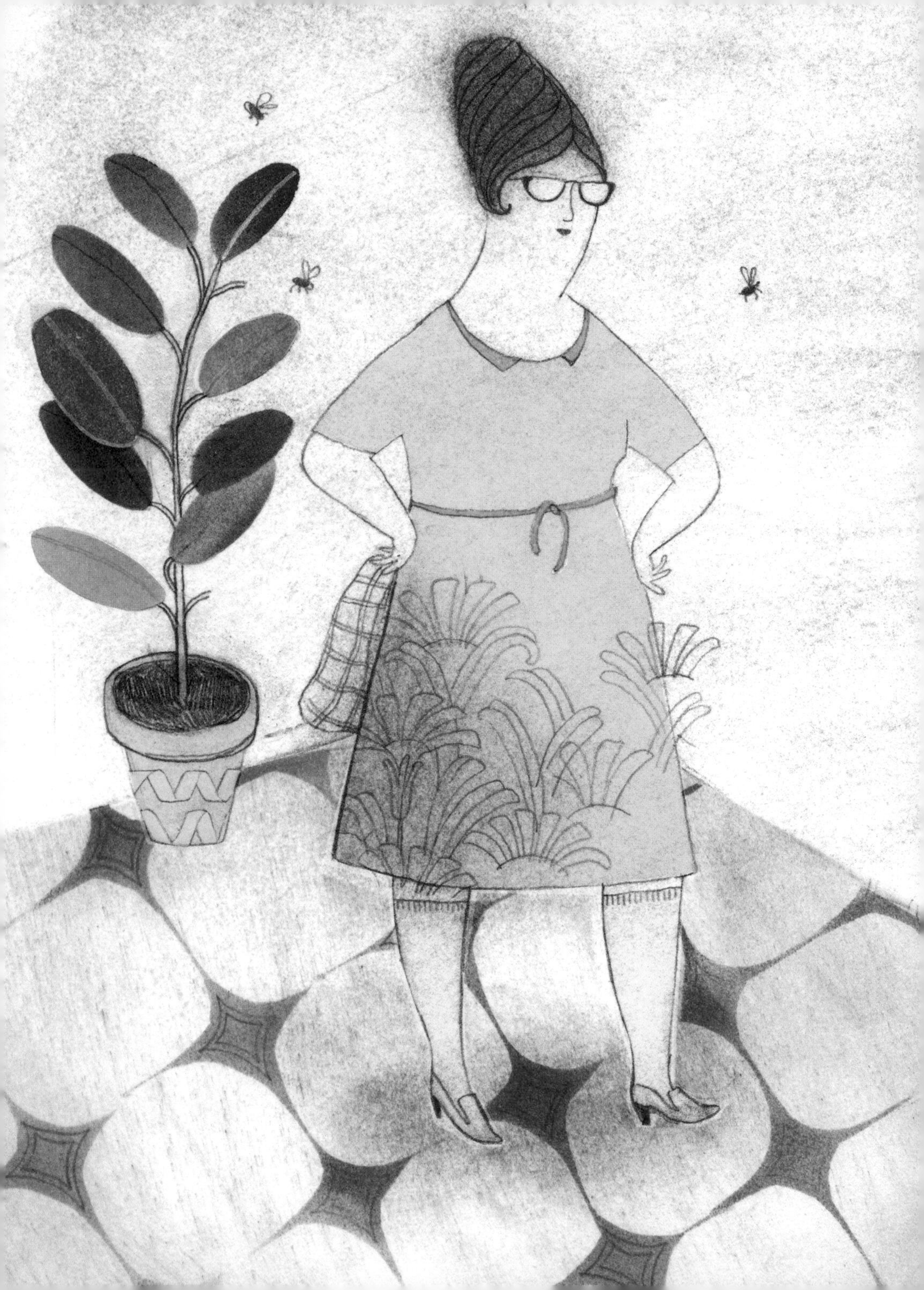

BUT FOR MY MOTHER, SPRING NUMBER ONE, I'M SURE, IS THE DAMN SPRING OF BLACK SNOW PILED ON THE SIDES OF THE ROAD, AND THE DAMN PUDDLES THAT COLLECT BY THE DOOR AND THE DAMN HORDES OF KIDS THAT TRACK IN THE WET, AND THE DAMN SAND AND DAMN SALT THAT GET INTO THE HOUSE AND THE DAMN BASEMENT THAT STARTS TO STINK OF DAMP. AND AFTER THIS FIRST SPRING WHEN EVERYTHING IS A PIG STY, AS SHE CALLS IT, COMES SPRING NUMBER TWO—A SPRING OF THE DAMN MUD AND THE DAMN BUGS THAT REAPPEAR RIGHT ABOUT THEN, AND THE DAMN BURNING OFF OF WEEDS IN THE FIELDS THAT SPREADS ITS DAMN SOOT EVERYWHERE.

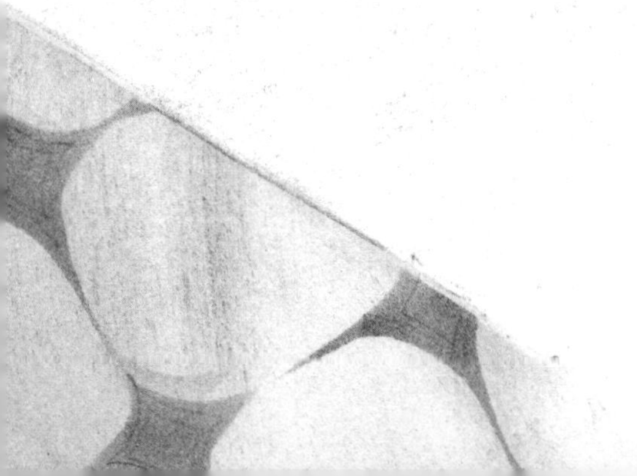

IT'S ALSO THE TIME FOR A BIG SPRING CLEANING.

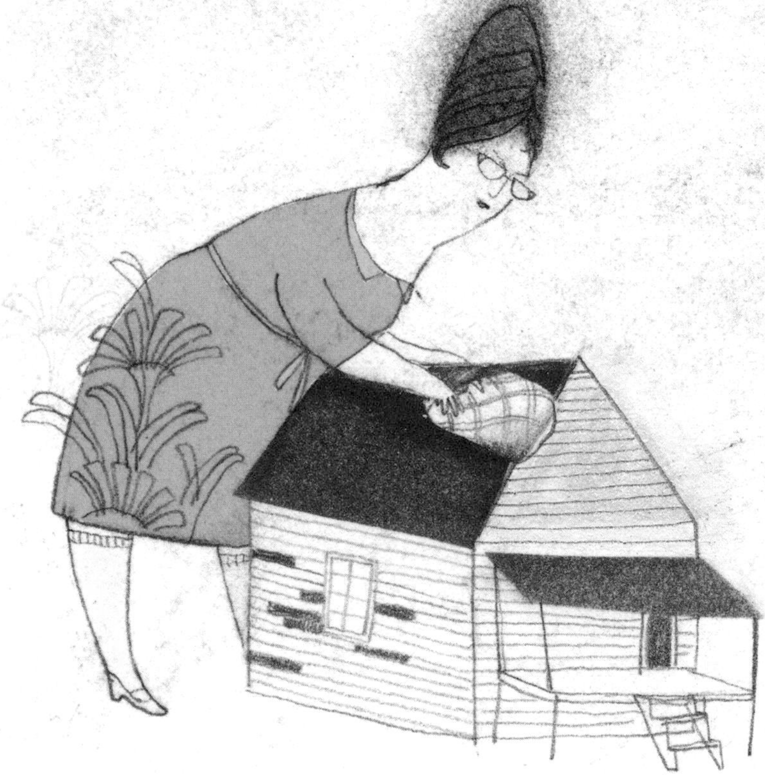

SPRING DOES NOT THRILL MY
MOTHER BOUILLON.

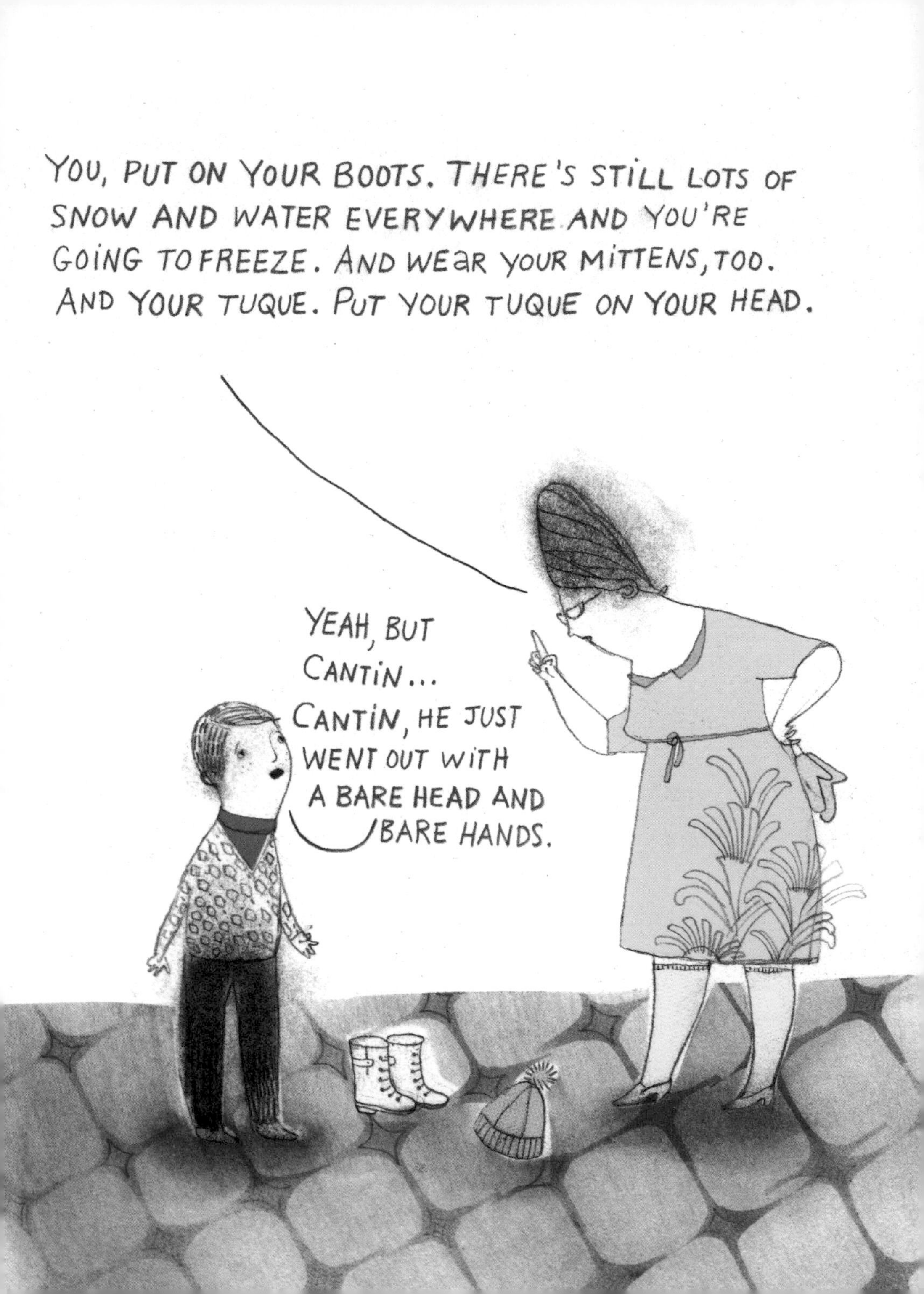
YOU, PUT ON YOUR BOOTS. THERE'S STILL LOTS OF SNOW AND WATER EVERYWHERE AND YOU'RE GOING TO FREEZE. AND WEAR YOUR MITTENS, TOO. AND YOUR TUQUE. PUT YOUR TUQUE ON YOUR HEAD.
YEAH, BUT CANTIN...
CANTIN, HE JUST WENT OUT WITH A BARE HEAD AND BARE HANDS.

CANTIN IS MY BROTHER. HE'S YOUNGER THAN ME.
BUT HE'S A WHOLE HEAD TALLER AND EVERYONE
THINKS I'M THE LITTLE BOUILLON. AND EVERY-
THING I WEAR HE WORE FIRST.

CANTIN

ME

MY MOTHER BUGS
ME WITH HER ORDERS.
YOU SHOULD HEAR HER.

FORGET ABOUT YOUR "BUT CANTIN!"
YOU ARE YOU AND HE IS HE.

FOR ME, THE FIRST SPRING IS THE TIME WHEN MY BOOTS GET HEAVY AND SLOW ME DOWN.

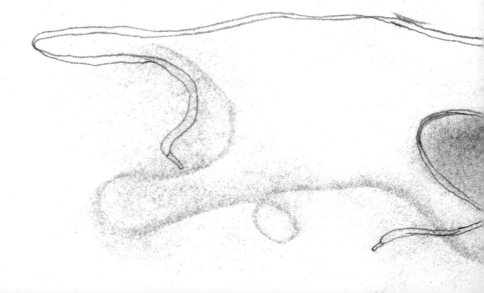

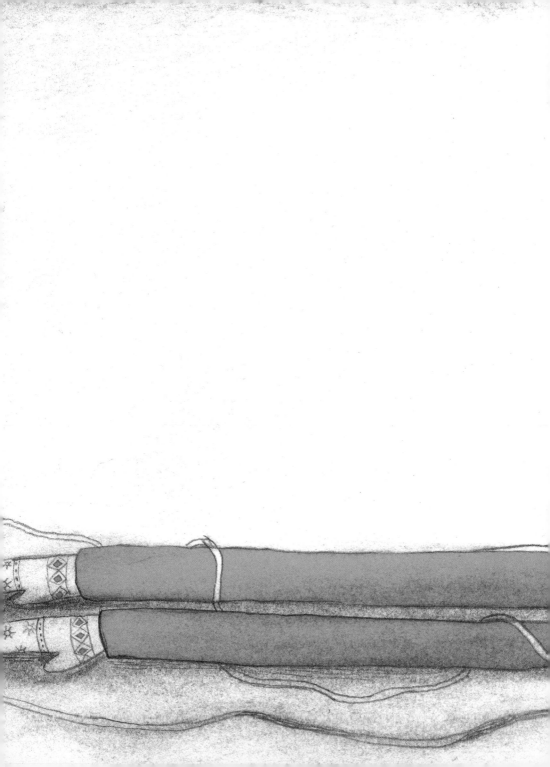

I DON'T KNOW HOW IT HAPPENS, BUT WHEN SPRING COMES, THEY SUDDENLY GET TOO BIG, THE LACES GROW AND HANG DOWN AND MY FEET DRAG WITH EVERY STEP.

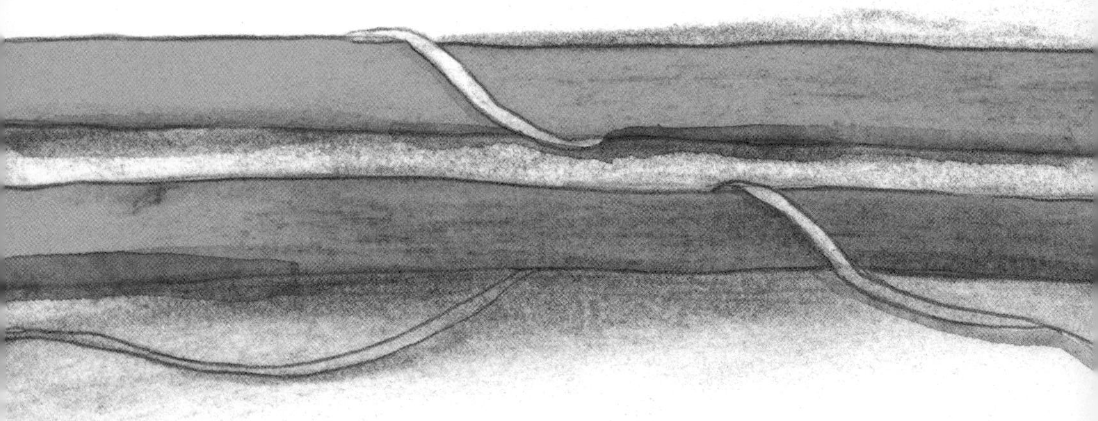

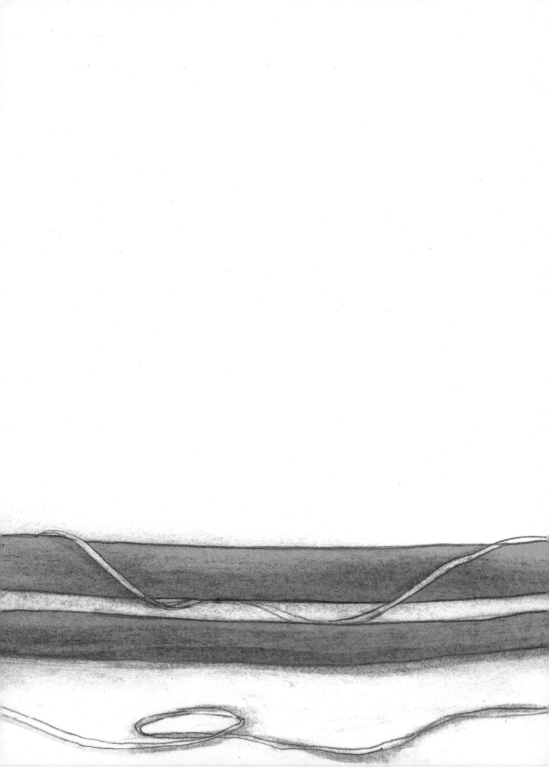

AND I'M HOT AND IT EVEN SEEMS THAT MY SLEEVES GET LONGER. BUT THIS TIME OF FIRST SPRING IS ALSO THE TIME FOR THE RACES IN THE GUTTERS. AND IT'S ALSO THE TIME WHEN CANTIN AND I LOST OUR FATHER BOUILLON. AND IT'S THE TIME WHEN I BECAME INVISIBLE. SO THERE ARE LOTS OF THINGS TO TELL.

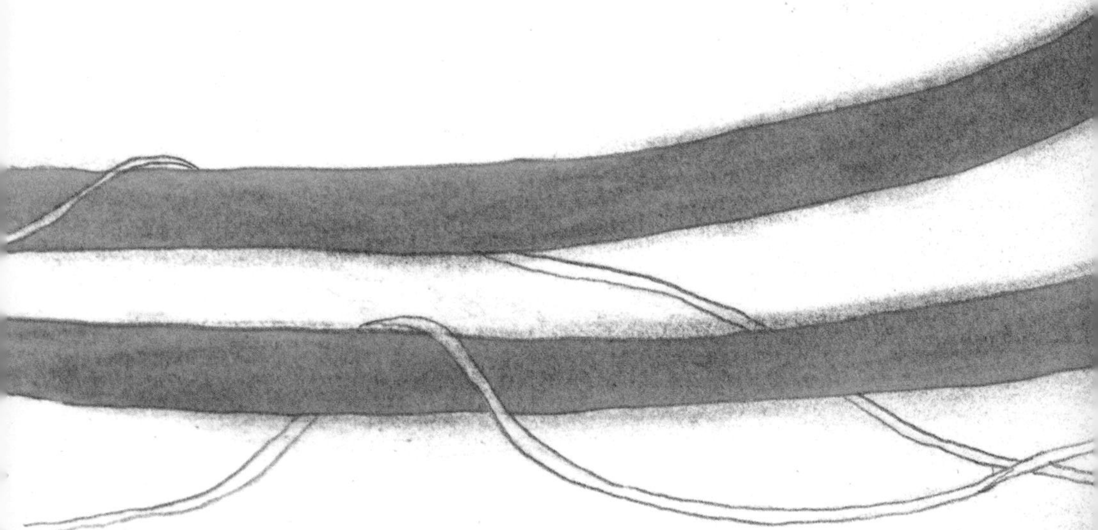

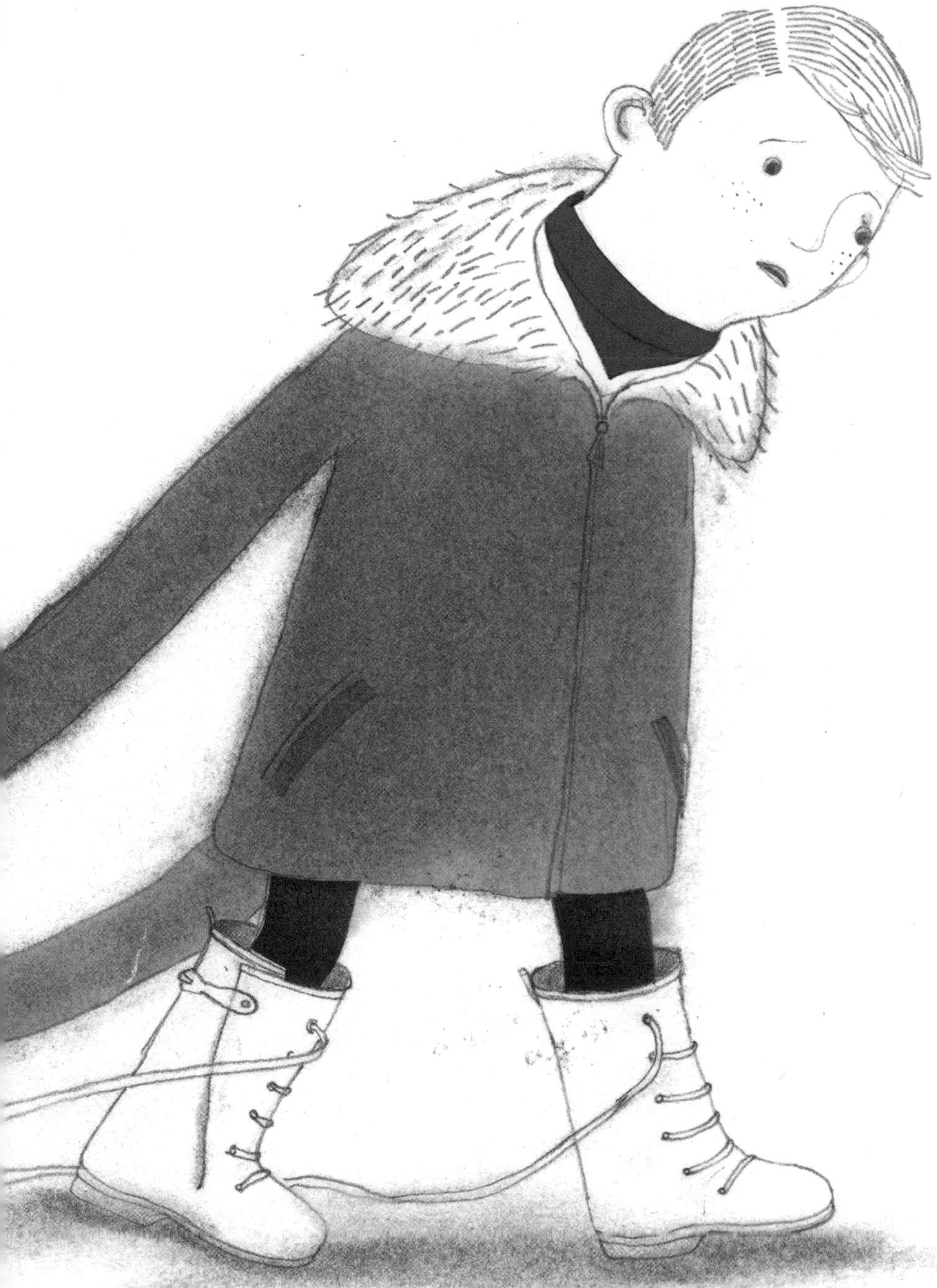

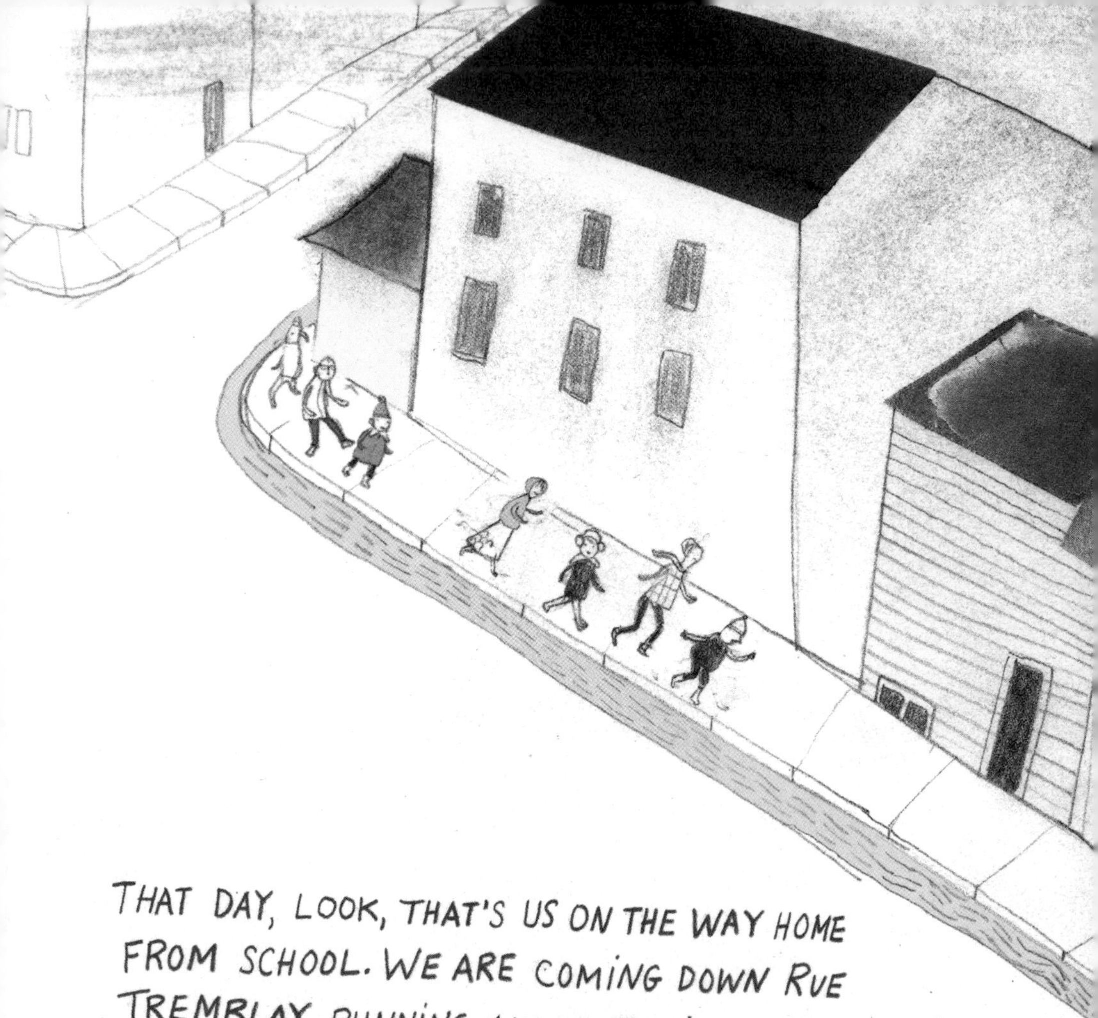

THAT DAY, LOOK, THAT'S US ON THE WAY HOME FROM SCHOOL. WE ARE COMING DOWN RUE TREMBLAY RUNNING ALONG BESIDE OUR TOOTHPICKS THAT ARE FLOATING NEXT TO US IN THE GUTTER.

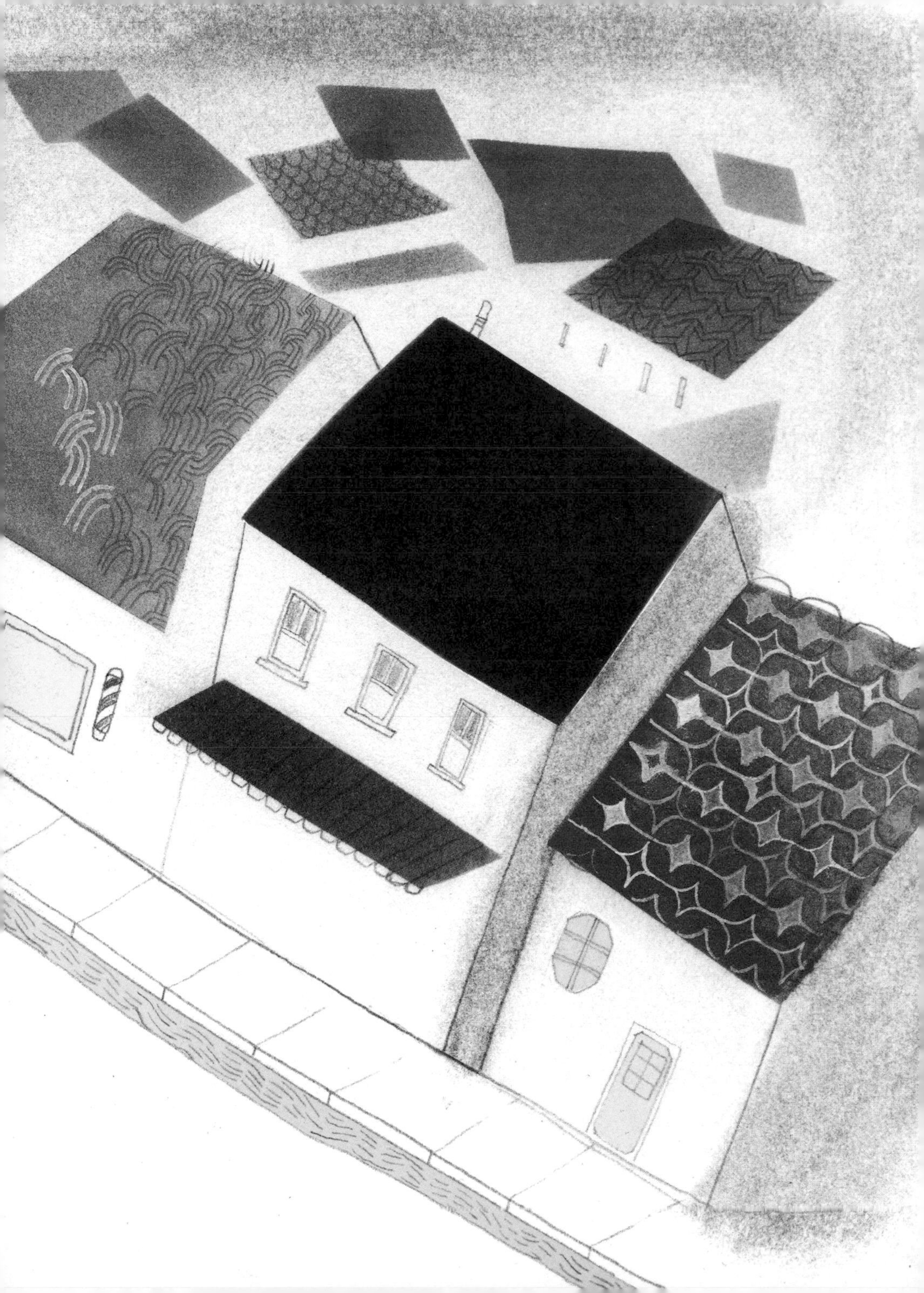

WE,

MEANS <u>ME</u> AND MY BROTHER CANTIN,

AND ALSO POULOURDE AND CHIQUETTE,

AND LOUISON CAYER AND MARCO BARBEAU,

AND NIC SAINT-GELAIS AND OTHERS WITH OTHER NAMES. THEY ALL LIVE NEARBY US.

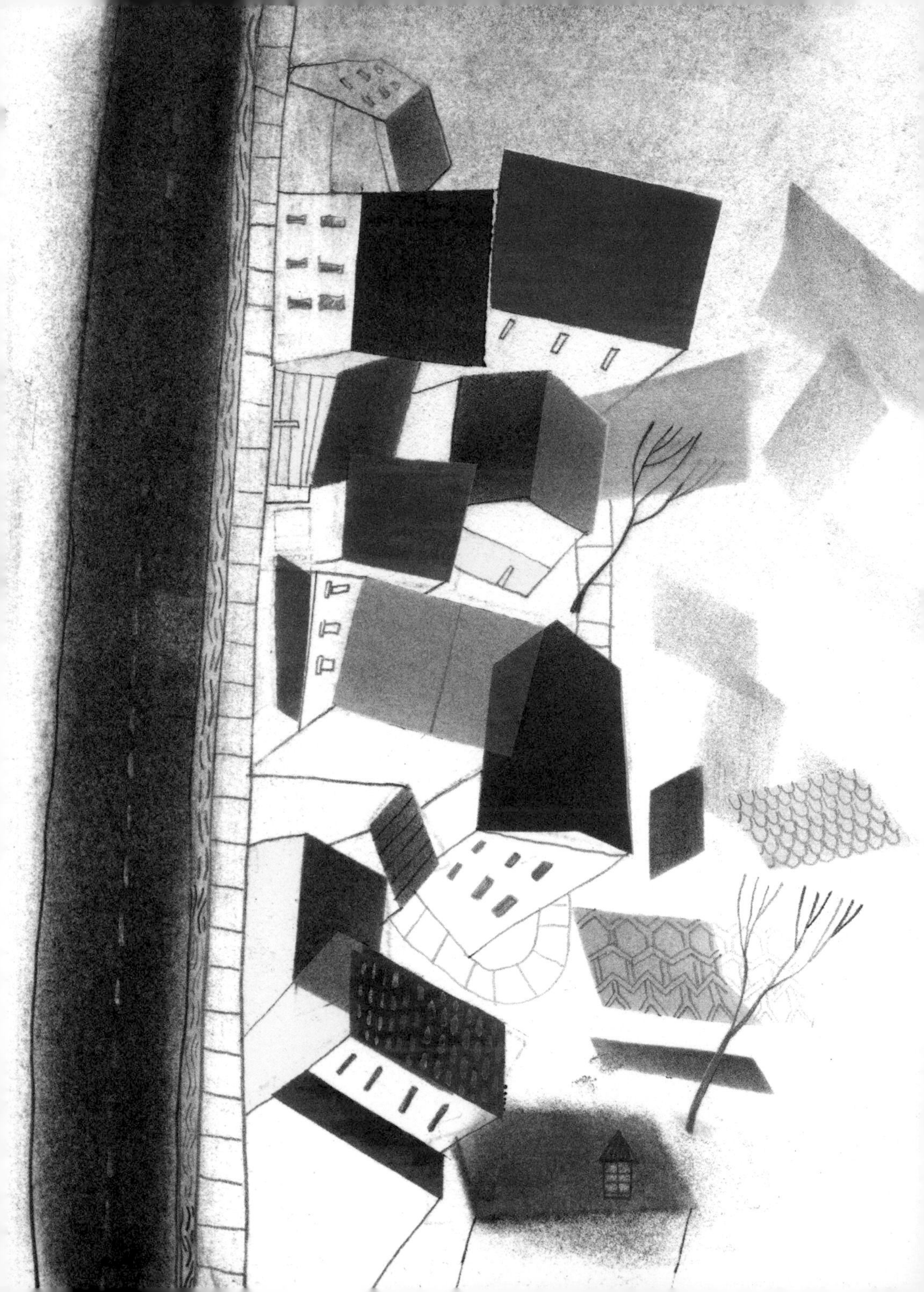

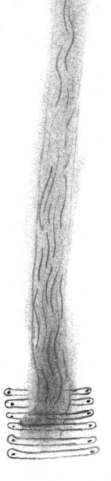

RUE TREMBLAY IS THE BEST STREET FOR THE
RACE BECAUSE IT'S LONG AND STRAIGHT AND
BECAUSE IT'S STEEP AND HAS A DRAIN
AT THE BOTTOM.

THE DRAIN IS THE GREAT WATERFALL WHERE ALL SHIPS COME TO AN END, FROM THE FIRST TO THE LAST. THE STARTING POINT IS THE CORNER OF RUE LAPOINTE, UP AT THE TOP. THERE ARE SHEETS OF ICE ON THE SIDEWALK, SO IT'S A ROUGH COURSE, LIKE A RIVER WITH CLIFFS ALONGSIDE IT, OR ONE WITH LOTS OF CAVES THAT SHIPS SAIL PAST. IT'S KIND OF LIKE A LITTLE VERSION OF SOMETHING REAL.

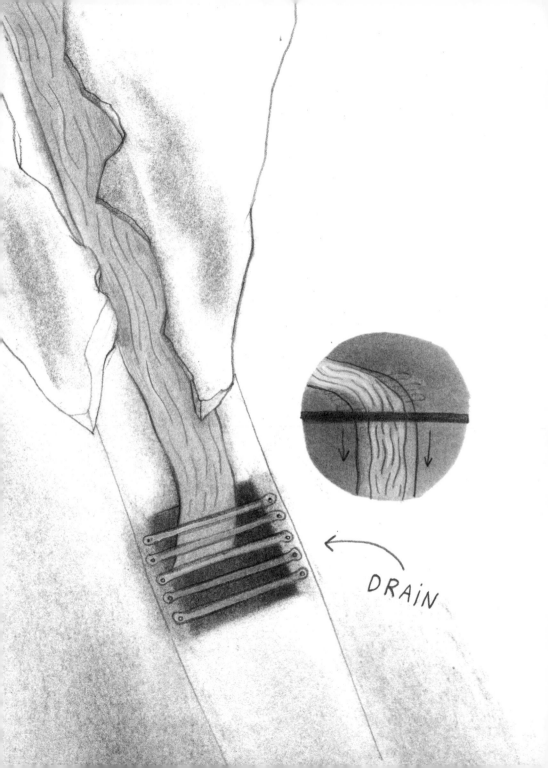

DRAIN

I COLORED THE END OF MY TOOTHPICK RED SO
I COULD TELL IT FROM THE OTHERS AND I PUT A
TINY GRAY DOT RIGHT IN THE MIDDLE. THE GRAY
DOT IS SCOTT CAREY. I'M THE ONE IN CHARGE OF
COLORING EVERYONE'S TOOTHPICKS SO THAT
EACH ONE IS DIFFERENT.

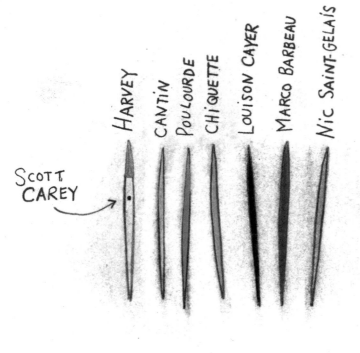

SCOTT
CAREY

HARVEY
CANTIN
POULOURDE
CHIQUETTE
LOUISON CAYER
MARCO BARBEAU
NIC SAINT-GELAIS

HERE, CANTIN. HERE'S YOUR BOAT. IT'S BLUE. DON'T LOSE SIGHT OF IT.

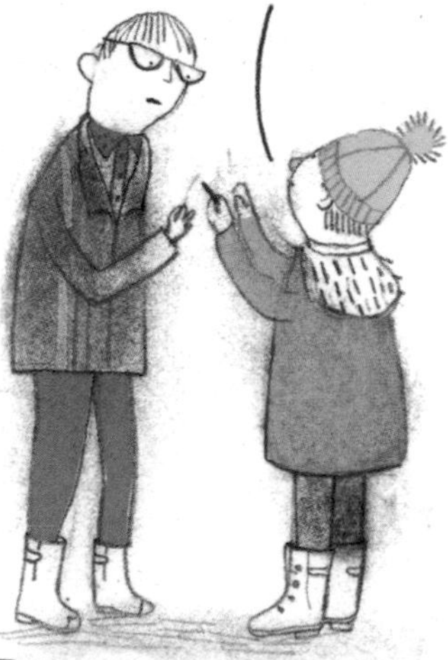

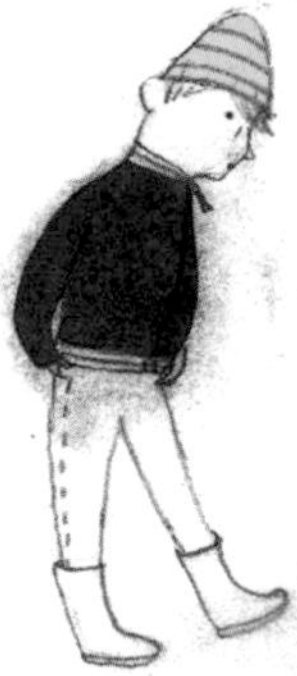

HE DIDN'T ANSWER BUT HE LOOKED AT ME AS THOUGH I THOUGHT HE WAS AN IDIOT. IT COULD BE.

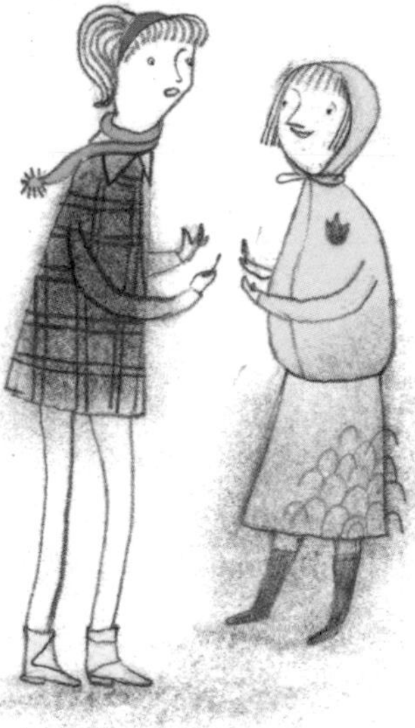

POULOURDE AND CHIQUETTE WANTED TO TRADE BOATS, SO THEY DID AND THEN WE GOT STARTED.

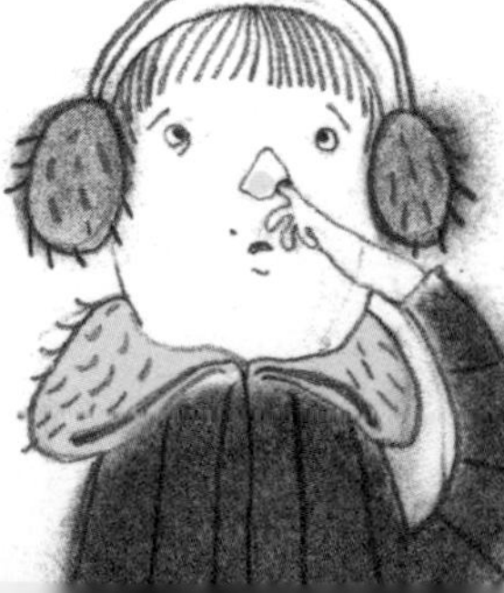

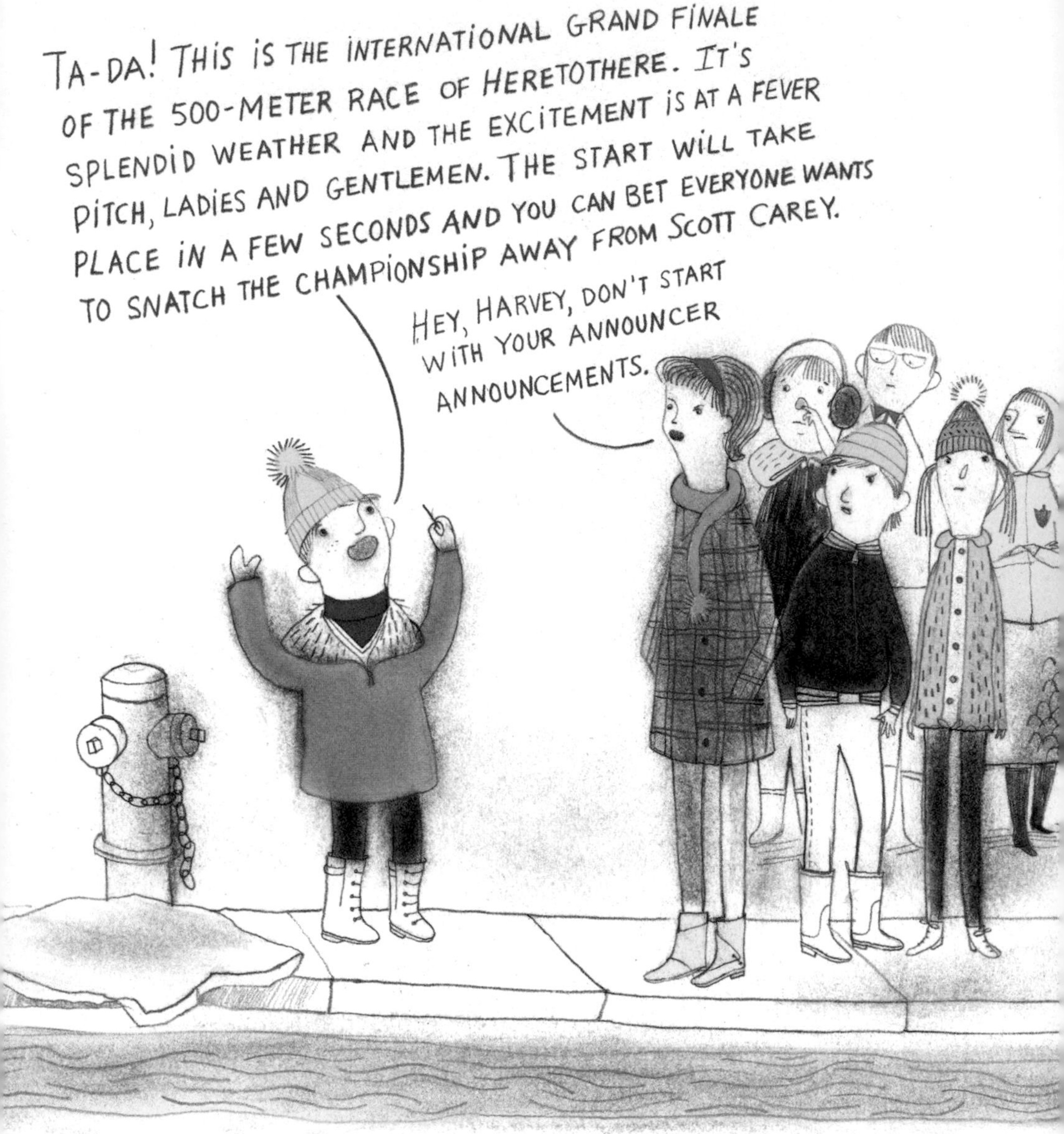
TA-DA! THIS IS THE INTERNATIONAL GRAND FINALE OF THE 500-METER RACE OF HERETOTHERE. IT'S SPLENDID WEATHER AND THE EXCITEMENT IS AT A FEVER PITCH, LADIES AND GENTLEMEN. THE START WILL TAKE PLACE IN A FEW SECONDS AND YOU CAN BET EVERYONE WANTS TO SNATCH THE CHAMPIONSHIP AWAY FROM SCOTT CAREY.
HEY, HARVEY, DON'T START WITH YOUR ANNOUNCER ANNOUNCEMENTS.

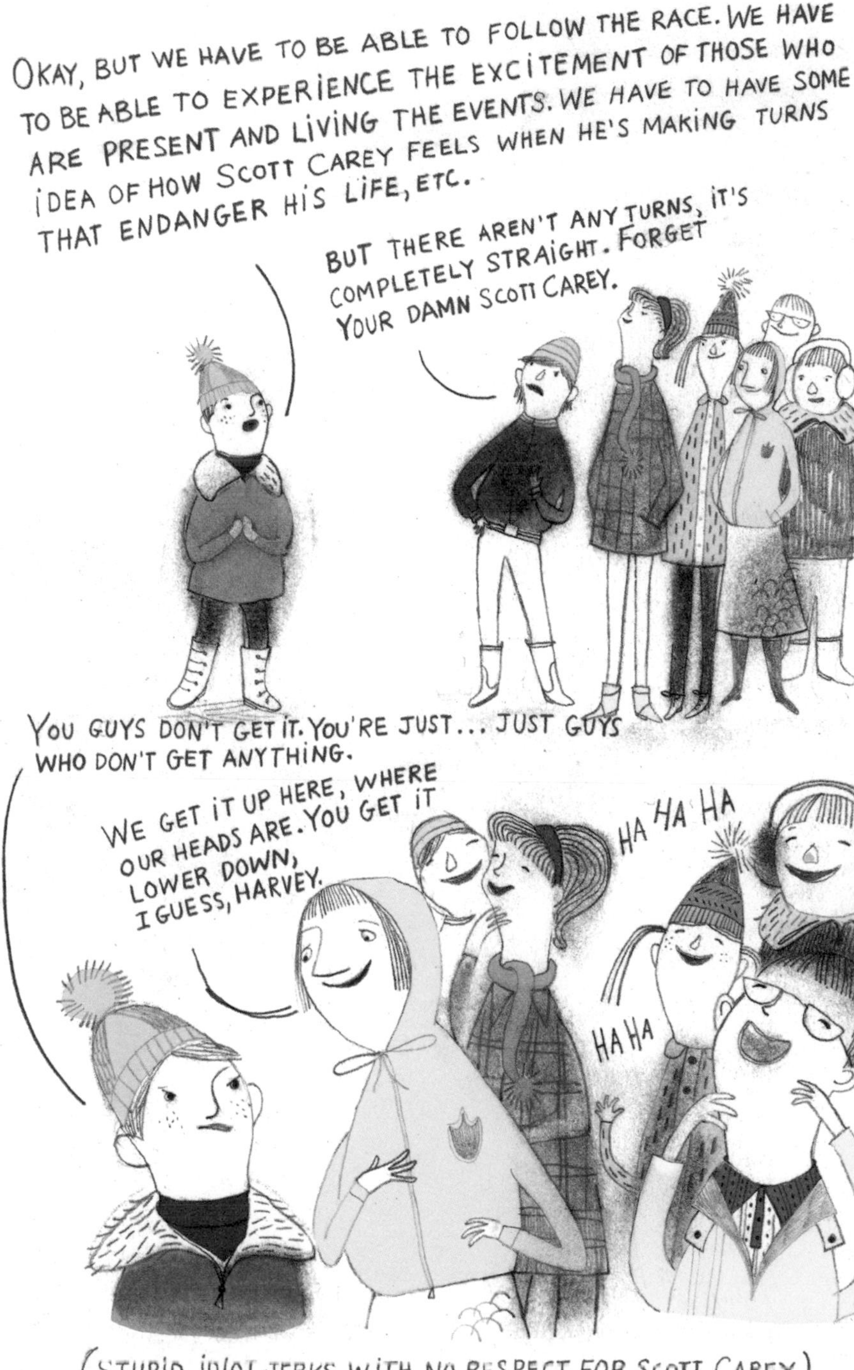
OKAY, BUT WE HAVE TO BE ABLE TO FOLLOW THE RACE. WE HAVE TO BE ABLE TO EXPERIENCE THE EXCITEMENT OF THOSE WHO ARE PRESENT AND LIVING THE EVENTS. WE HAVE TO HAVE SOME IDEA OF HOW SCOTT CAREY FEELS WHEN HE'S MAKING TURNS THAT ENDANGER HIS LIFE, ETC.
BUT THERE AREN'T ANY TURNS, IT'S COMPLETELY STRAIGHT. FORGET YOUR DAMN SCOTT CAREY.
YOU GUYS DON'T GET IT. YOU'RE JUST... JUST GUYS WHO DON'T GET ANYTHING.
WE GET IT UP HERE, WHERE OUR HEADS ARE. YOU GET IT LOWER DOWN, I GUESS, HARVEY.
HA HA HA
HA HA
(STUPID IDIOT JERKS WITH NO RESPECT FOR SCOTT CAREY.)

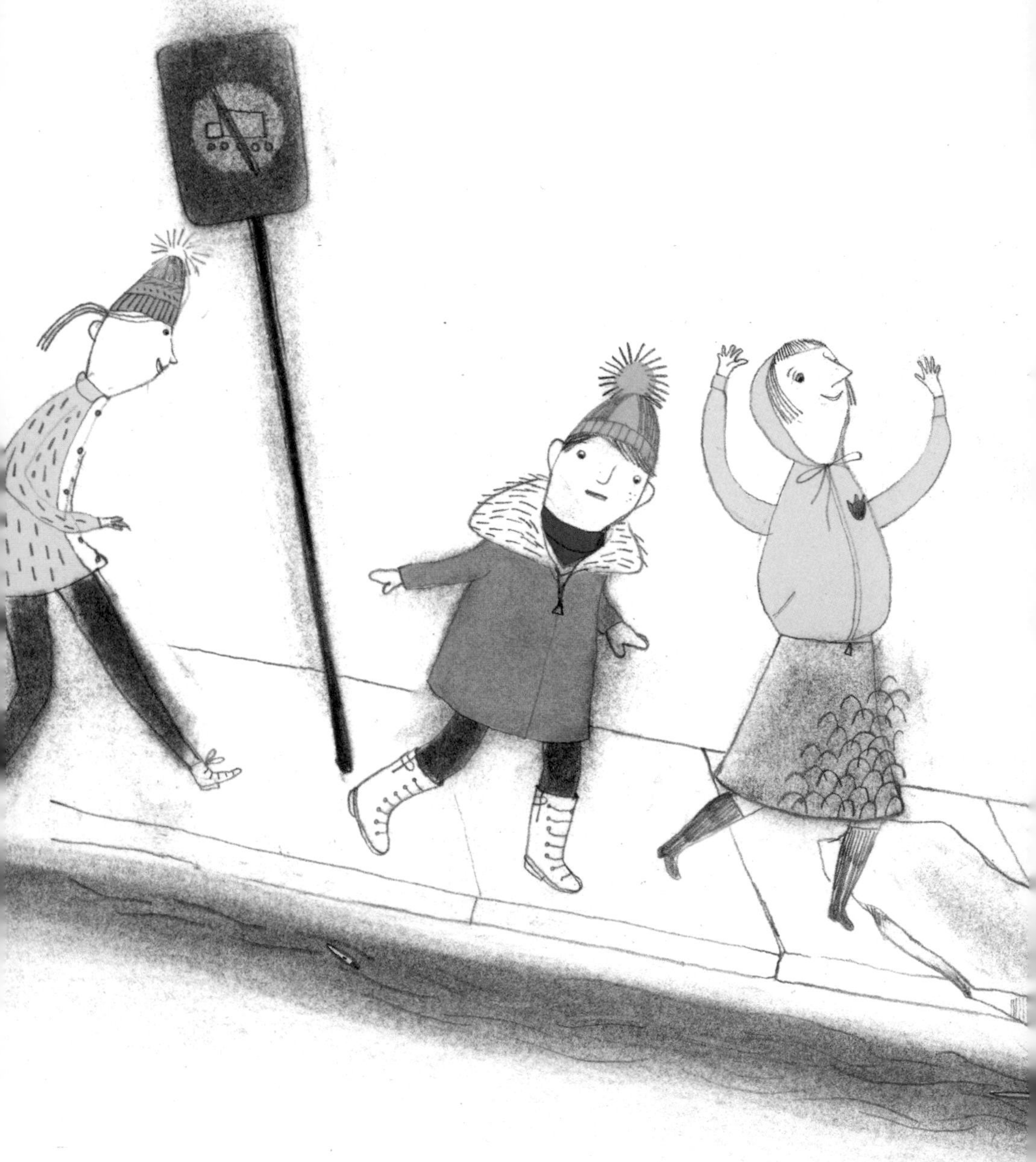

THE RACE BEGAN UNDER A MAGNIFICENT APRIL SUN.

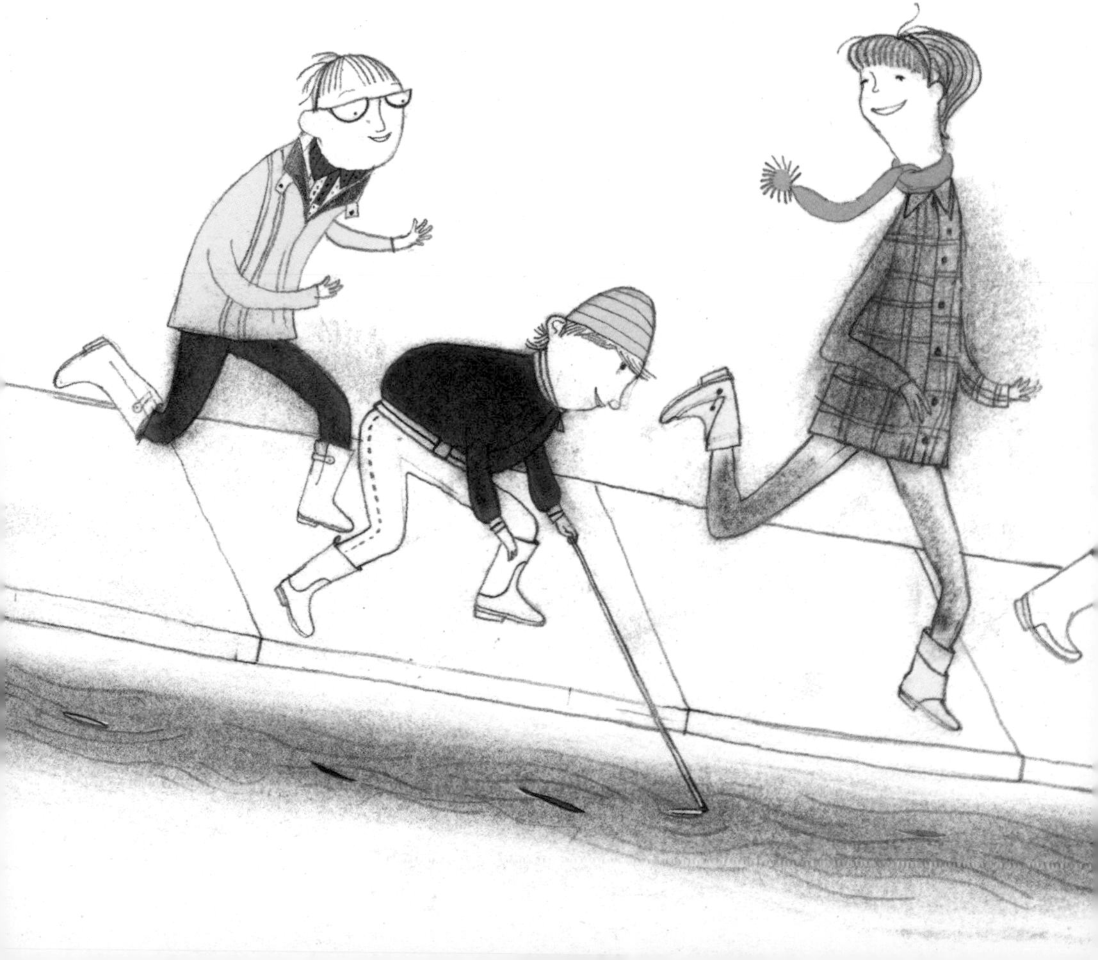

ALL SEVEN OF US FOLLOWED IT TO THE END.

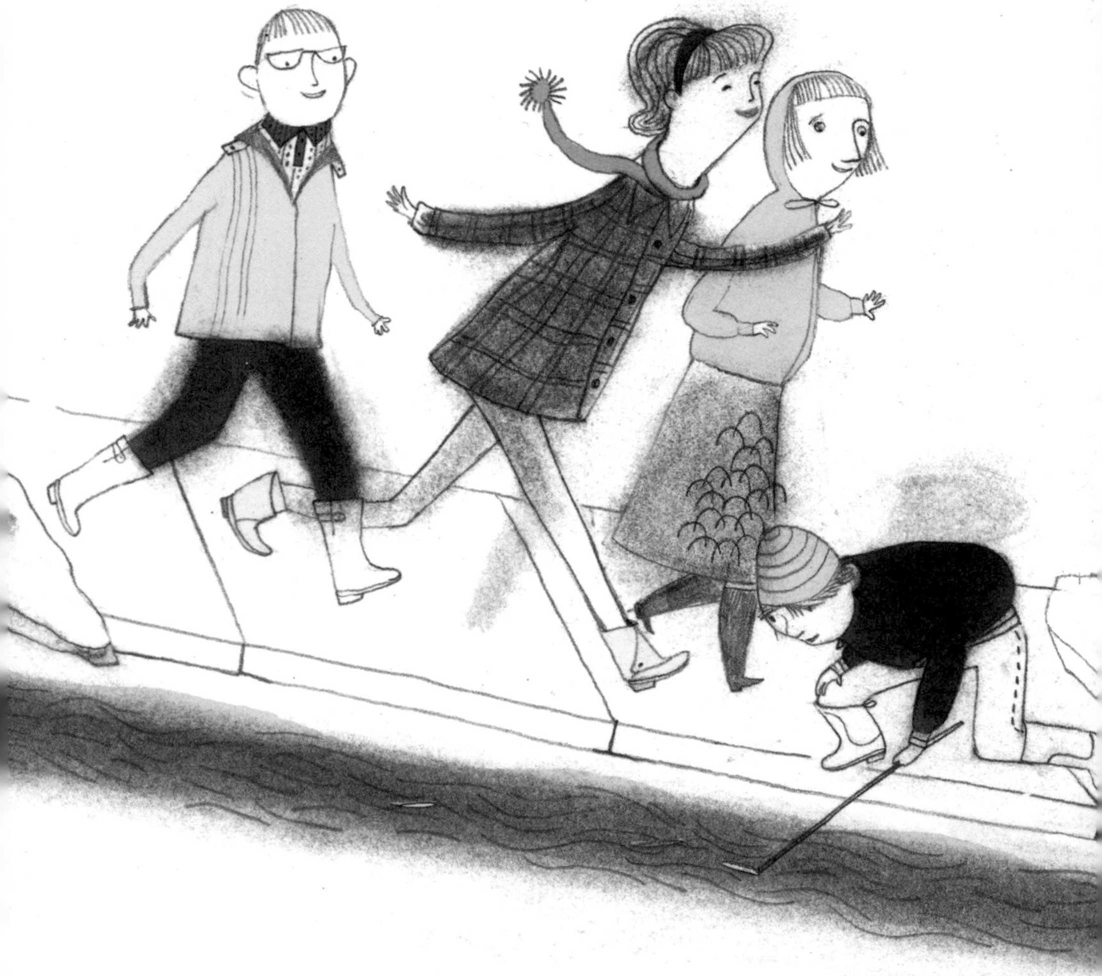

I ANNOUNCED THE RACE INSIDE MY HEAD JUST FOR ME, MAKING SCOTT CAREY LOOK GOOD.

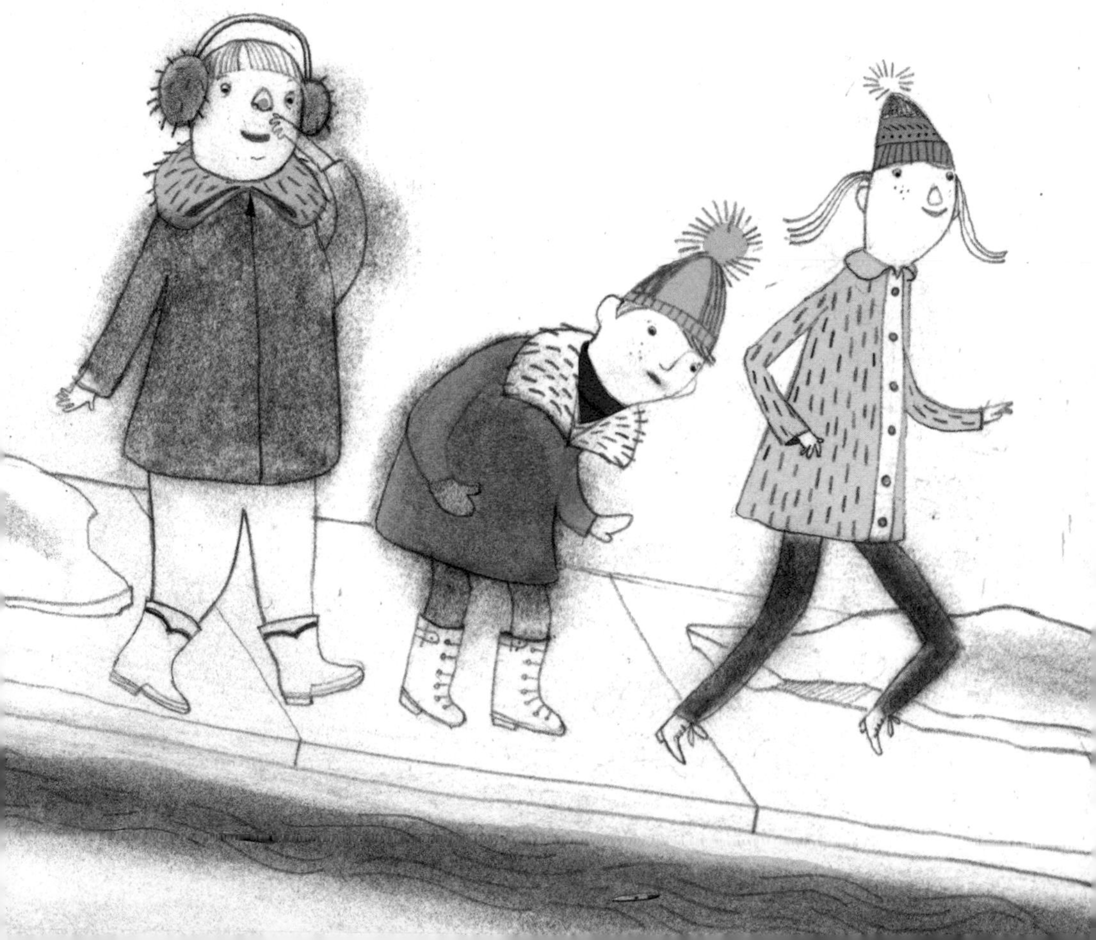

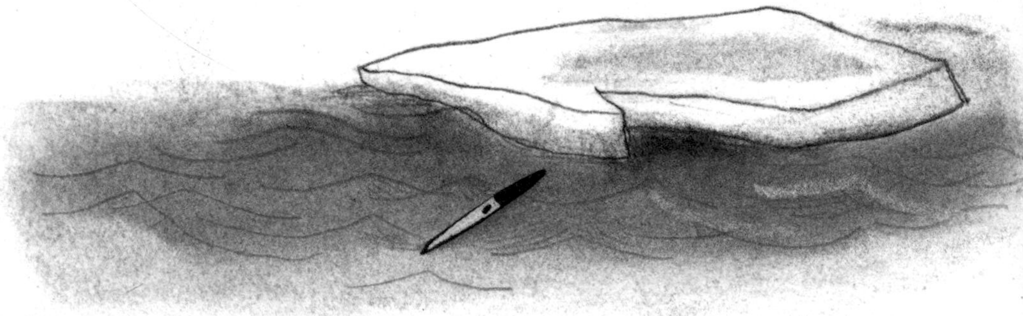

BUT ACTUALLY THE RACE DIDN'T GO SO WELL FOR HIM. HE HAD TROUBLE CONTROLLING HIS BOAT.

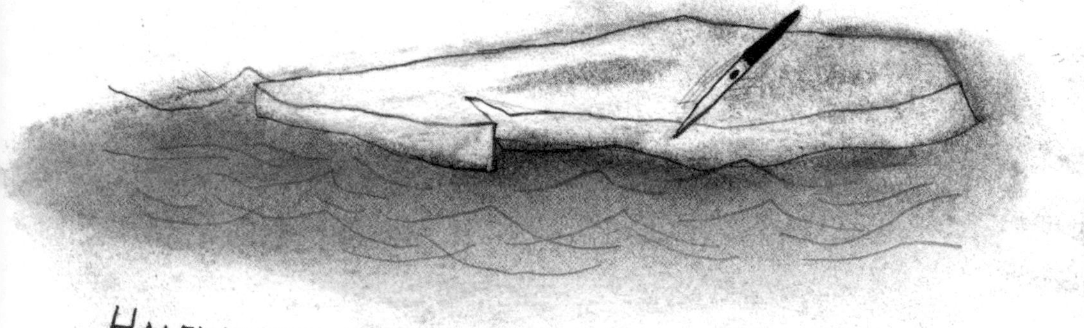

HALFWAY THROUGH, IN FRONT OF CHEZ LALANCETTE, HE STOPPED FOR QUITE A WHILE, HIS WHOLE HULL STUCK ON A CHUNK OF ICE. IF HE COULD HAVE GOTTEN OFF HIS SHIP TO LIFT IT UP AND FREE IT, HE WOULD HAVE.

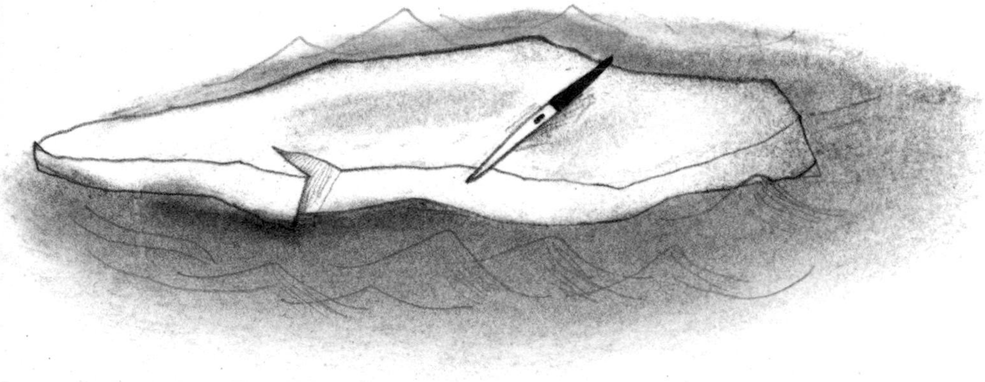

BUT THE CURRENT WAS VERY STRONG THERE,
AND HE THOUGHT IT WOULD BE TOO DANGEROUS.

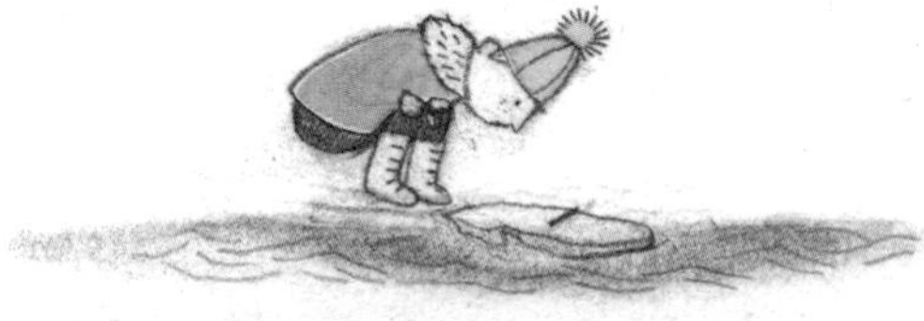

AFTER A WHILE THE BOAT SLID OFF THE ICE FLOE BY ITSELF, AND THE REST OF THE RACE TOOK PLACE WITH NO MORE PROBLEMS.

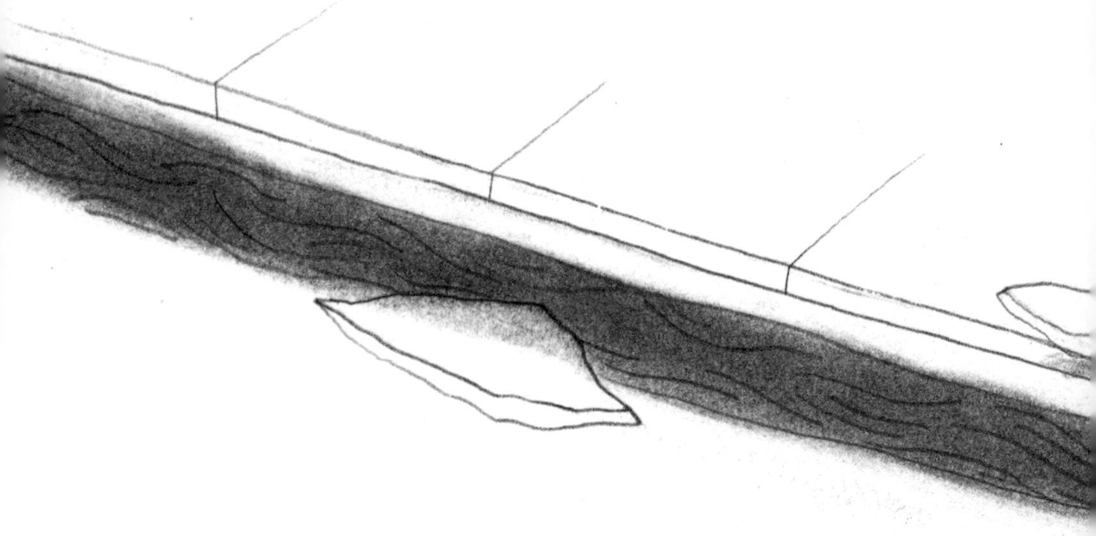

AT THE BOTTOM OF RUE TREMBLAY, THE OTHERS HAD ALREADY LEFT, EXCEPT FOR MY BROTHER CANTIN, WHO WAS WAITING FOR ME. TOGETHER WE WATCHED SCOTT CAREY PLUNGE INTO THE DRAIN, AND THEN WE HEADED HOME.

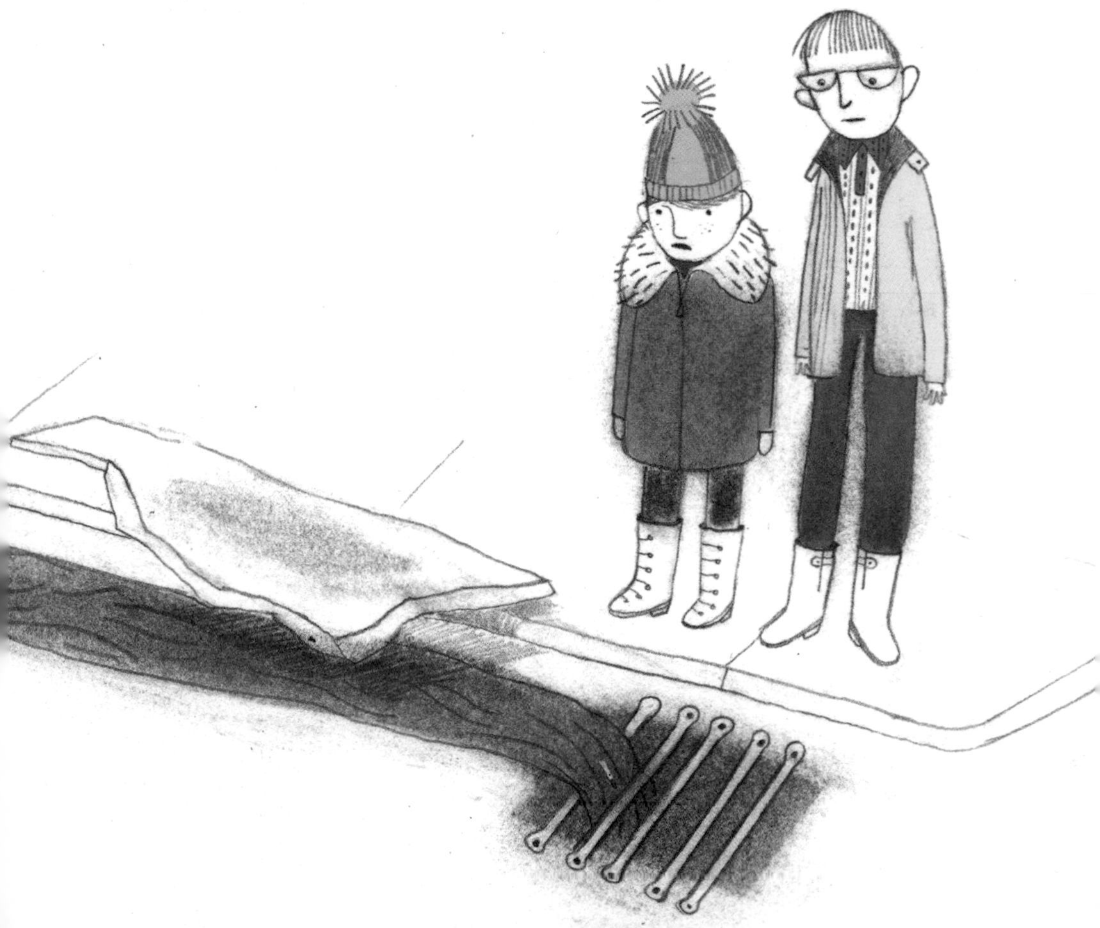

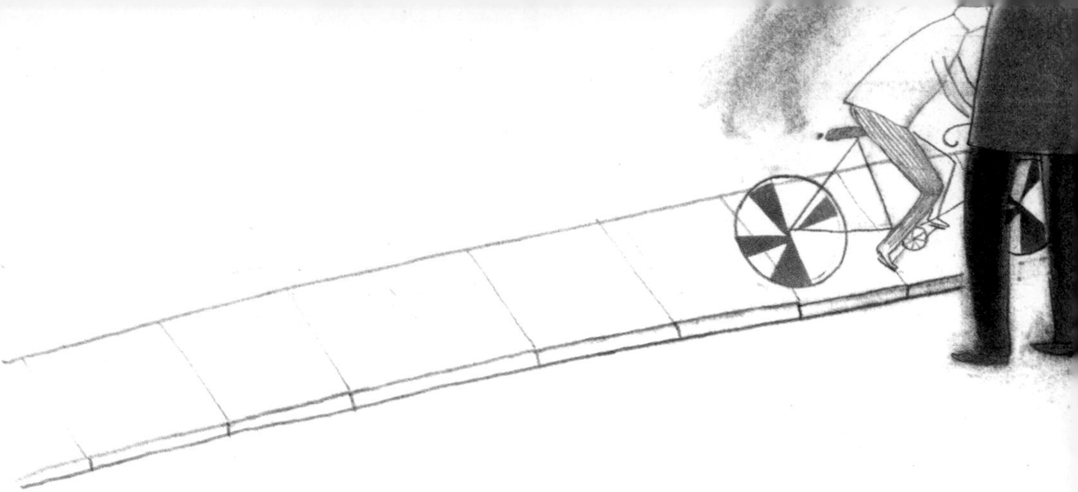

THERE WERE TONS OF PEOPLE ON THE STREET IN FRONT OF OUR HOUSE. WHEN I SAW THEM ALL I FELT THAT SOMETHING WAS HAPPENING.

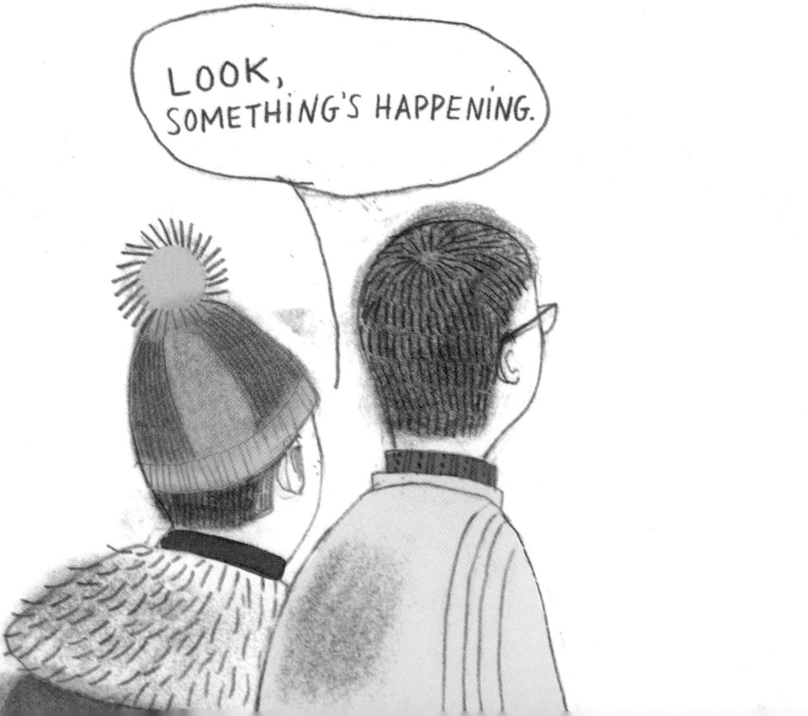
LOOK, SOMETHING'S HAPPENING.

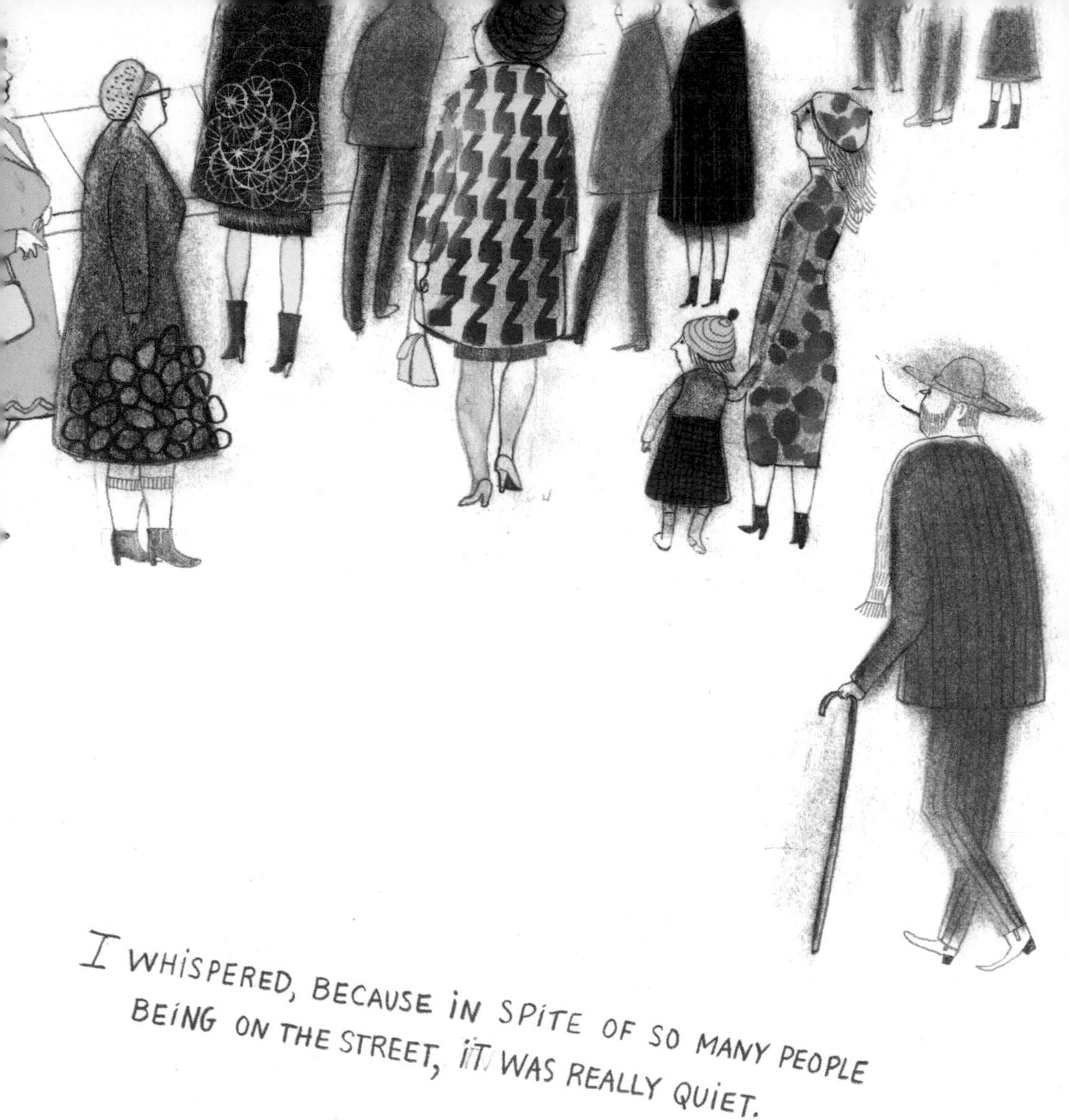

I WHISPERED, BECAUSE IN SPITE OF SO MANY PEOPLE BEING ON THE STREET, IT WAS REALLY QUIET.

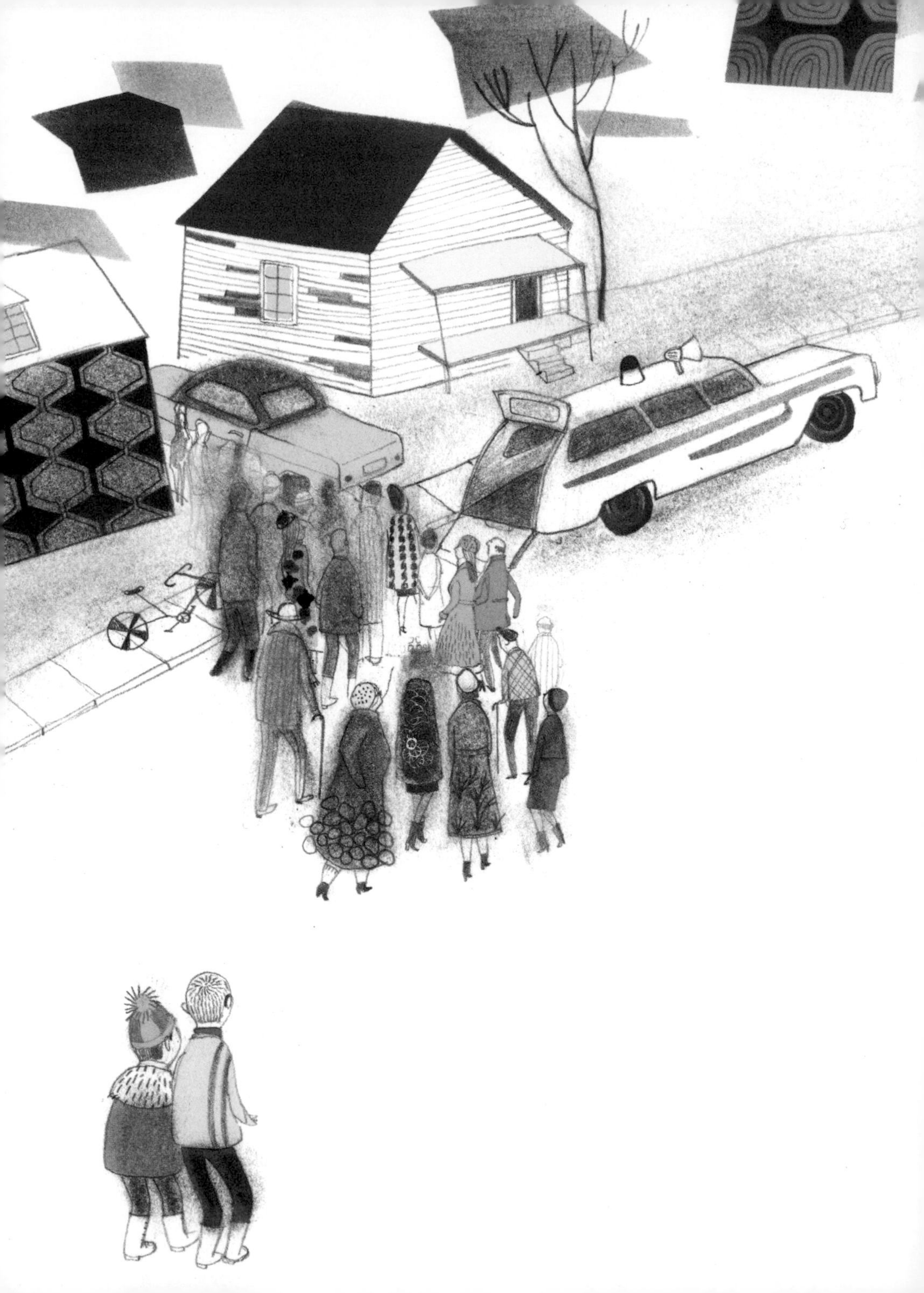

AN AMBULANCE STOOD IN FRONT OF THE HOUSE WITH
ITS LIGHT FLASHING. I MADE THE SOUND OF A SIREN
IN MY HEAD. AND AS IF HE HAD HEARD ME, CANTIN MADE
THE SOUND, TOO, BUT OUT LOUD. THAT WAS KIND OF
CREEPY. THERE WERE OTHER CARS I DIDN'T RECOGNIZE
AND STRANGERS STANDING AROUND WATCHING.

THE CHIQUETTES SAT ON THEIR PORCH
ACROSS THE STREET.

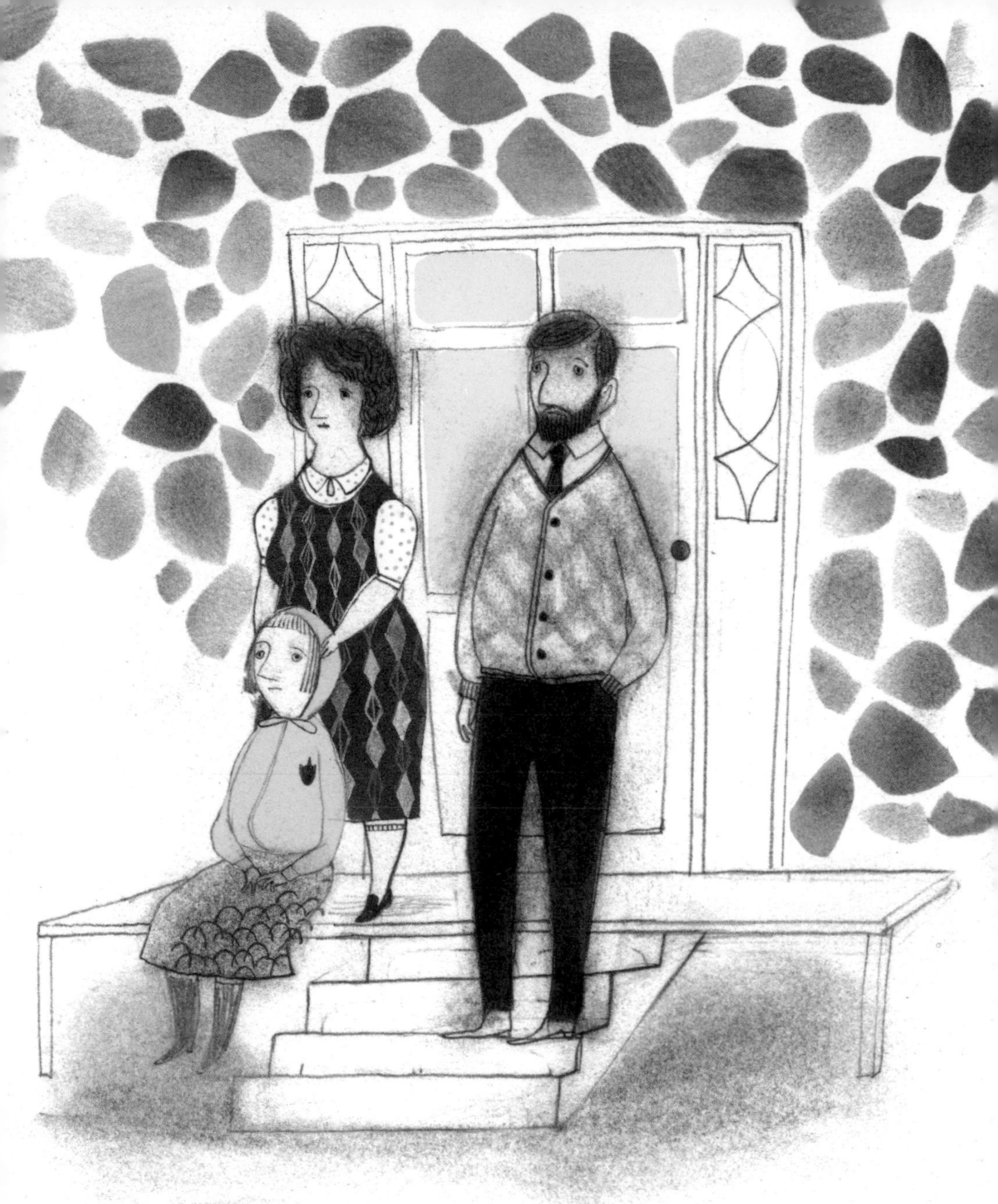

I SAW MOTHER CAYER WITH LOUISON.

BARBEAU HAD ALREADY GOTTEN OUT HIS BIKE.

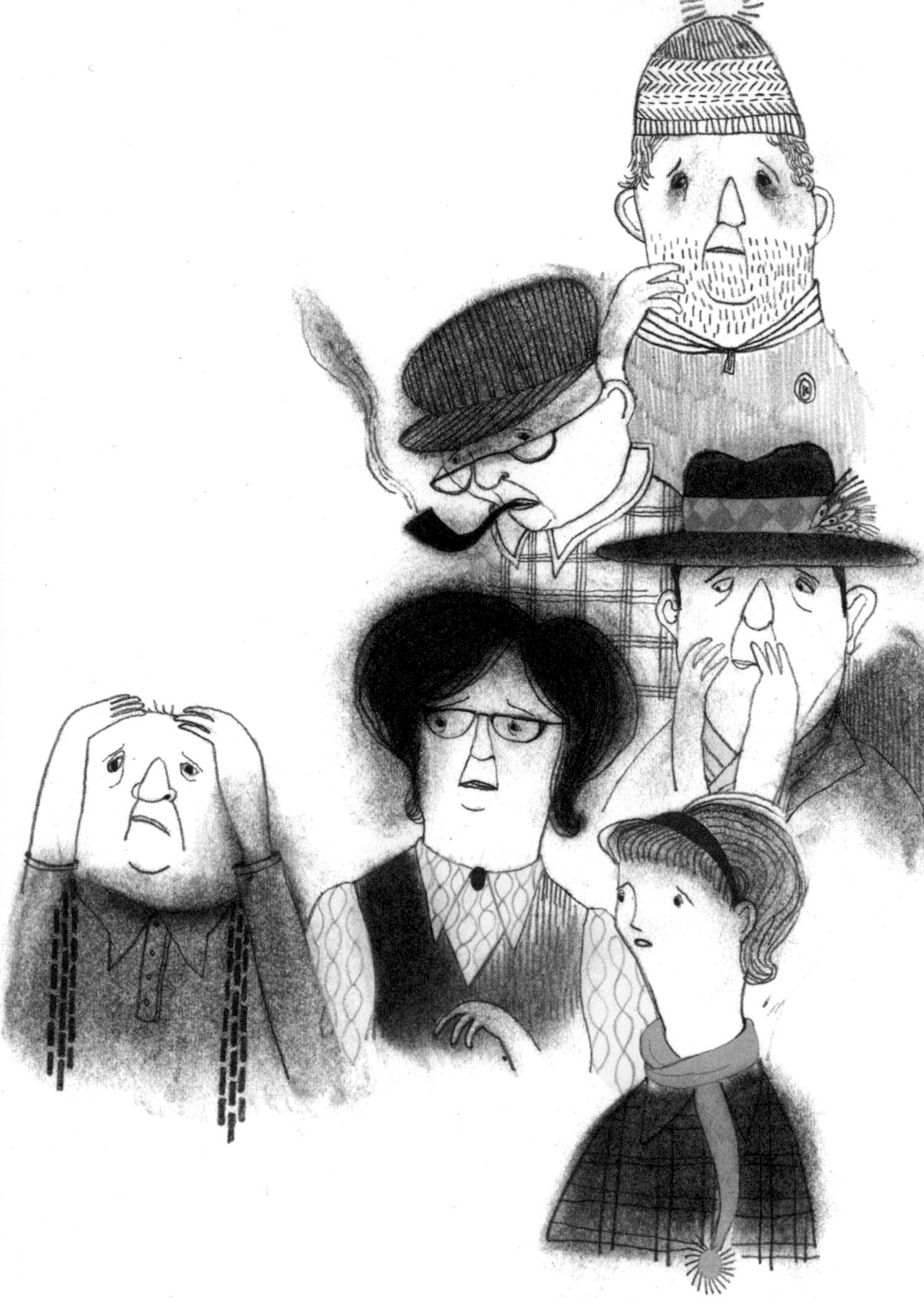

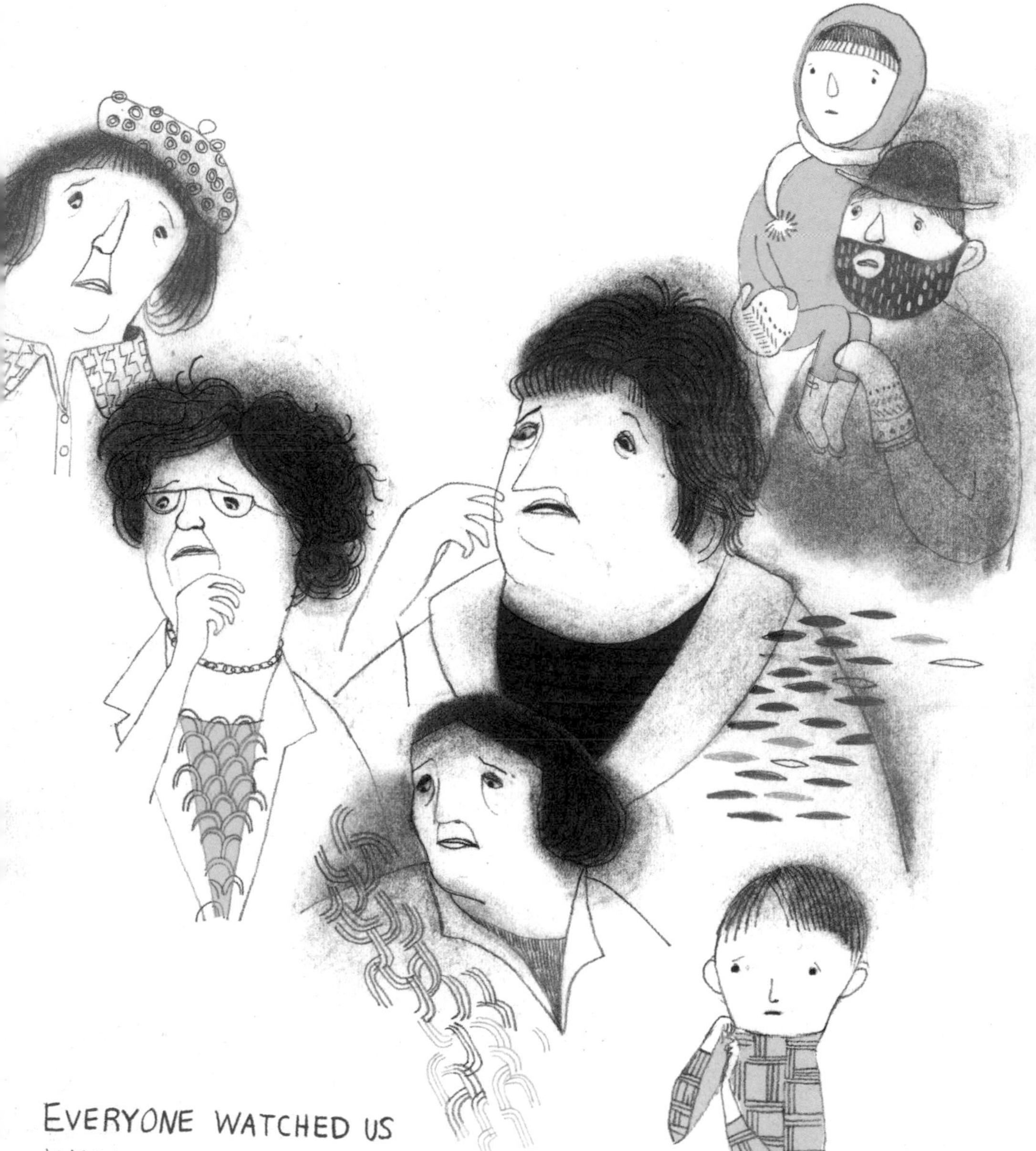

EVERYONE WATCHED US
WALK UP.

WE WERE WALKING UP THE SIDEWALK BESIDE OUR DRIVEWAY, BUT THE PRIEST WAS STANDING THERE IN THE MIDDLE. HE STOPPED US.

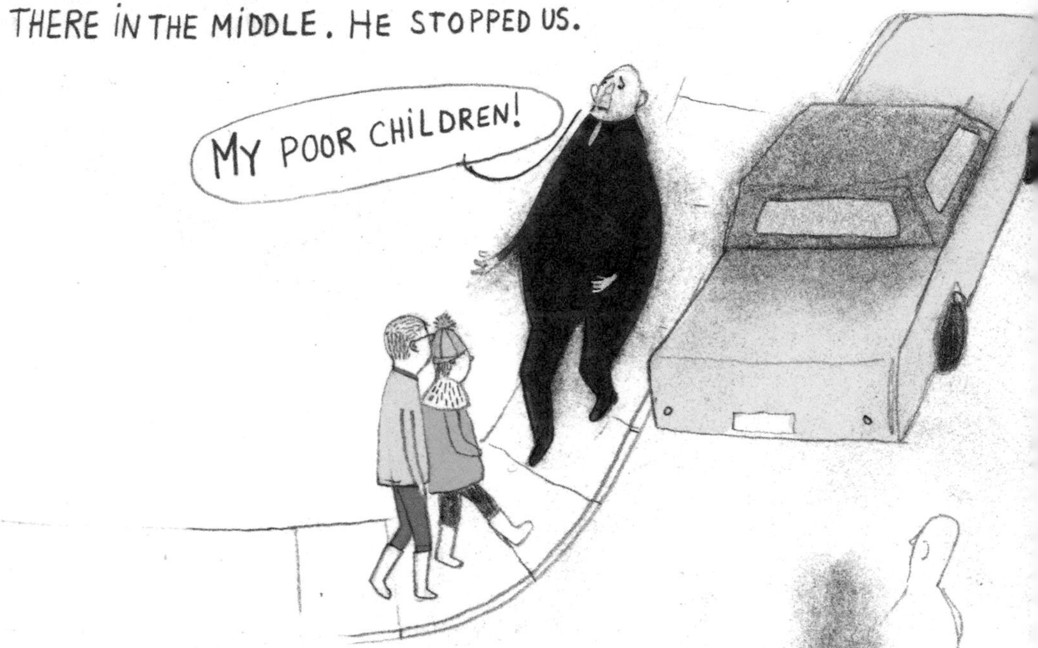
MY POOR CHILDREN!

WE KNEW HIM. IT WAS THE PRIEST.

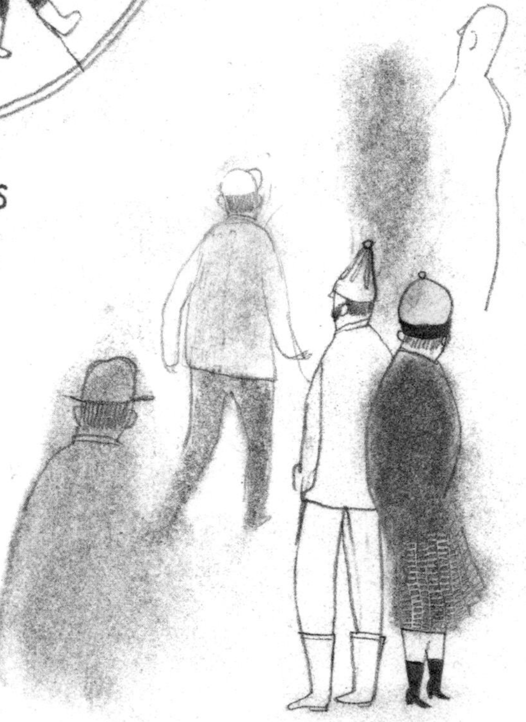

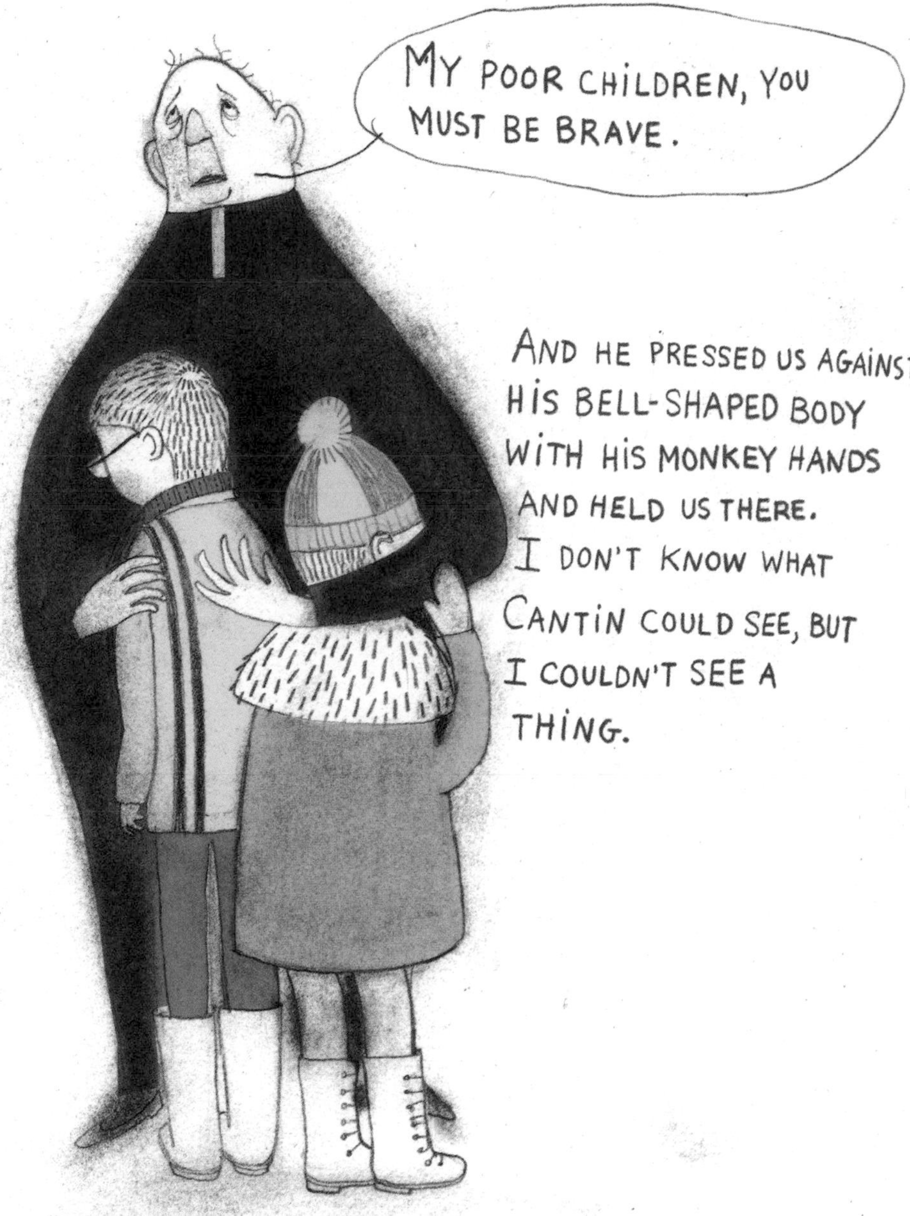

AND HE PRESSED US AGAINST HIS BELL-SHAPED BODY WITH HIS MONKEY HANDS AND HELD US THERE. I DON'T KNOW WHAT CANTIN COULD SEE, BUT I COULDN'T SEE A THING.

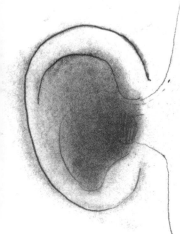

I HEARD OUR DOOR OPEN
WITH A CRASH AND THEN MY MOTHER
BOUILLON CALLING OUT THE NAME OF
MY FATHER BOUILLON. AND I HEARD
A THUMPING DOWN THE WOODEN
PORCH STEPS AND SOMETHING ROLLING
ALONG THE WALK RIGHT BESIDE US.
AND I HEARD MEN'S VOICES
THAT I DIDN'T RECOGNIZE
AND OTHER SOUNDS OF DOORS.

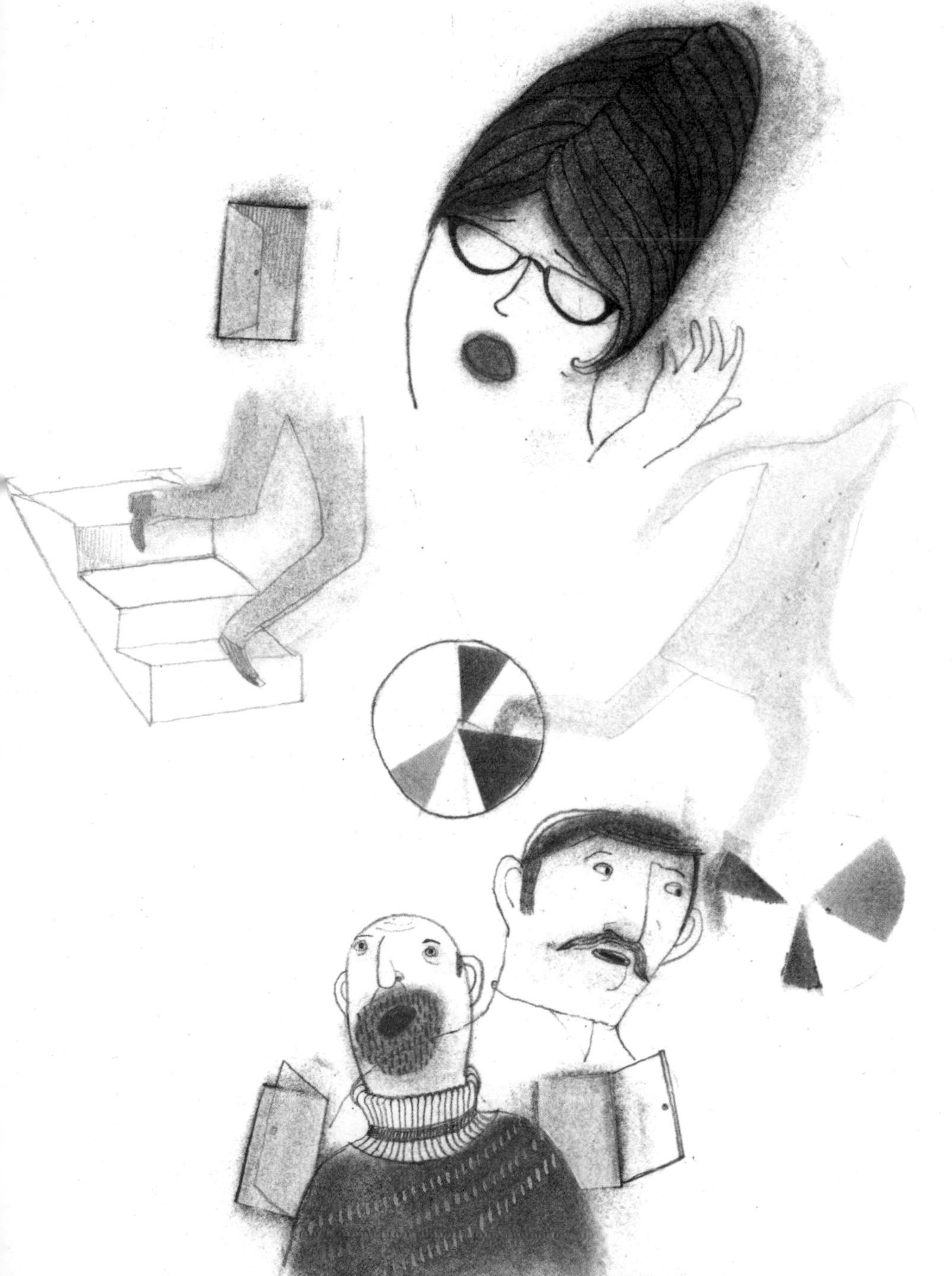

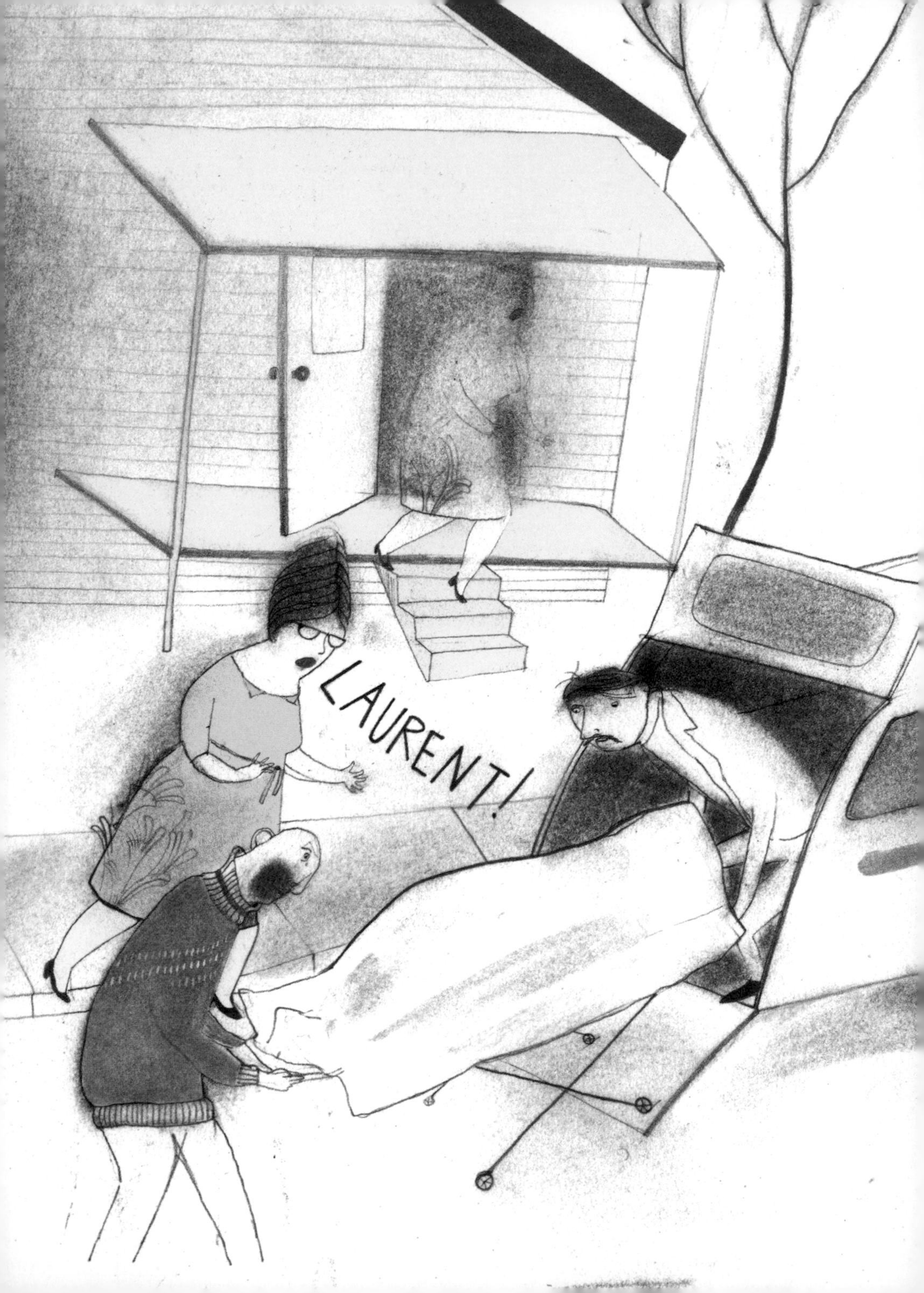
LAURENT!

I MANAGED TO ESCAPE FROM THE PRIEST'S GRIP. I TURNED MY HEAD, AND RIGHT THERE I SAW TWO AMBULANCE GUYS PUTTING A STRETCHER INTO THE AMBULANCE. A BLANKET COMPLETELY COVERED A BODY. MY MOTHER BOUILLON, SHE WAS LIKE A CRAZY WOMAN. SHE WAS SCREAMING MY FATHER'S NAME AS LOUD AS SHE COULD BUT HIM, MY FATHER BOUILLON, WE COULDN'T SEE. AND EVERYONE WAS THERE ON THE STREET IN FRONT OF OUR HOUSE, STARING AT THE GROUND.

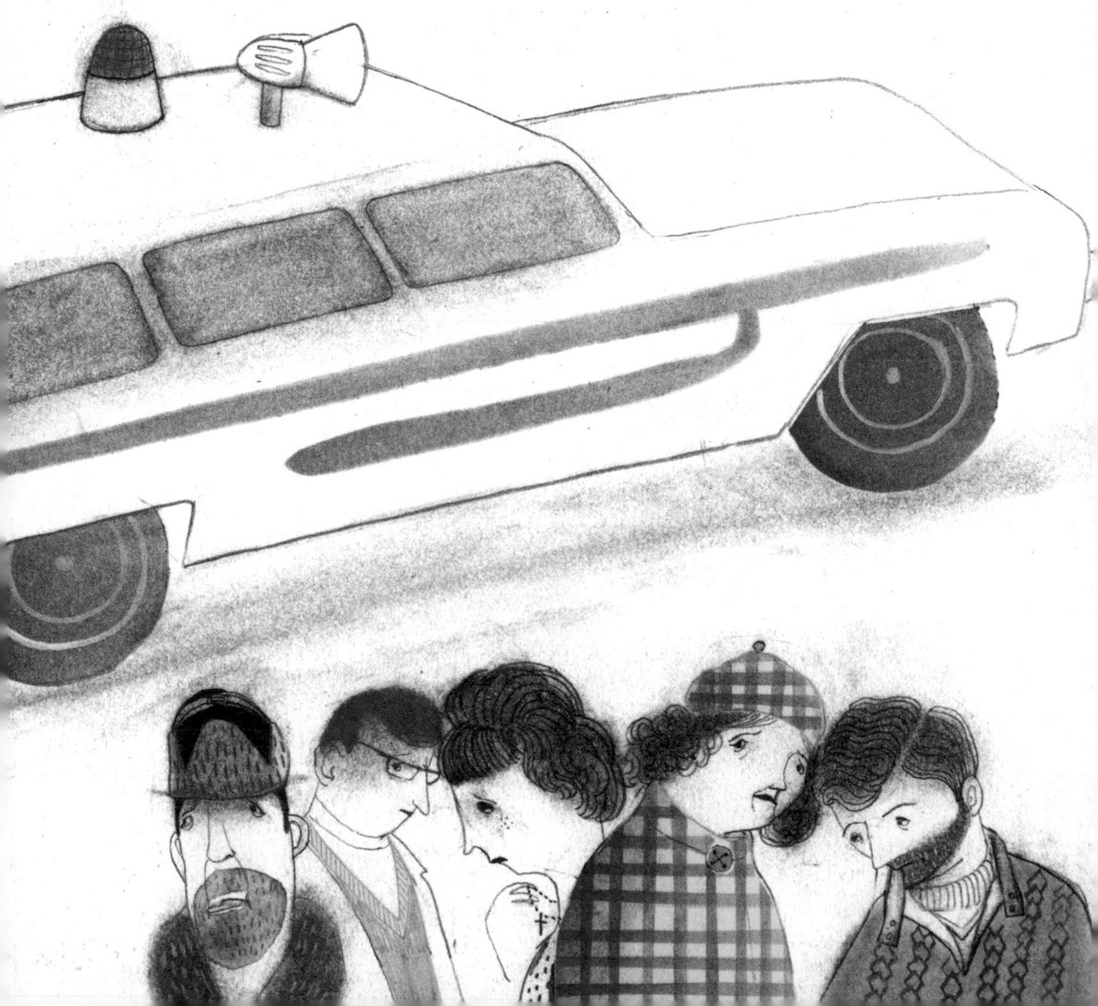

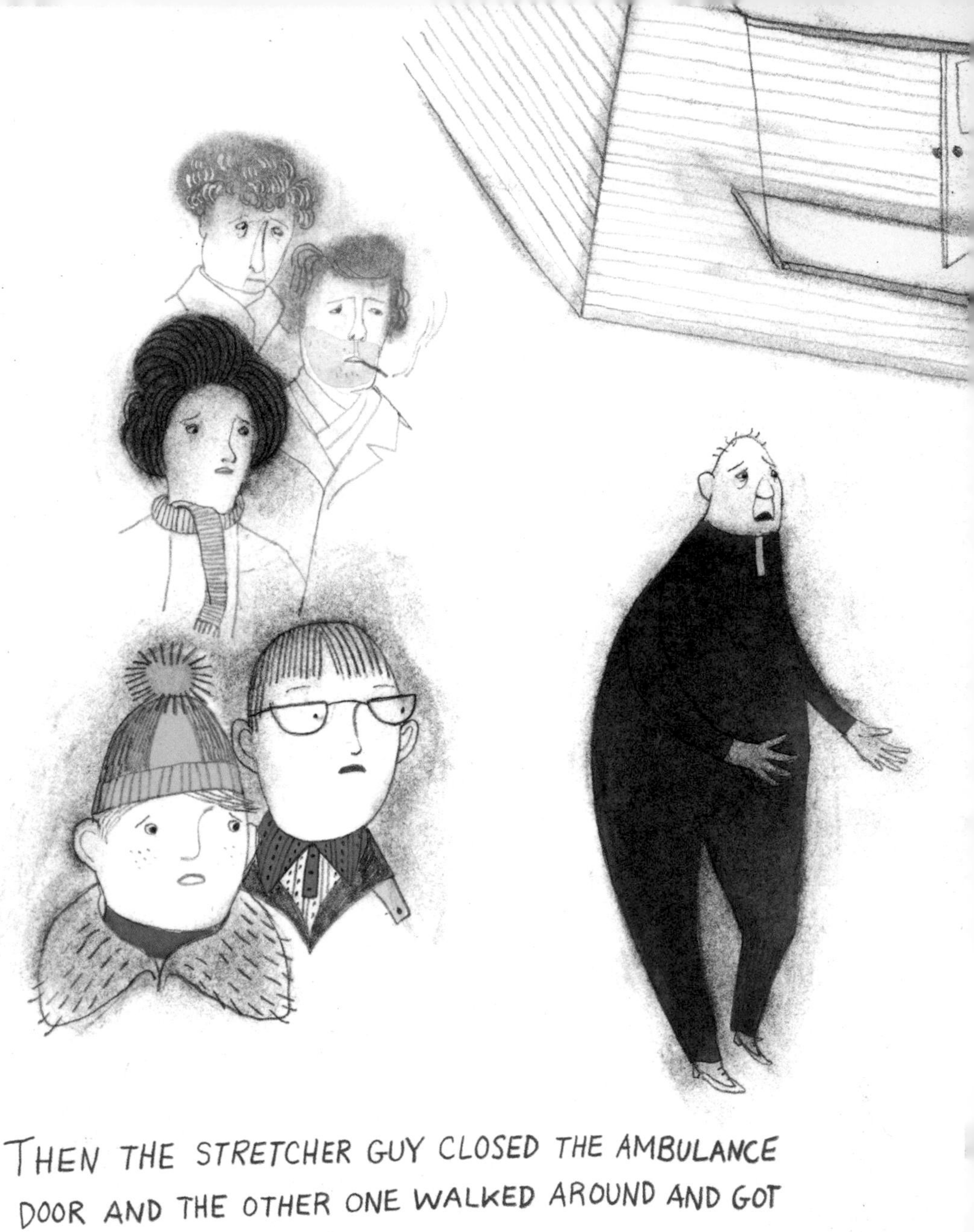

THEN THE STRETCHER GUY CLOSED THE AMBULANCE DOOR AND THE OTHER ONE WALKED AROUND AND GOT IN THE DRIVER'S SEAT.

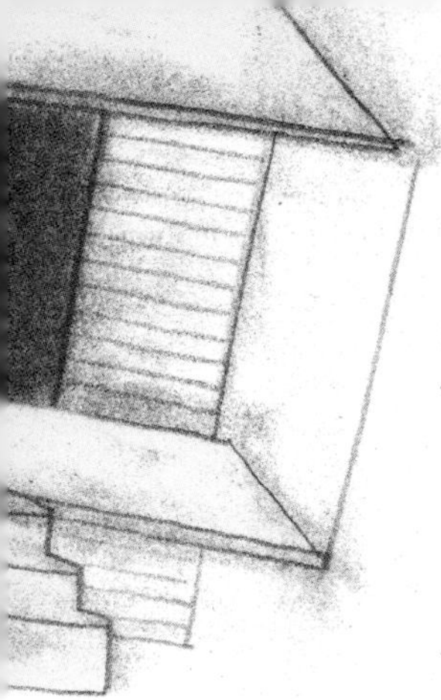

MY MOTHER WENT UP AND BEGAN BANGING ON THE BACK WINDOW OF THE AMBULANCE. IT WASN'T LONG BEFORE WE HEARD THE SIREN. I LOOKED AT MY BROTHER, THEN AT EVERYONE ELSE.

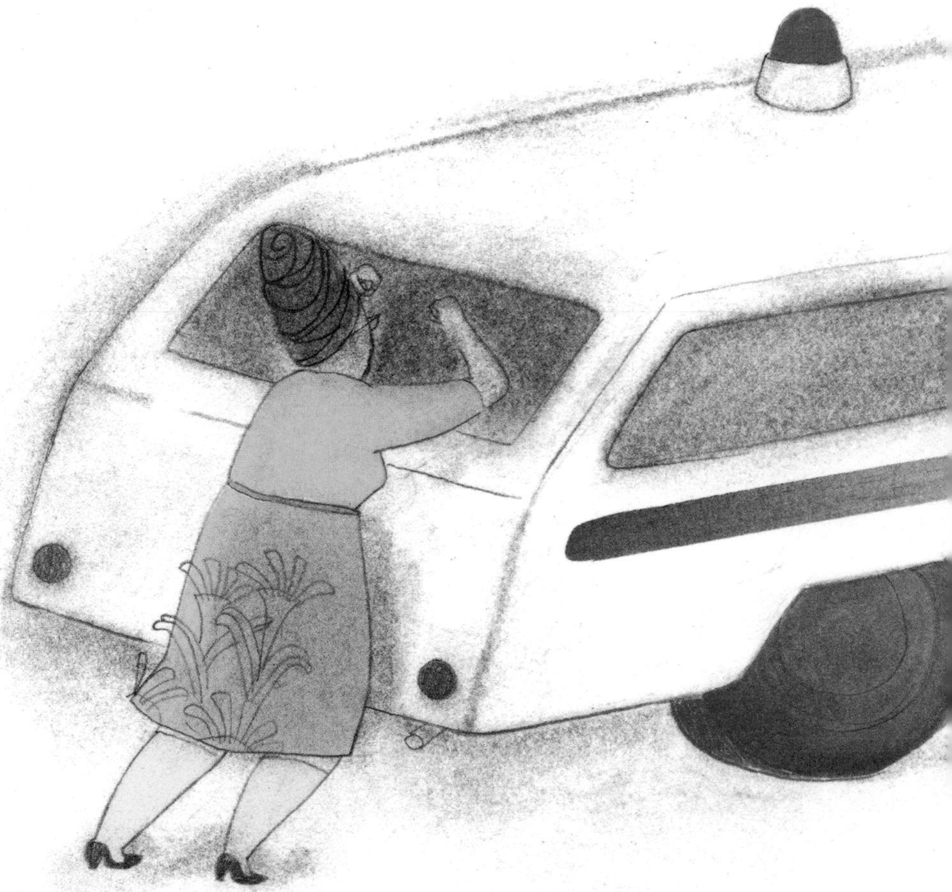

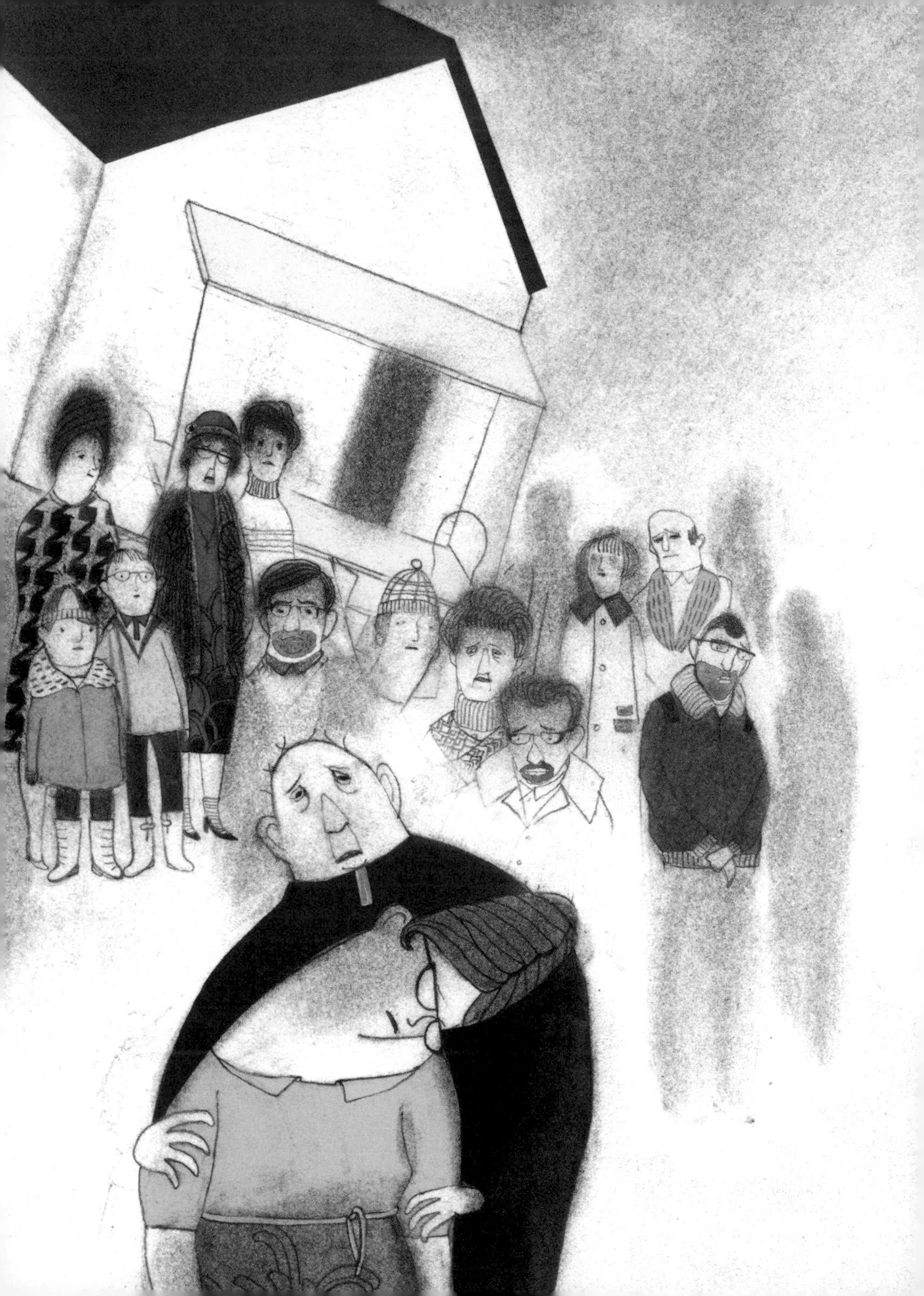

THE AMBULANCE LEFT WITH MY FATHER INSIDE.
MY MOTHER BOUILLON FELL INTO THE PRIEST'S ARMS.

PEOPLE FINALLY BEGAN TO MOVE AWAY.

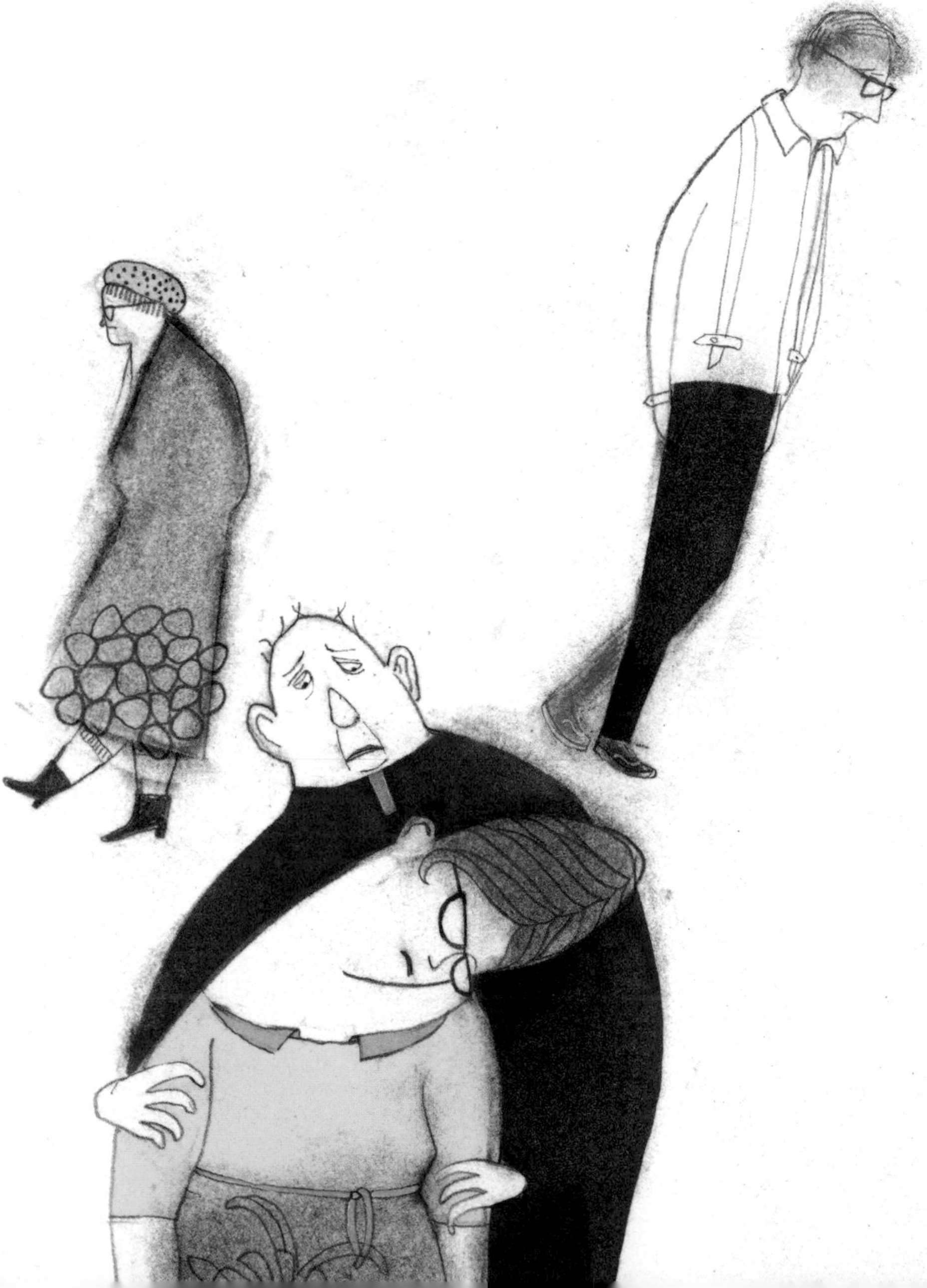

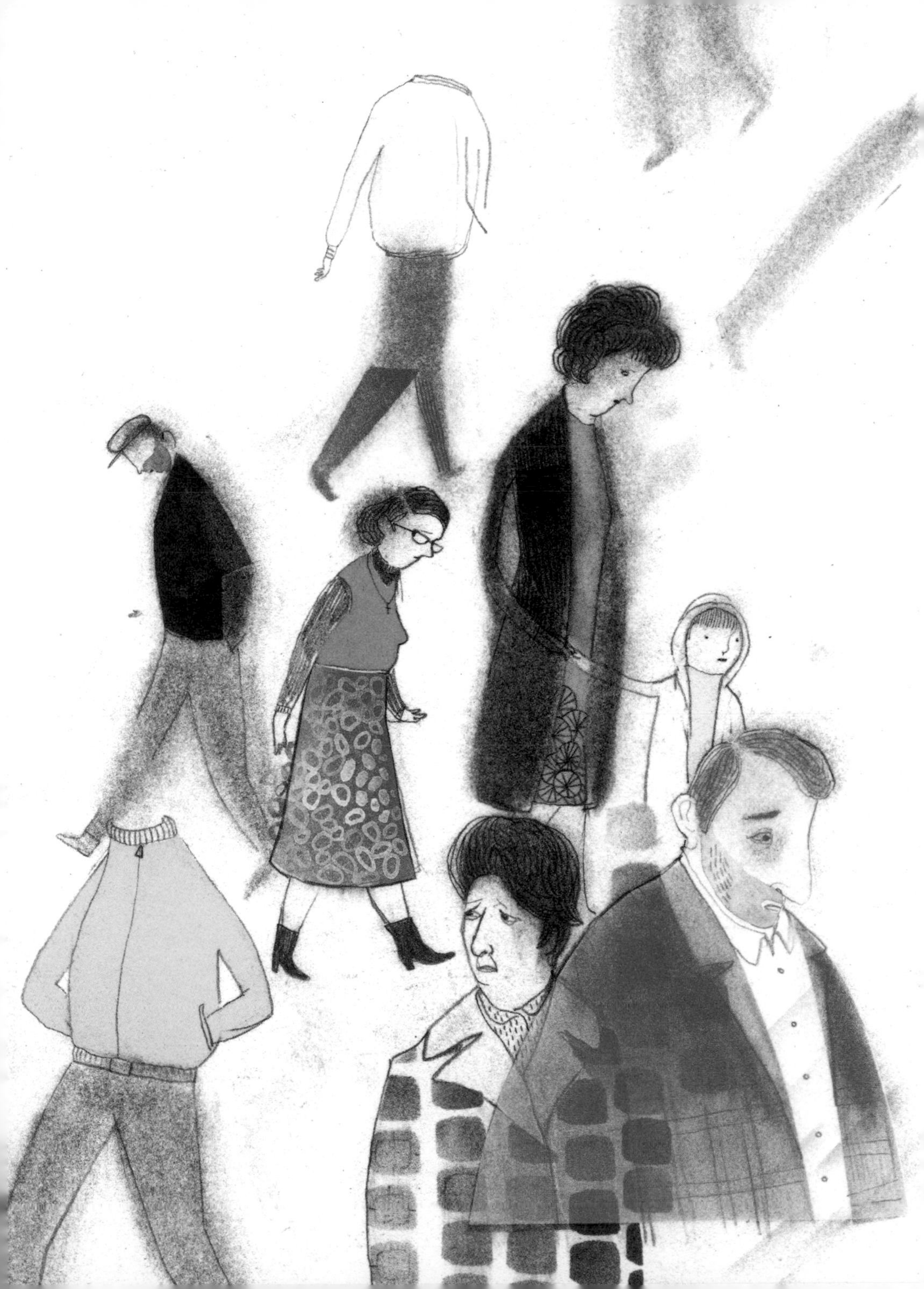

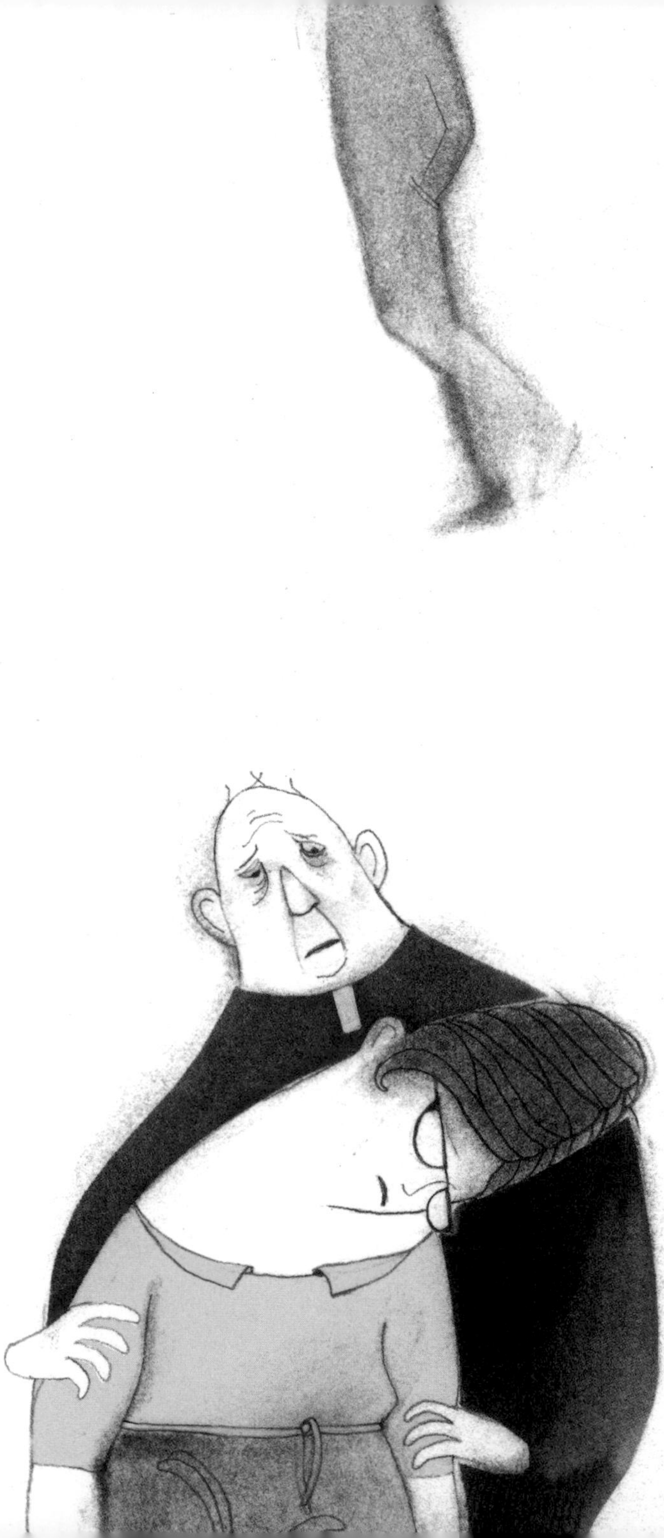

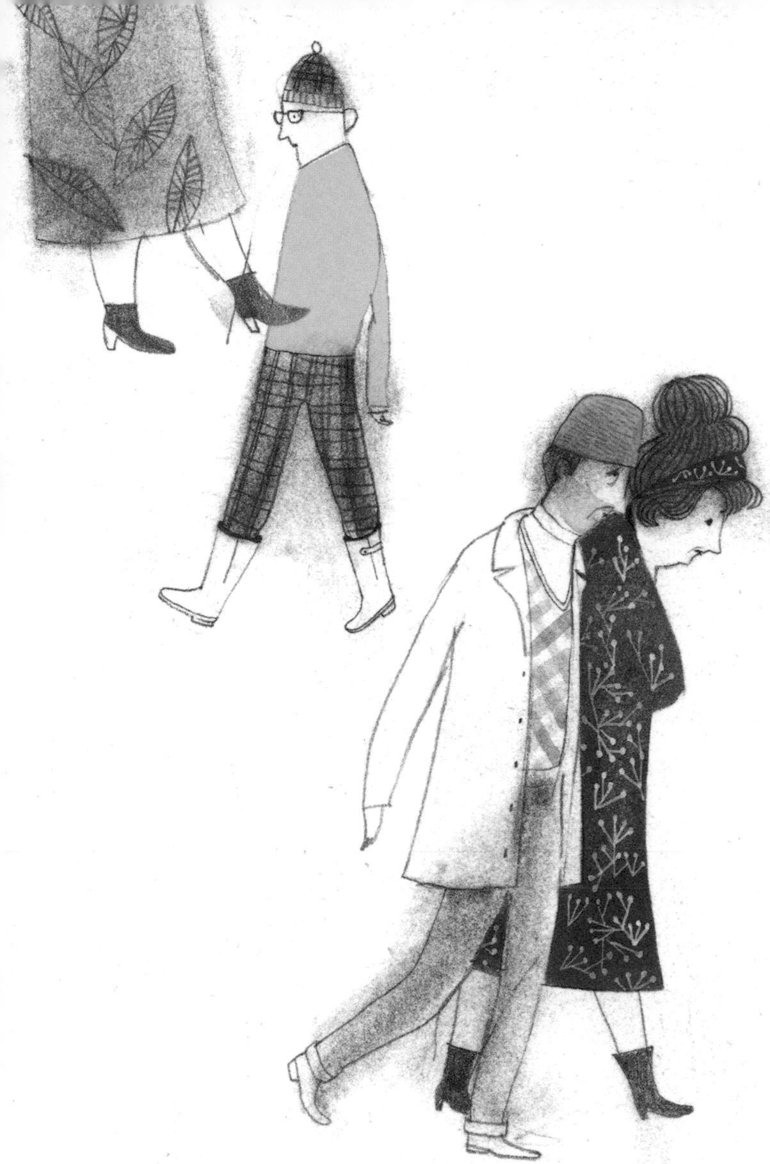

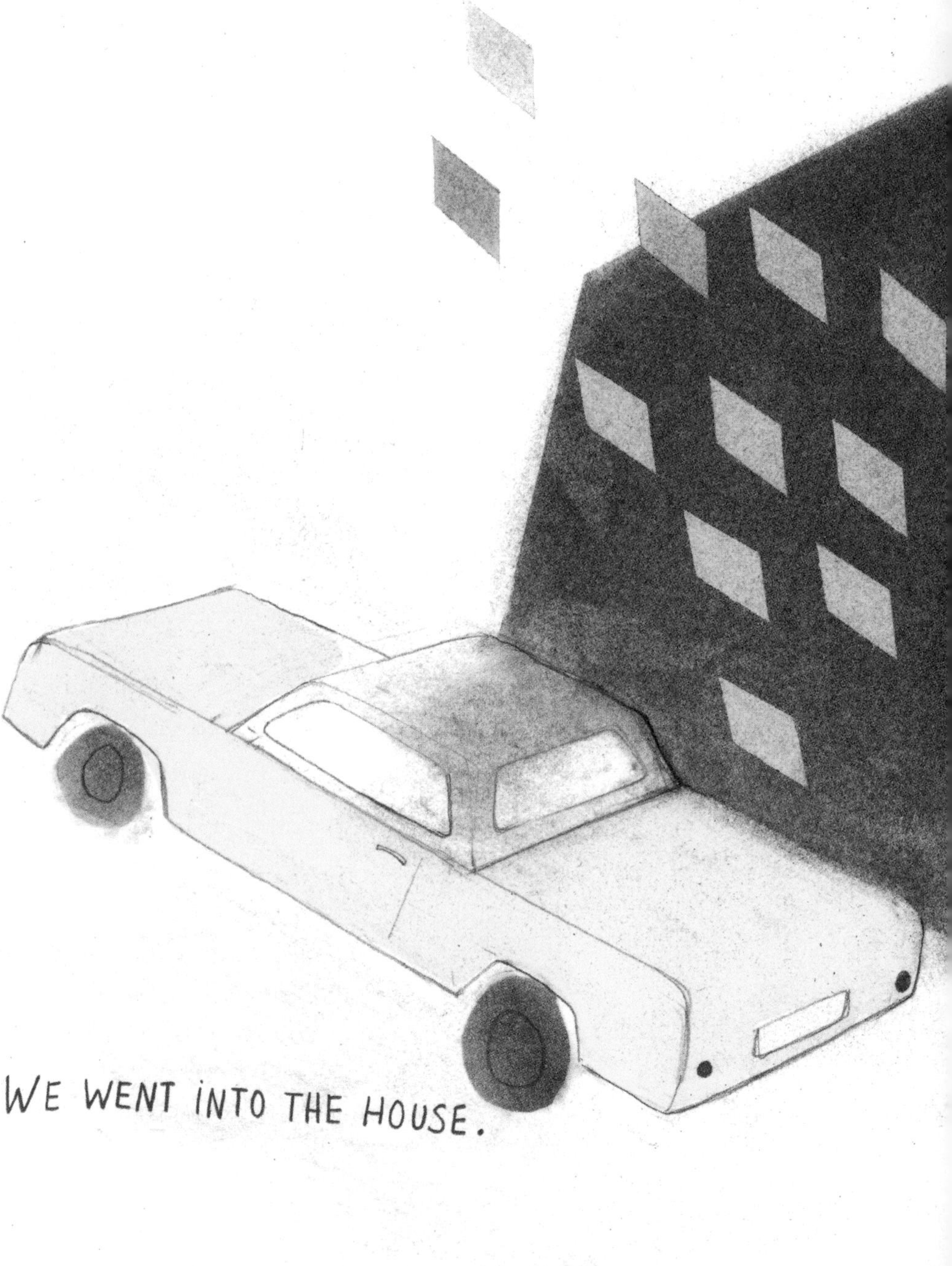
WE WENT INTO THE HOUSE.

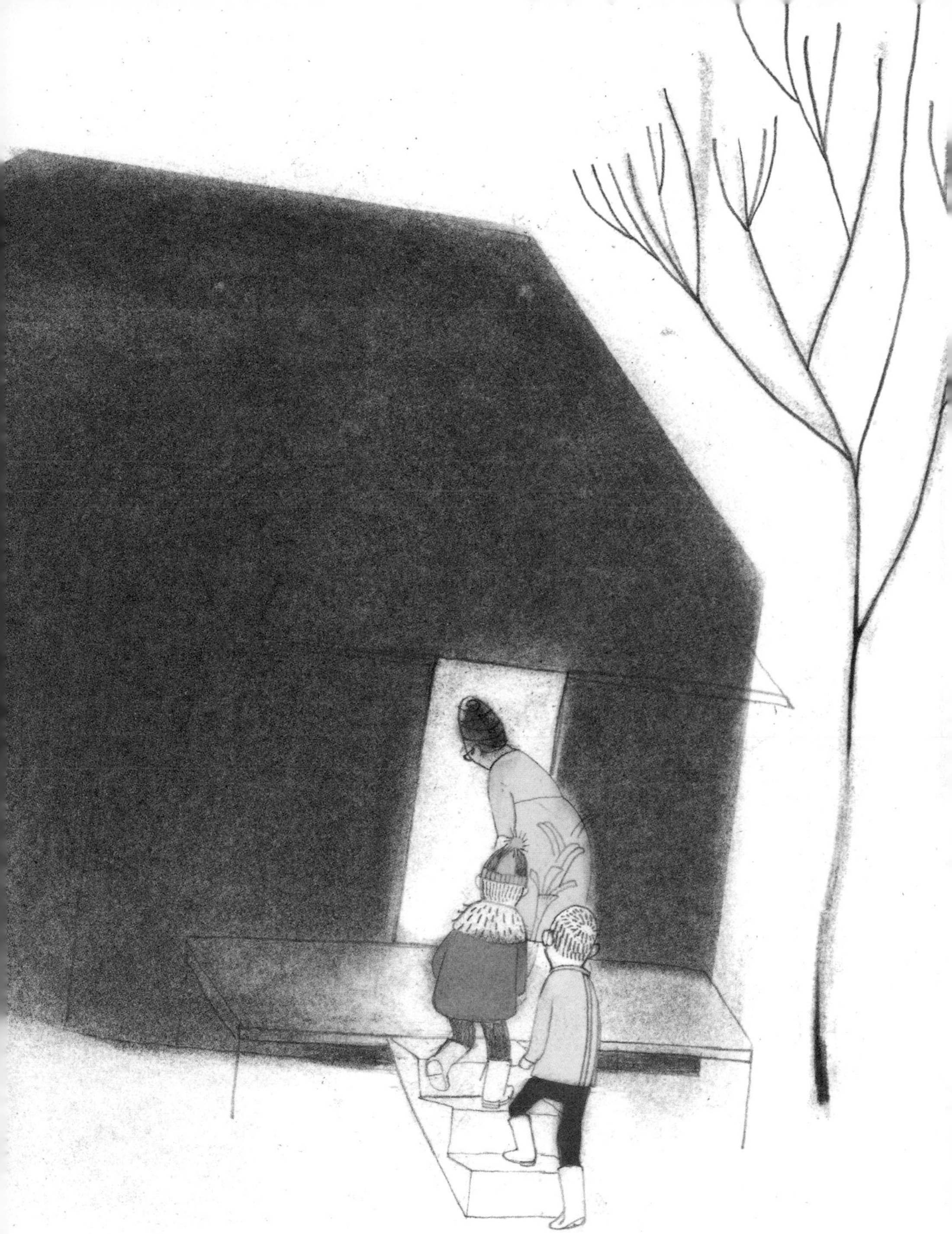

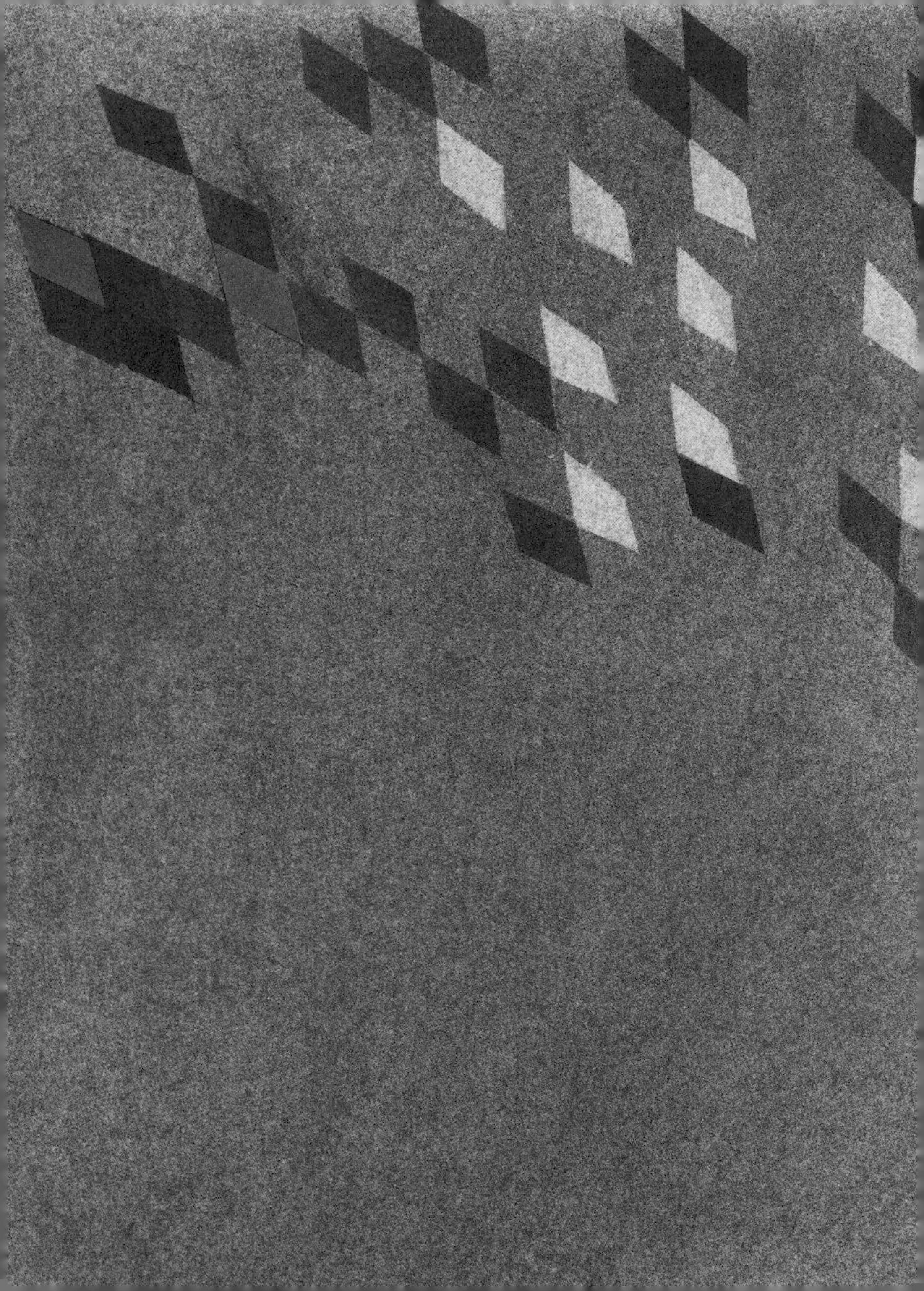

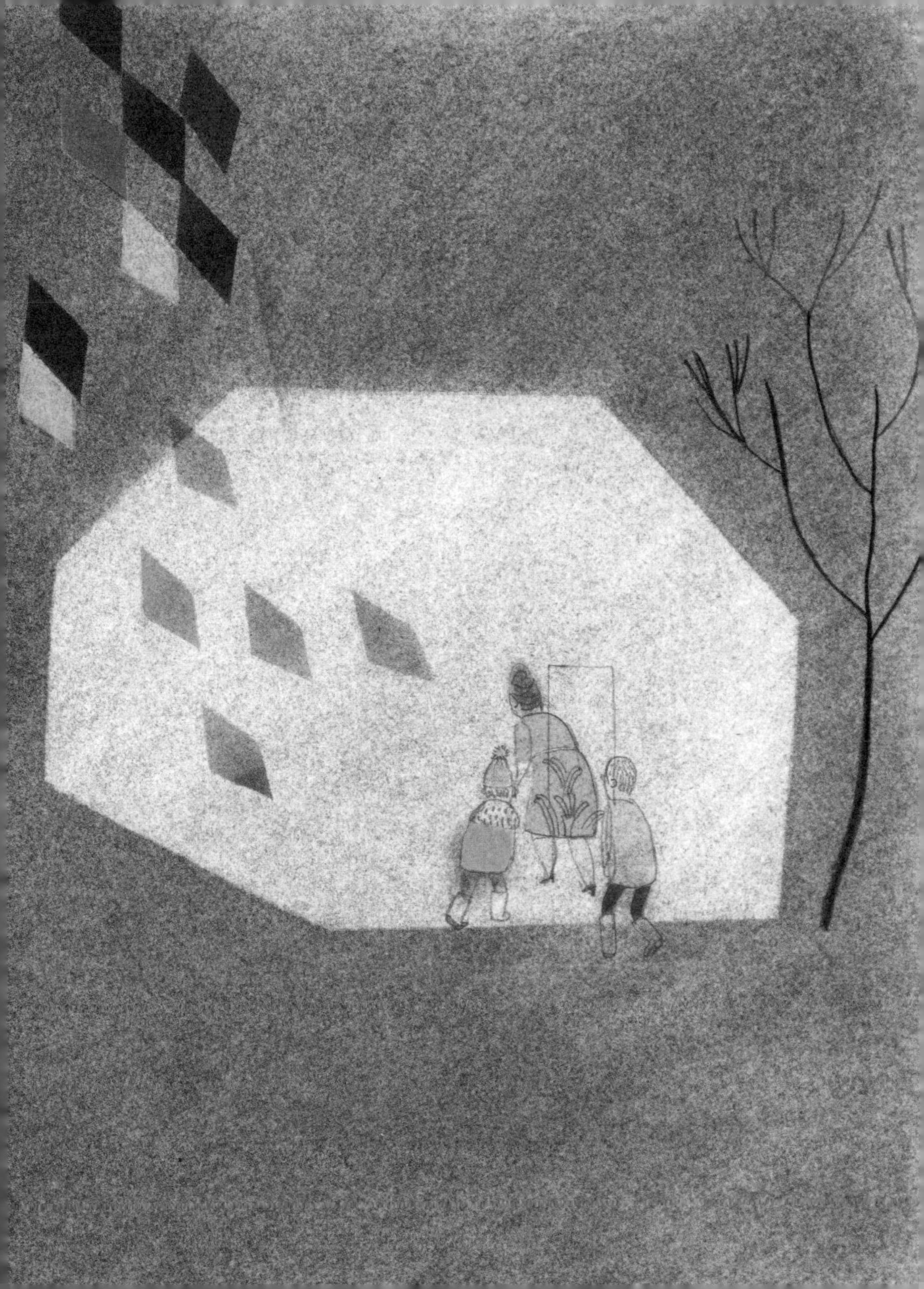

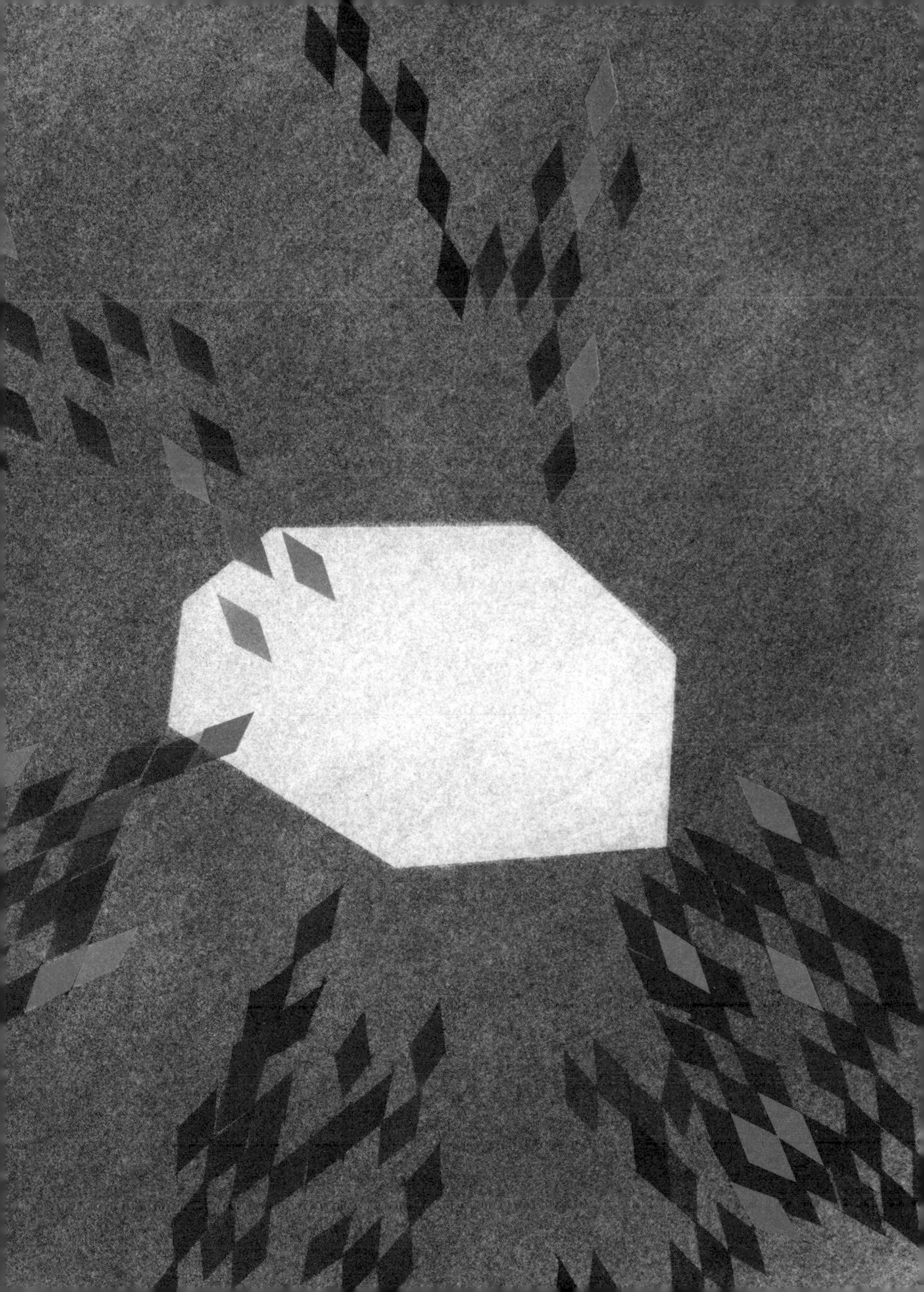

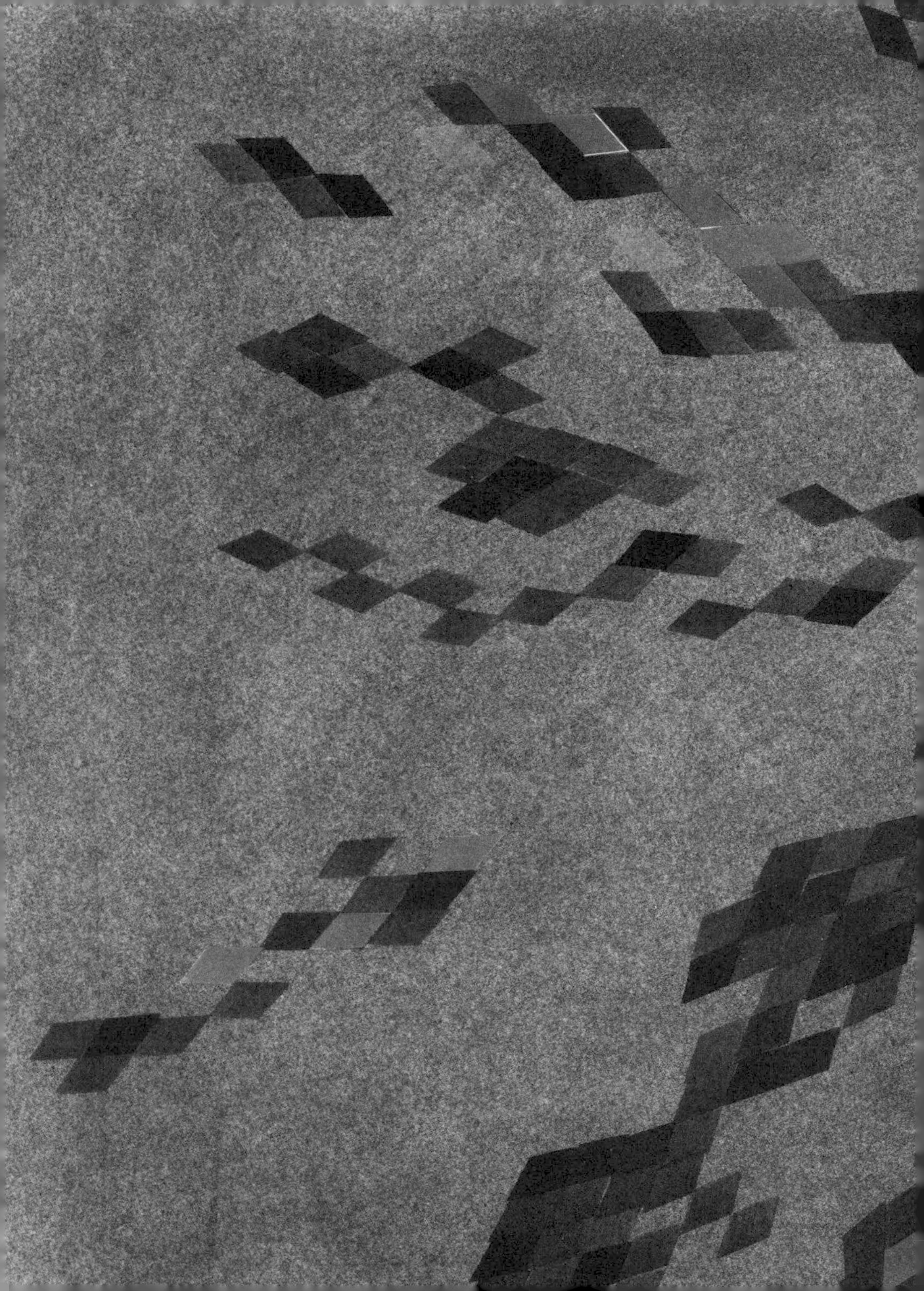

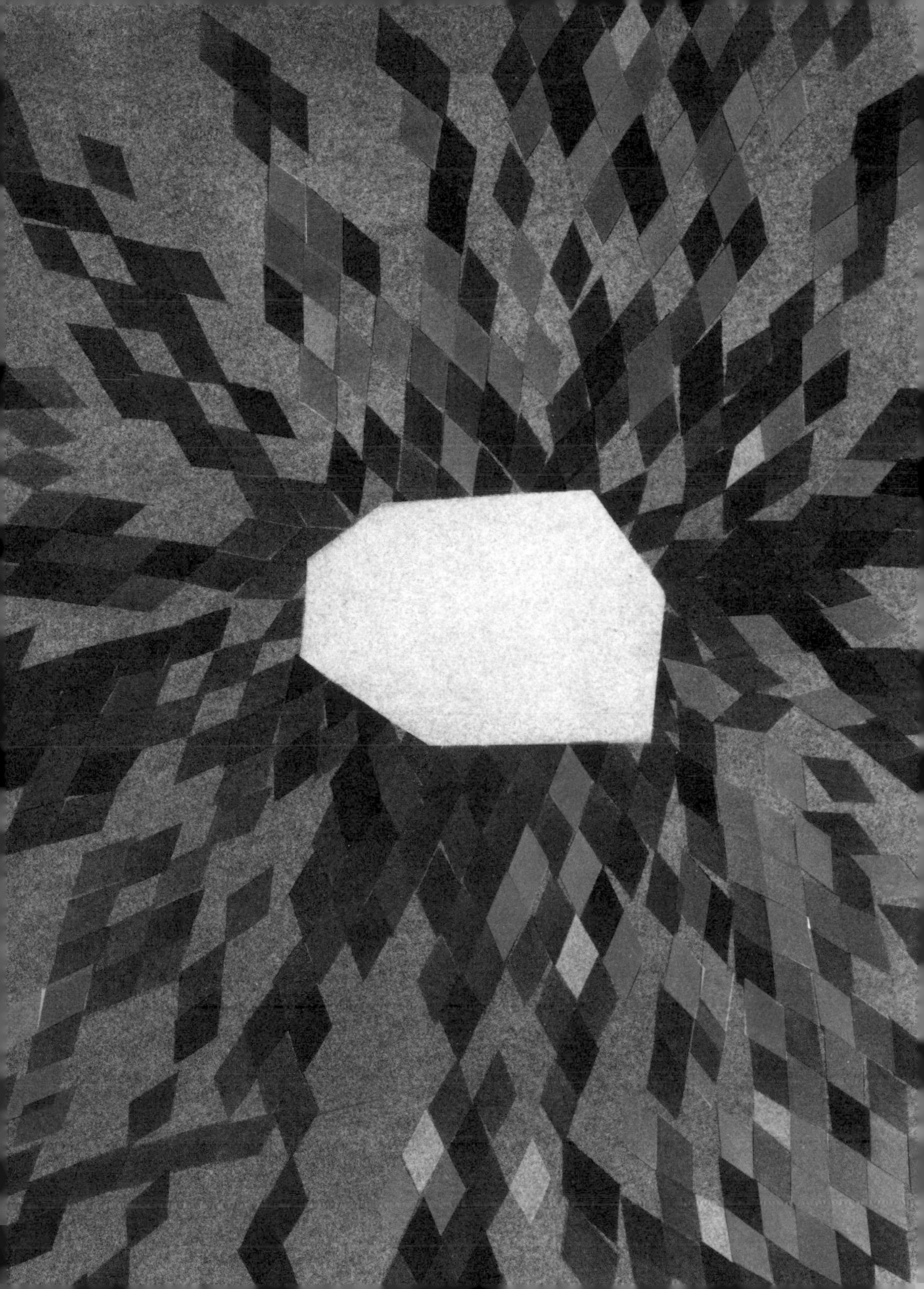

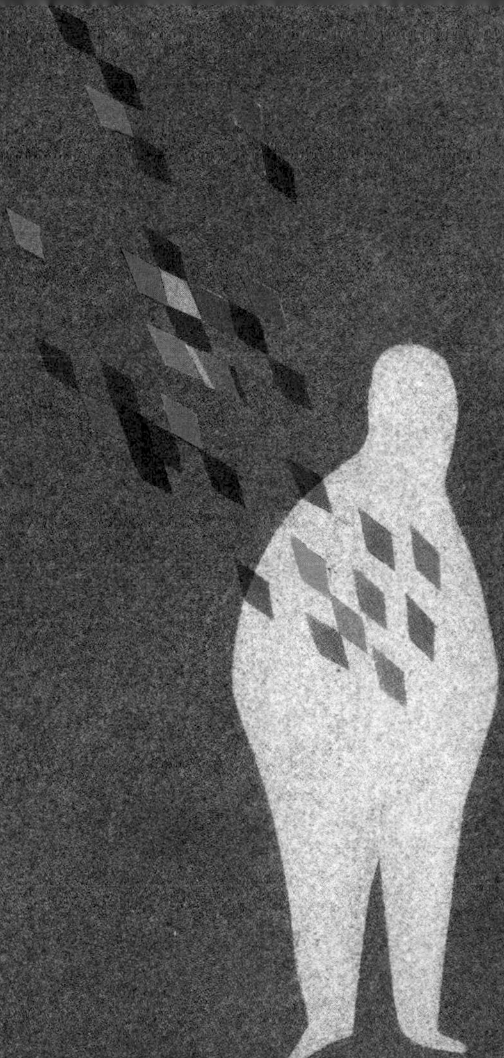

OF COURSE, MY FATHER BOUILLON WASN'T THERE.

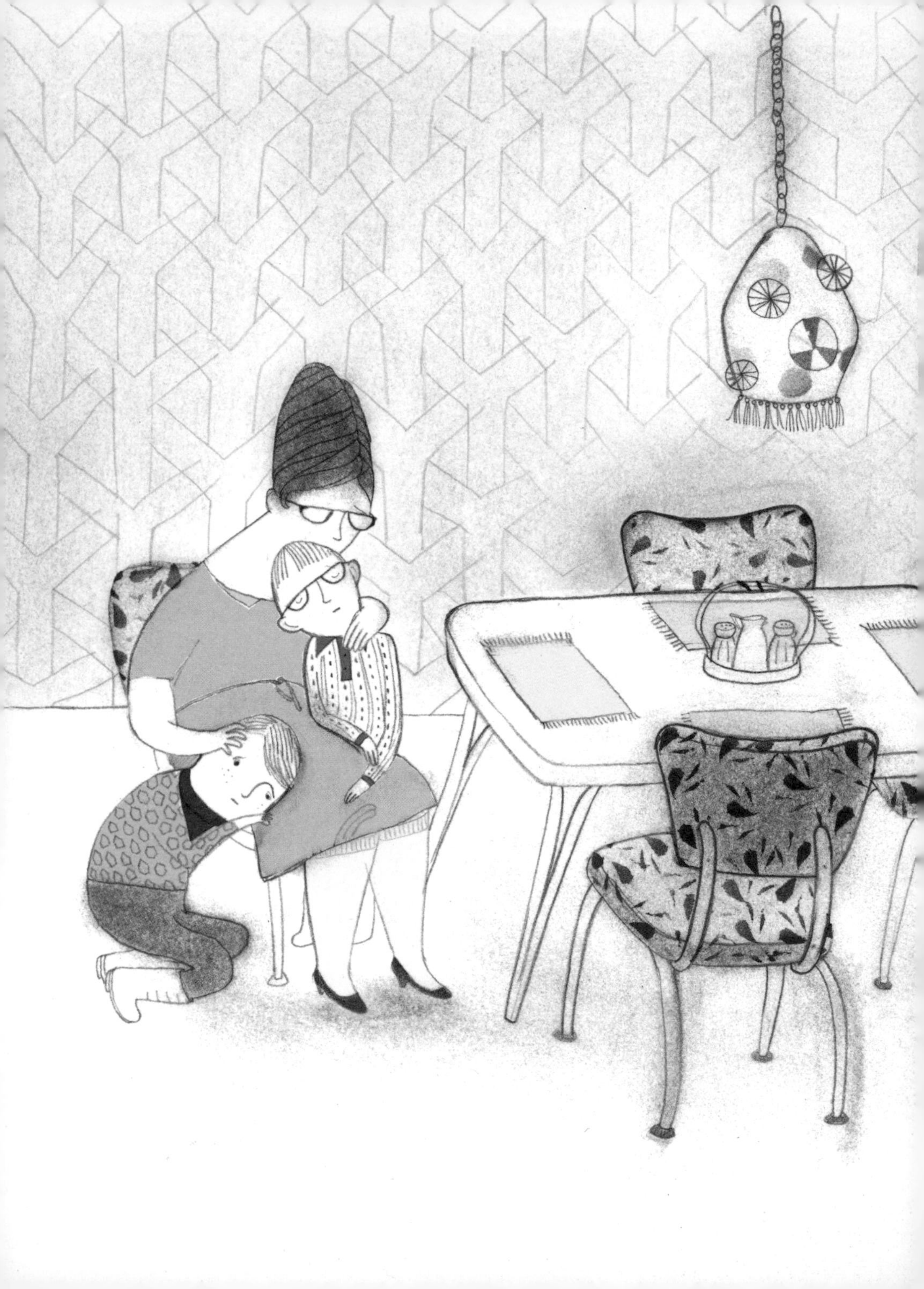

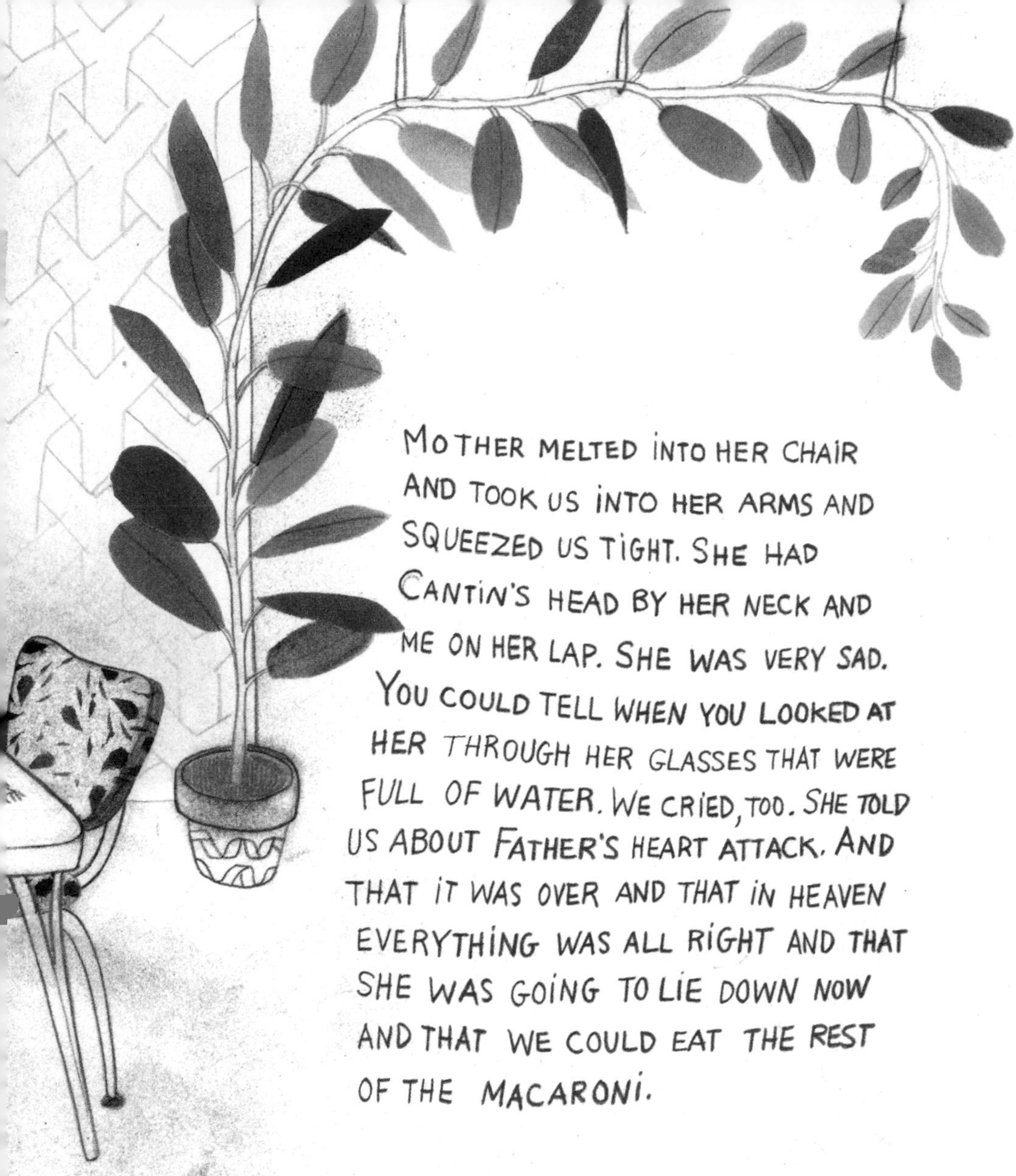

MOTHER MELTED INTO HER CHAIR AND TOOK US INTO HER ARMS AND SQUEEZED US TIGHT. SHE HAD CANTIN'S HEAD BY HER NECK AND ME ON HER LAP. SHE WAS VERY SAD. YOU COULD TELL WHEN YOU LOOKED AT HER THROUGH HER GLASSES THAT WERE FULL OF WATER. WE CRIED, TOO. SHE TOLD US ABOUT FATHER'S HEART ATTACK. AND THAT IT WAS OVER AND THAT IN HEAVEN EVERYTHING WAS ALL RIGHT AND THAT SHE WAS GOING TO LIE DOWN NOW AND THAT WE COULD EAT THE REST OF THE MACARONI.

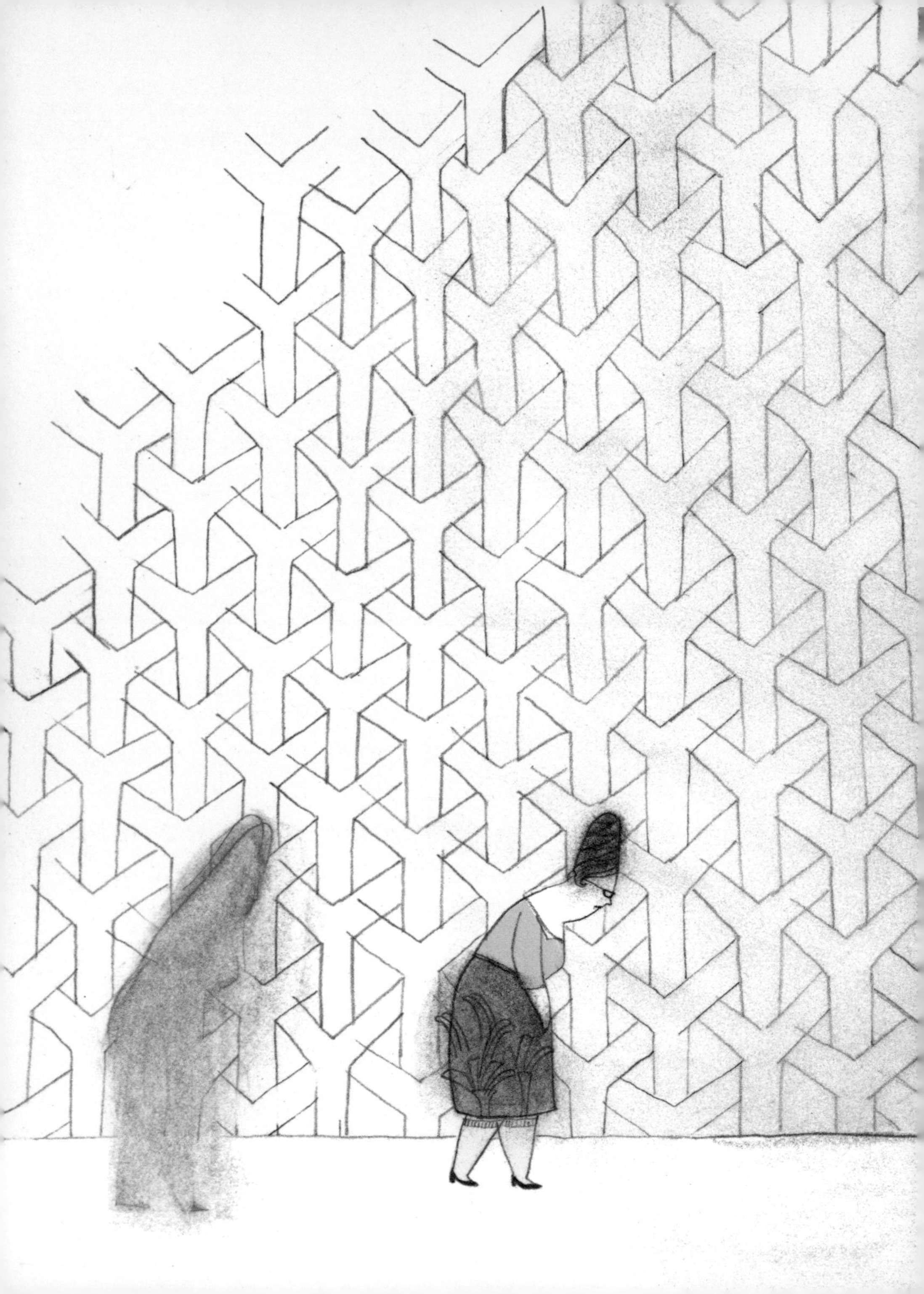

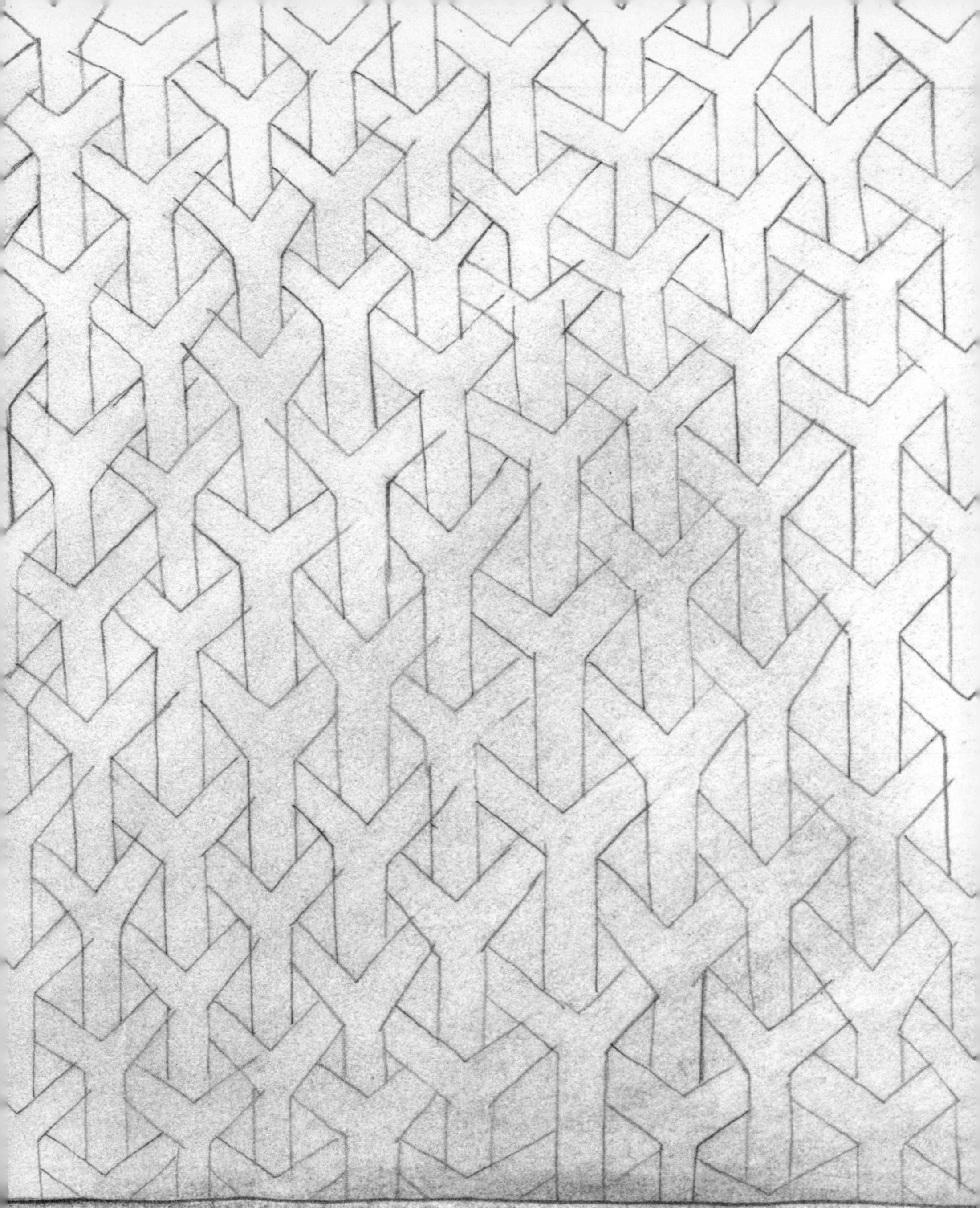

I HAD TO EXPLAIN TO CANTIN AGAIN WHY
OUR FATHER BOUILLON WASN'T THERE AND THAT
WE HAD SEEN HIM LEAVE A LITTLE WHILE AGO IN
THE AMBULANCE.

BUT, I DIDN'T SEE ANYTHING.

YES, BUT ANYHOW,
THAT WAS HIM UNDER
THE BLANKET.

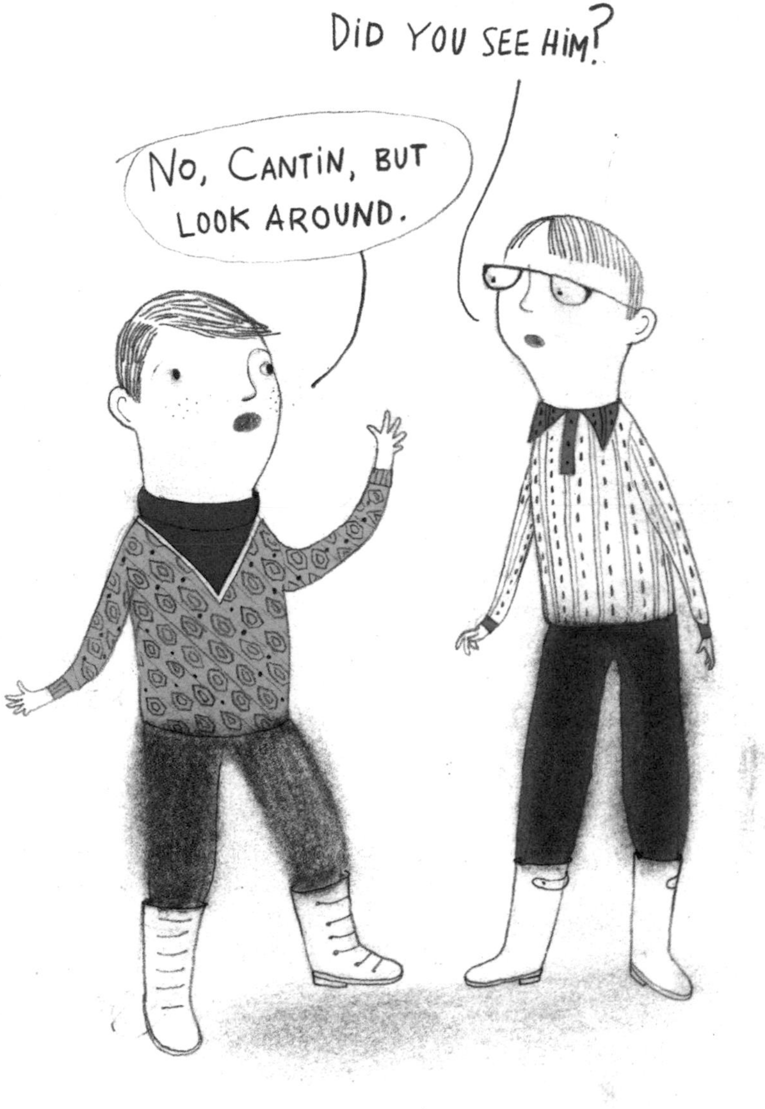
DID YOU SEE HIM?
NO, CANTIN, BUT LOOK AROUND.

WE WENT THROUGH THE WHOLE HOUSE. WE
WENT AND LOOKED IN THE SHED. WE EVEN
LOOKED IN THE CAR.

FOR THE CAR TO BE THERE BY THE DOOR WHEN
FATHER WAS GONE, THAT WAS THE HARDEST THING
TO EXPLAIN.

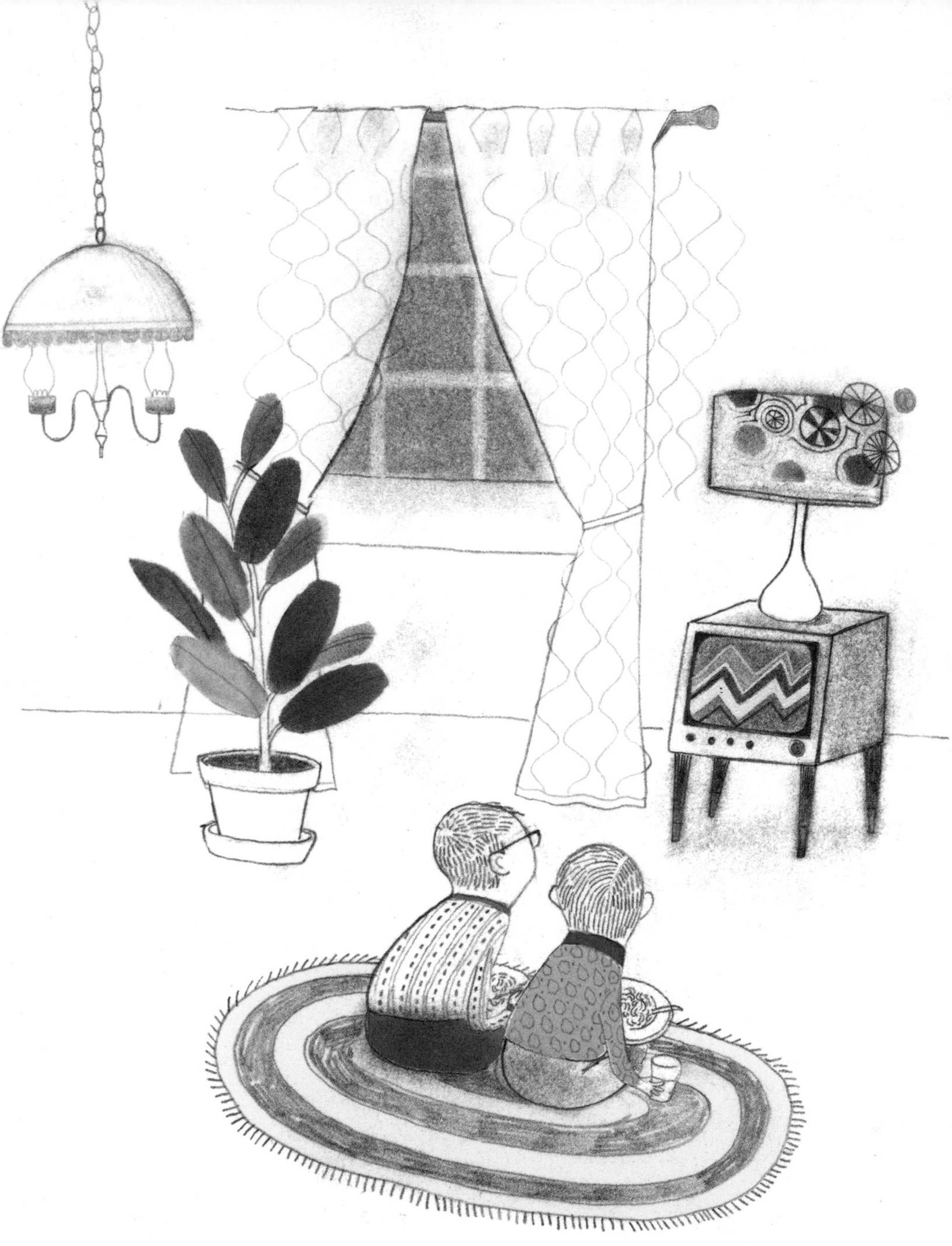

WE ATE IN FRONT OF THE TV. MOTHER WASN'T SLEEPING. SHE HAD SHUT HERSELF IN HER BEDROOM AND WE COULD HEAR HER TALKING. BUT WE COULDN'T HEAR WHAT SHE WAS SAYING.

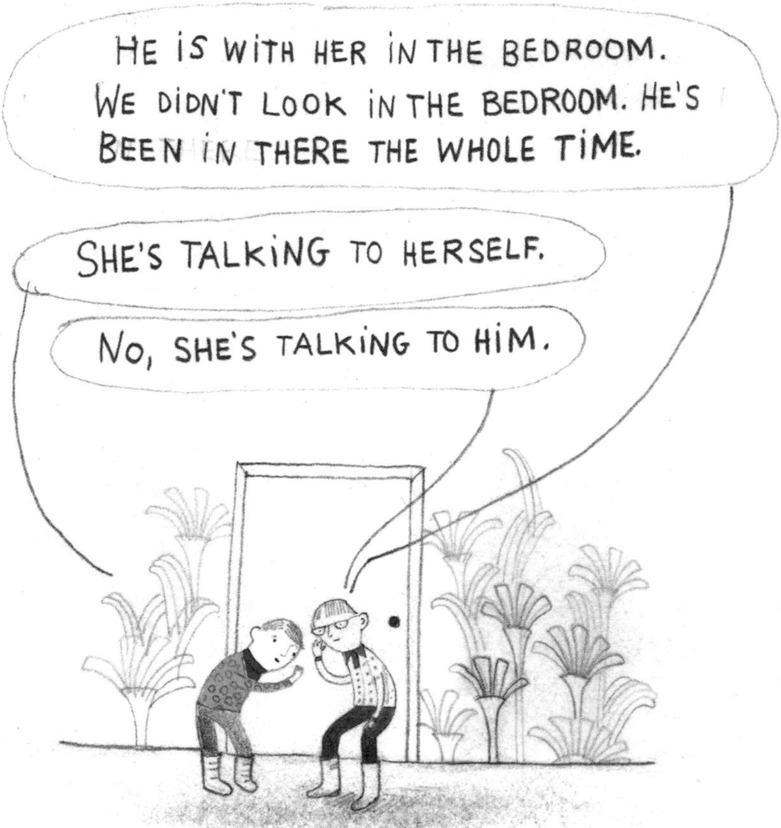
HE IS WITH HER IN THE BEDROOM. WE DIDN'T LOOK IN THE BEDROOM. HE'S BEEN IN THERE THE WHOLE TIME.
SHE'S TALKING TO HERSELF.
NO, SHE'S TALKING TO HIM.

WE WENT UP TO THE DOOR TO LISTEN.
WE COULD HEAR HER ASKING QUESTIONS
THAT NO ONE ANSWERED.

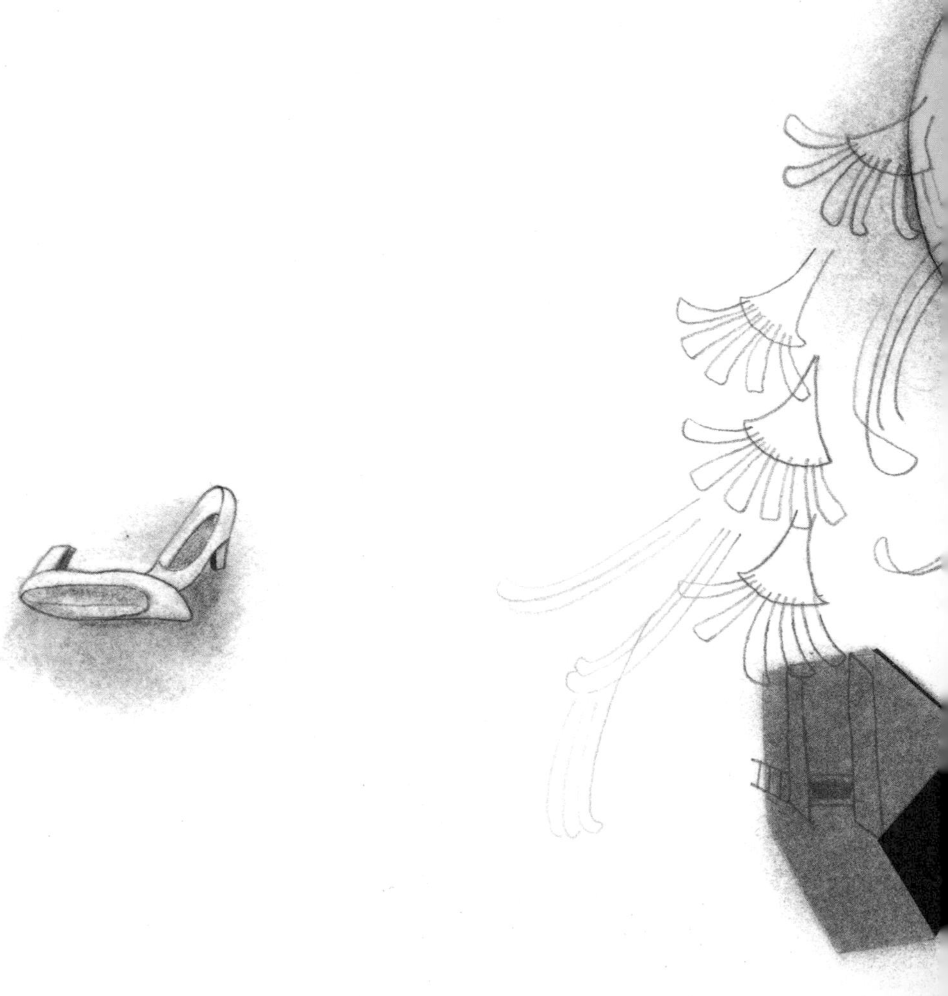

QUESTIONS ABOUT THE FUTURE.

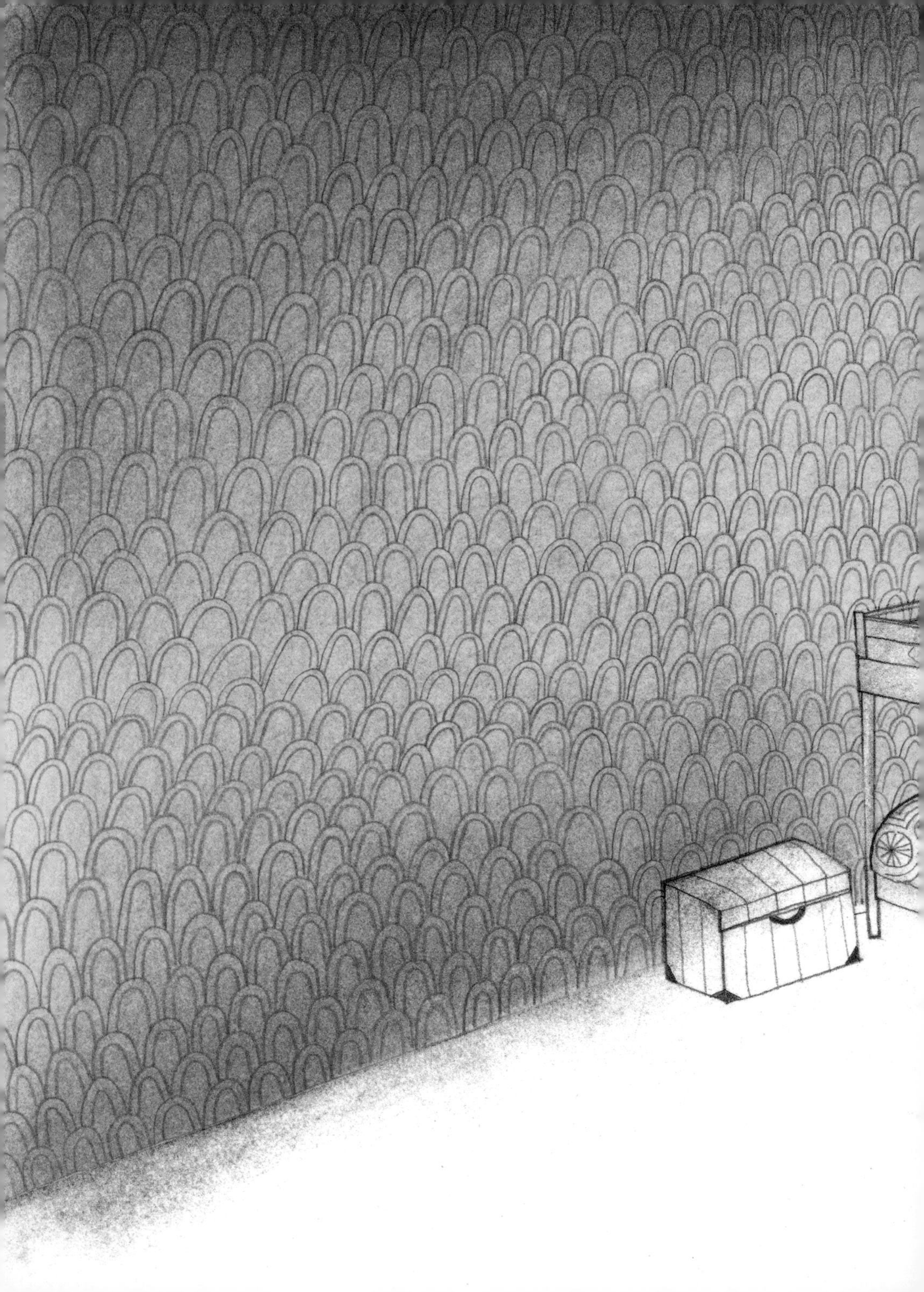

IN HIS BED ABOVE MINE, CANTIN WENT TO SLEEP QUICKLY. NOT ME. I KEPT MY EYES OPEN IN THE DARK. SOON I COULD MAKE OUT THINGS IN THE ROOM.

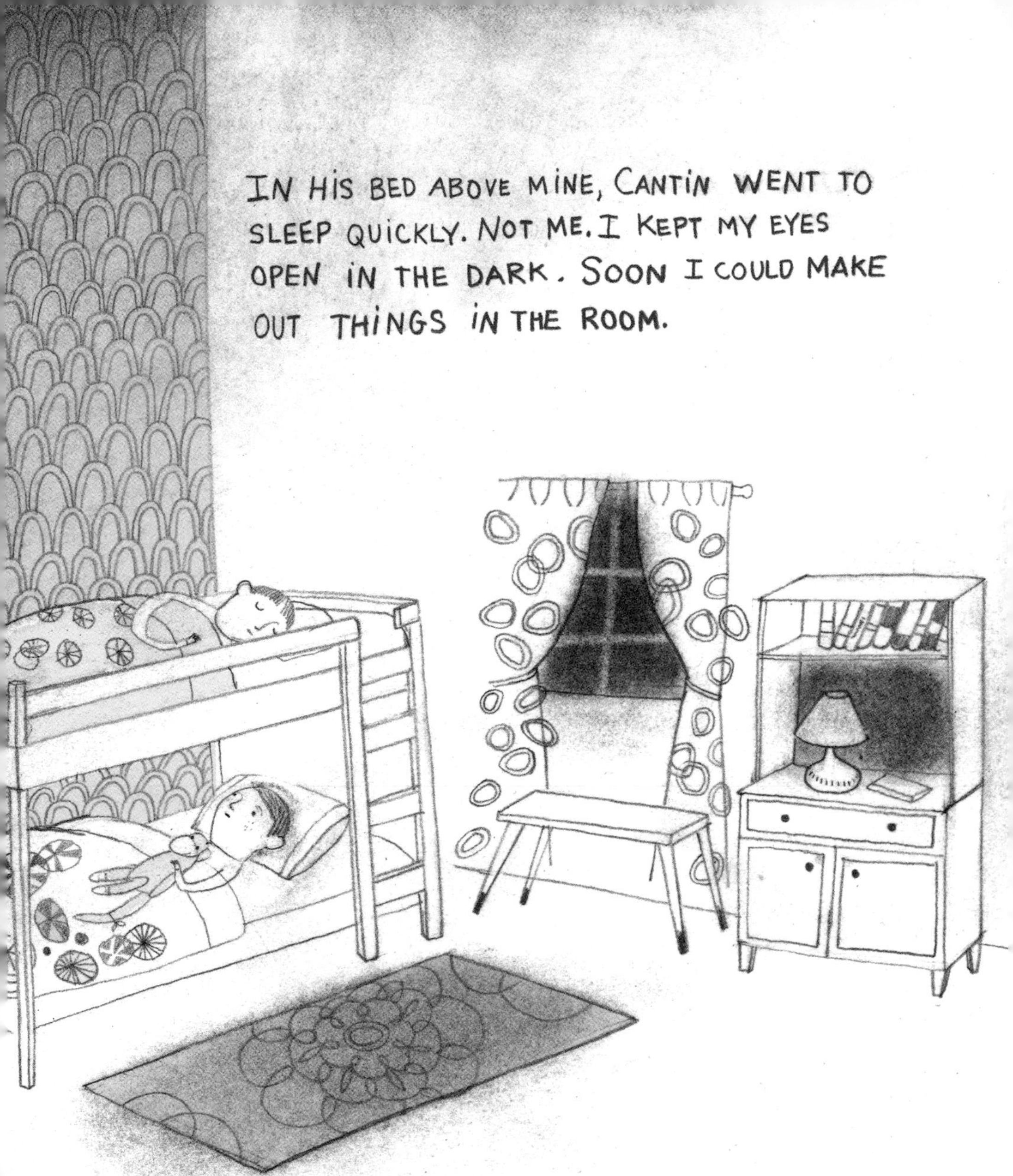

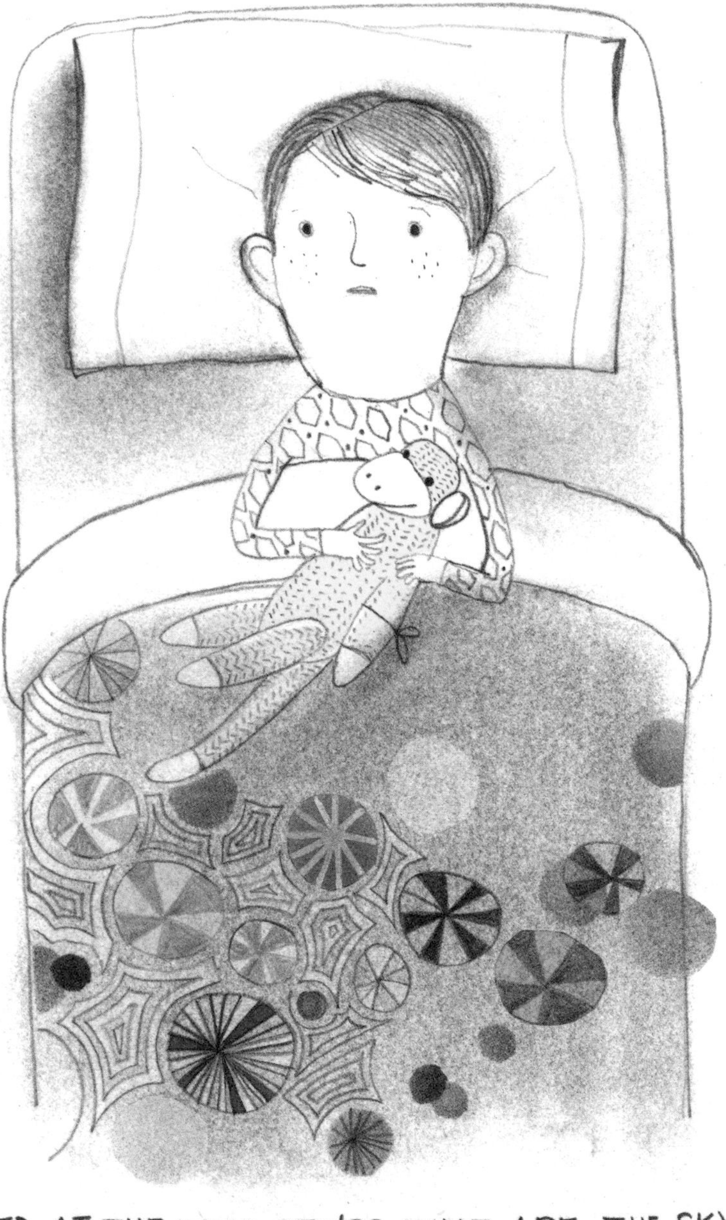

I STARED AT THE WOOD STRIPS THAT ARE THE SKY OF MY BED AND HOLD UP CANTIN'S MATTRESS.

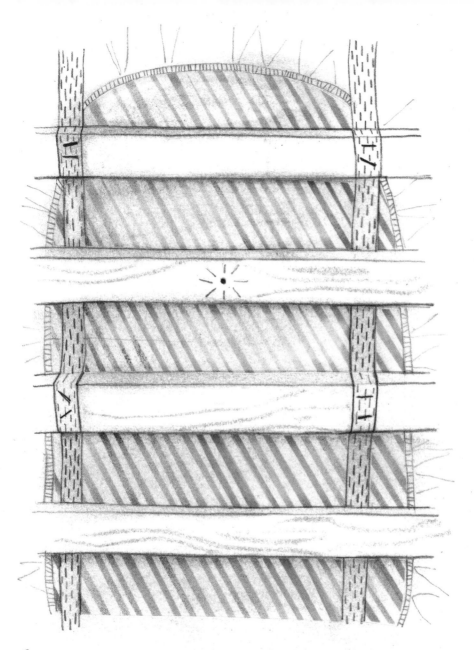

ON ONE OF THOSE STRIPS THERE IS A TINY DOT THAT
ONLY I RECOGNIZE. IT'S SCOTT CAREY.

SCOTT CAREY IS THE SHRINKING MAN. HE ONCE LIVED A NORMAL LIFE IN A SMALL CITY WITH HIS WIFE AND BABY DAUGHTER.

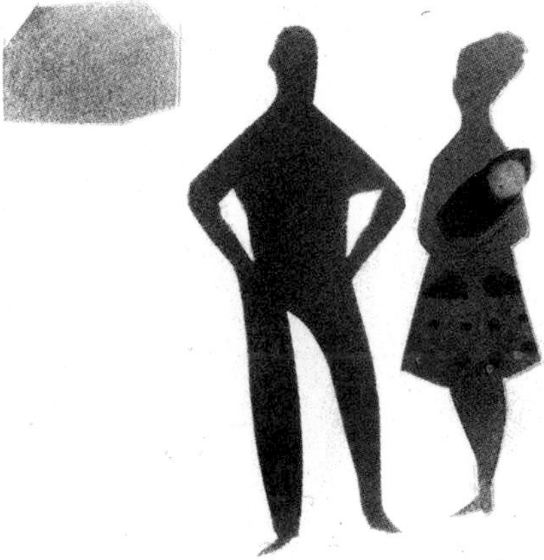

ONE DAY HE GOES FOR A BOAT RIDE ON A HUGE LAKE WHERE YOU CAN'T SEE THE SHORE.

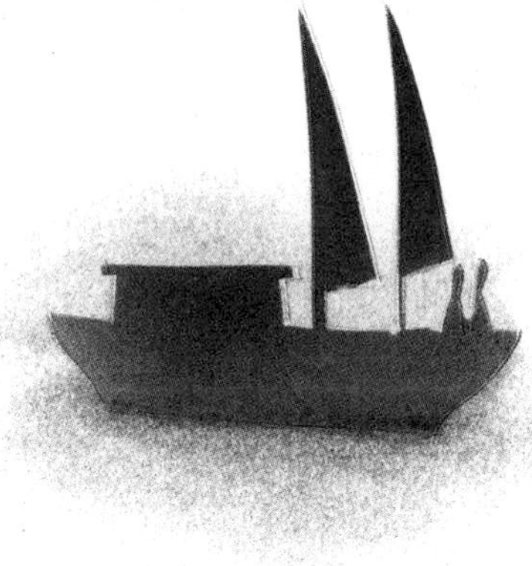

THE BABY GIRL ISN'T THERE. OR MAYBE SHE'S IN THE CABIN AT THE MOMENT WHEN YOU SEE SCOTT CAREY WITH HIS WIFE ON THE BOAT'S DECK. YOU CAN HEAR CRYING. IT MUST BE THE BABY.

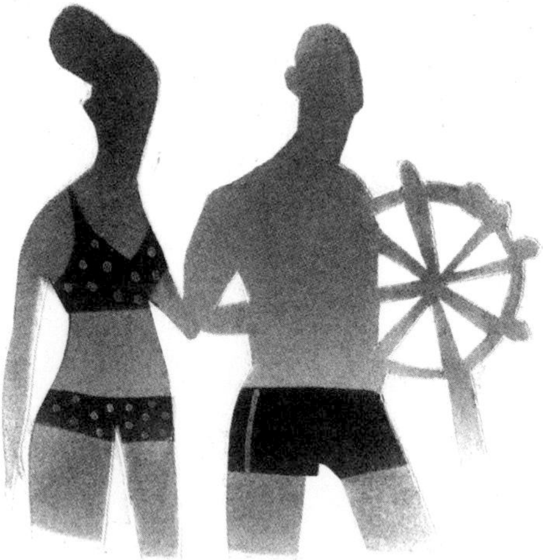

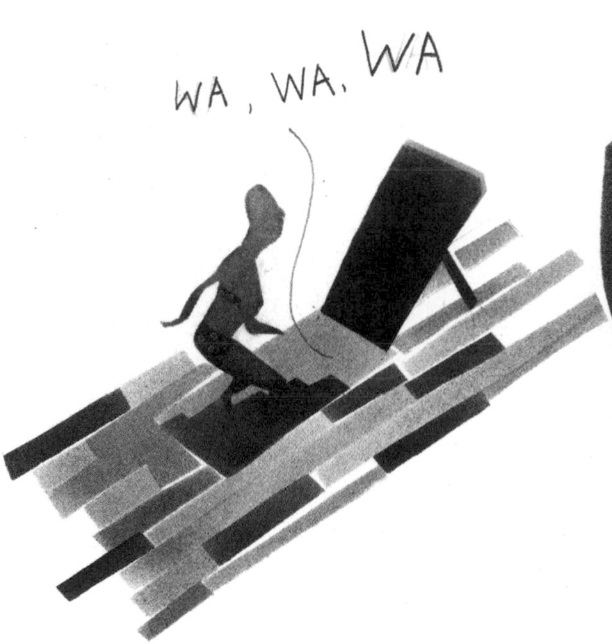
WA, WA, WA

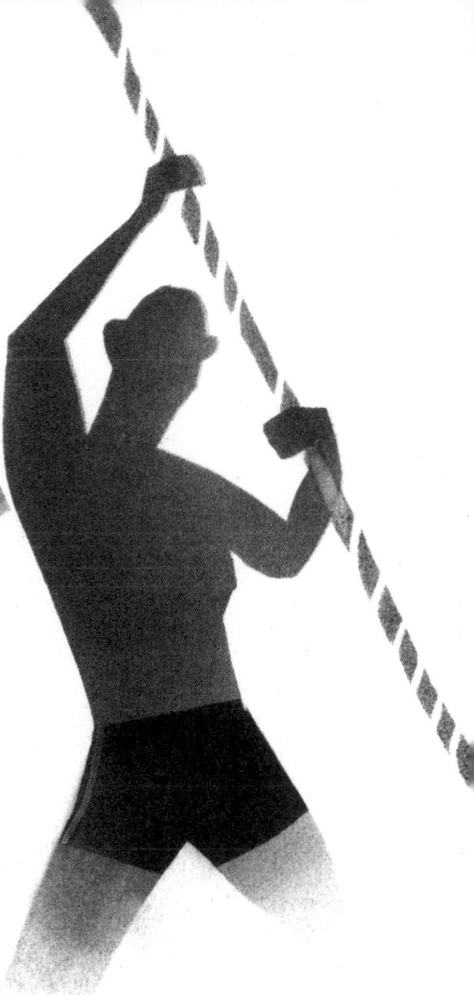

AND BECAUSE SHE'S CRYING, THE MOTHER GOES DOWN INTO THE CABIN TO SEE WHAT'S WRONG. SCOTT CAREY STAYS ON THE DECK, DEALING WITH THE ROPES. THE SUN IS SHINING VERY BRIGHT, YOU CAN SEE THAT, AND THE LAKE IS ALL WHITE AND SCOTT CAREY SQUINCHES HIS EYES WHEN HE LOOKS AT THE WATER AND HE HOLDS HIS HAND OVER HIS BROW TO SEE BETTER THE WAY INDIANS DO TO SEE FAR AWAY, BECAUSE SCOTT CAREY JUST LIKE THE INDIANS DOESN'T WEAR A HAT NO MATTER HOW SUNNY IT IS. HE'S BARE-CHESTED, TOO.

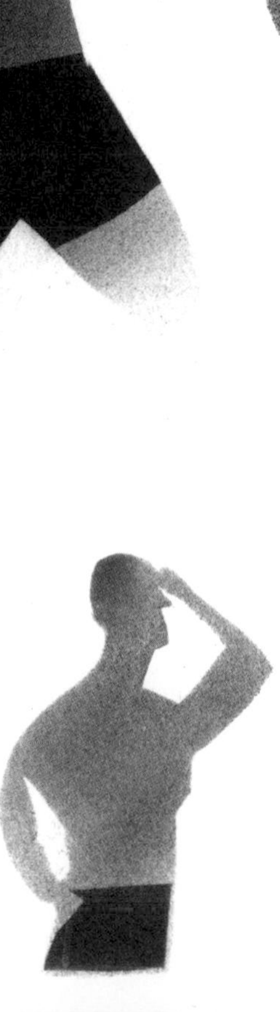

IT'S A BEAUTIFUL SUMMER DAY AND SCOTT CAREY IS
WEARING A BATHING SUIT, YOU CAN SEE HIS GRAY CHEST.
OKAY, HIS CHEST ISN'T REALLY GRAY. I GUESS IT'S
FLESH-COLORED. WELL, TANNED-WHITE-MAN COLOR, THAT
IS TO SAY GRAY LIKE THE WATER.

I'VE GOT TO SAY THAT SCOTT CAREY'S
STORY IS VERY OLD. I SAW IT IN A
BLACK-AND-WHITE MOVIE LONG AGO.

I SAW IT IN SECRET. I'D
GOTTEN OUT OF BED QUIETLY
AND GONE OUT INTO THE HALL
AND THERE, HIDING AGAINST
THE WALL, WHEN EVERYONE
THOUGHT I WAS IN BED, I
WATCHED SCOTT CAREY'S STORY
ON TV.

So he's on the deck all alone.

Suddenly, a cloud passes in front of the sun and casts a shadow everywhere. For a second it's like night and everything is dark gray.

And there's serious music— Baboom! Baboom! Baboom!

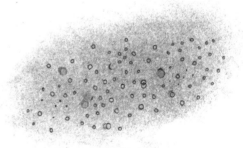

Then the cloud disappears, the light returns and a breeze picks up, scattering little specks of sparkling dust above the surface of the lake.

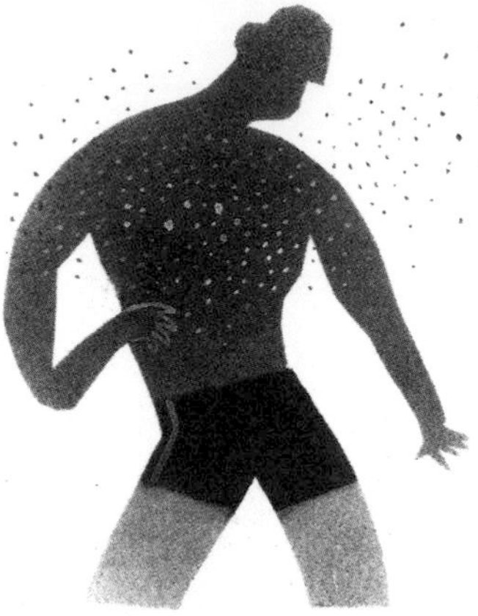

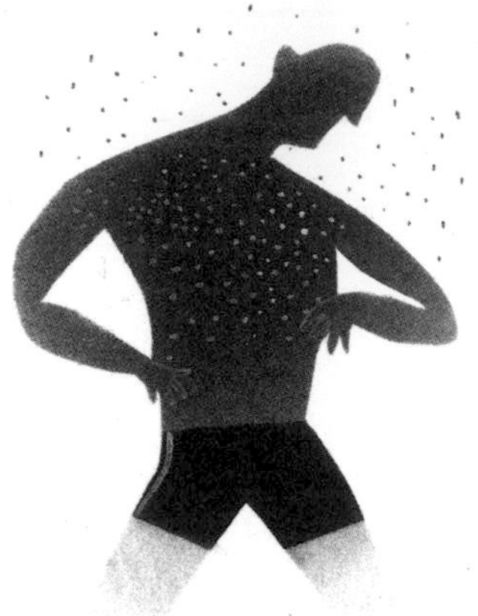

As for Scott Carey, the breeze ruffles his hair a bit, and the specks of dust stick to his body and arms. You can see the shiny specks on Scott Carey's gray skin.

He looks fascinated. You'd think he was saying, "It's strange, all these specks of shiny dust on my gray skin." And you can see him brushing off his chest, his shoulders, his arms, his stomach. With his hands.

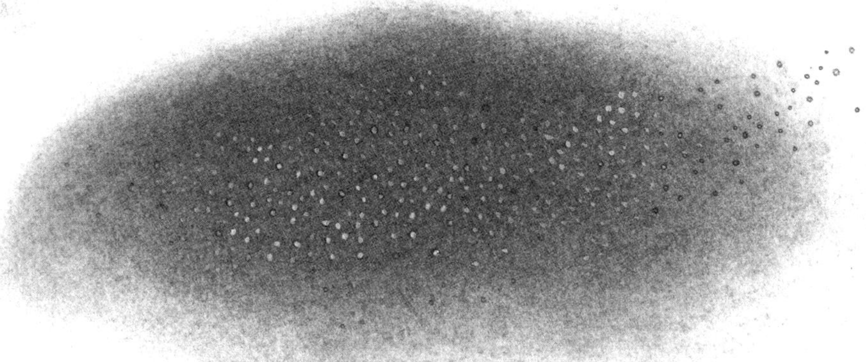

You can't see his legs, but you're sure he has them on his legs, those specks. He must be brushing them off while they're showing us the cloud of dust disappearing into the infinity that we can't see.

THEN IT'S CALM AGAIN. YOU CAN TELL BY THE MUSIC, WHICH SOUNDS SWEET THE WAY IT DOES BEFORE DARK. AND BECAUSE IT'S CALM THE BABY STOPS CRYING AND SCOTT CAREY'S WIFE CLIMBS BACK UP TO THE DECK.

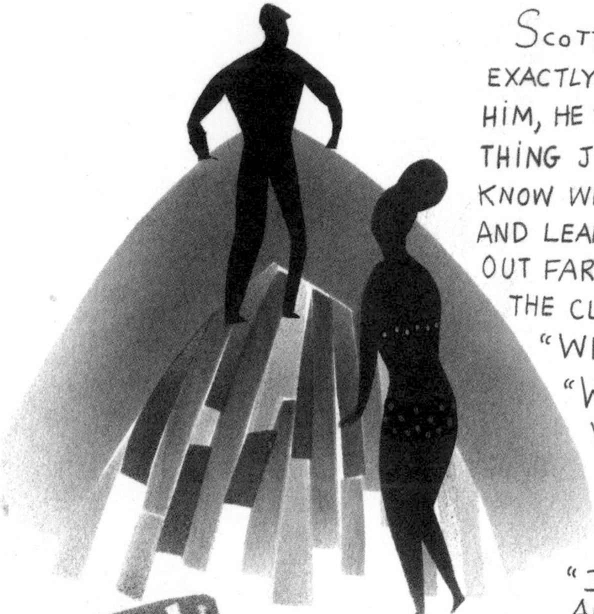

SCOTT CAREY DOESN'T KNOW EXACTLY WHAT JUST HAPPENED TO HIM, HE SAYS SO TO HIS WIFE. "SOMETHING JUST HAPPENED BUT I DON'T KNOW WHAT," HE SAYS. HE TURNS AWAY AND LEANS ON THE RAILING, LOOKING OUT FAR AWAY INTO INFINITY WHERE THE CLOUD HAS DISAPPEARED.

"WHAT? WHAT?" ASKS HIS WIFE. "WHAT'S THE MATTER WITH YOU? WHAT HAPPENED TO YOU?"

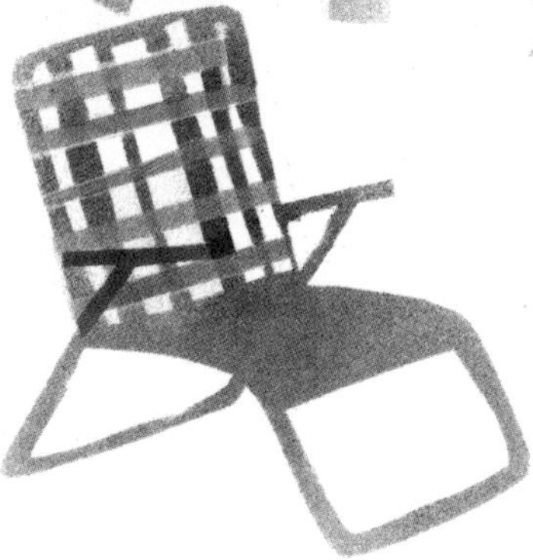

"I DON'T KNOW WHAT HAPPENED." AND AS HE SAYS THAT SCOTT CAREY TURNS TOWARD HIS WIFE. SHE SEES HIS CONFUSED LOOK.

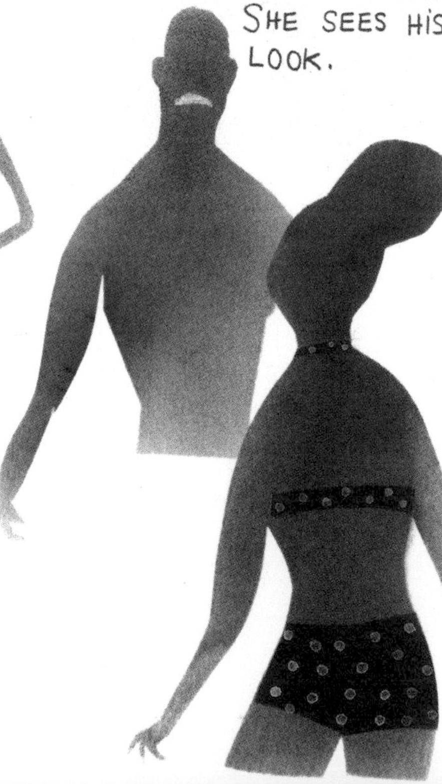

HE LOOKS AT THE GRAY SKIN ON HIS ARMS. HE EXAMINES HIS HANDS, TURNING THEM OVER AND OVER. THERE IS NO TRACE OF THE SPECKS OF DUST. "I DON'T KNOW," SCOTT CAREY SAYS. " PROBABLY NOTHING, NOTHING BUT A CLOUD."

IT SEEMS LIKE SHE DOESN'T UNDERSTAND A THING. AFTER ALL, SHE DIDN'T NOTICE ANYTHING. SHE WAS CALMING THE BABY DOWN IN THE CABIN WHILE HER HUSBAND WAS BEING COVERED WITH DUST. SHE DIDN'T NOTICE A THING. BUT THE BABY FELT IT, THAT THERE WAS DANGER THERE ON THE LAKE.

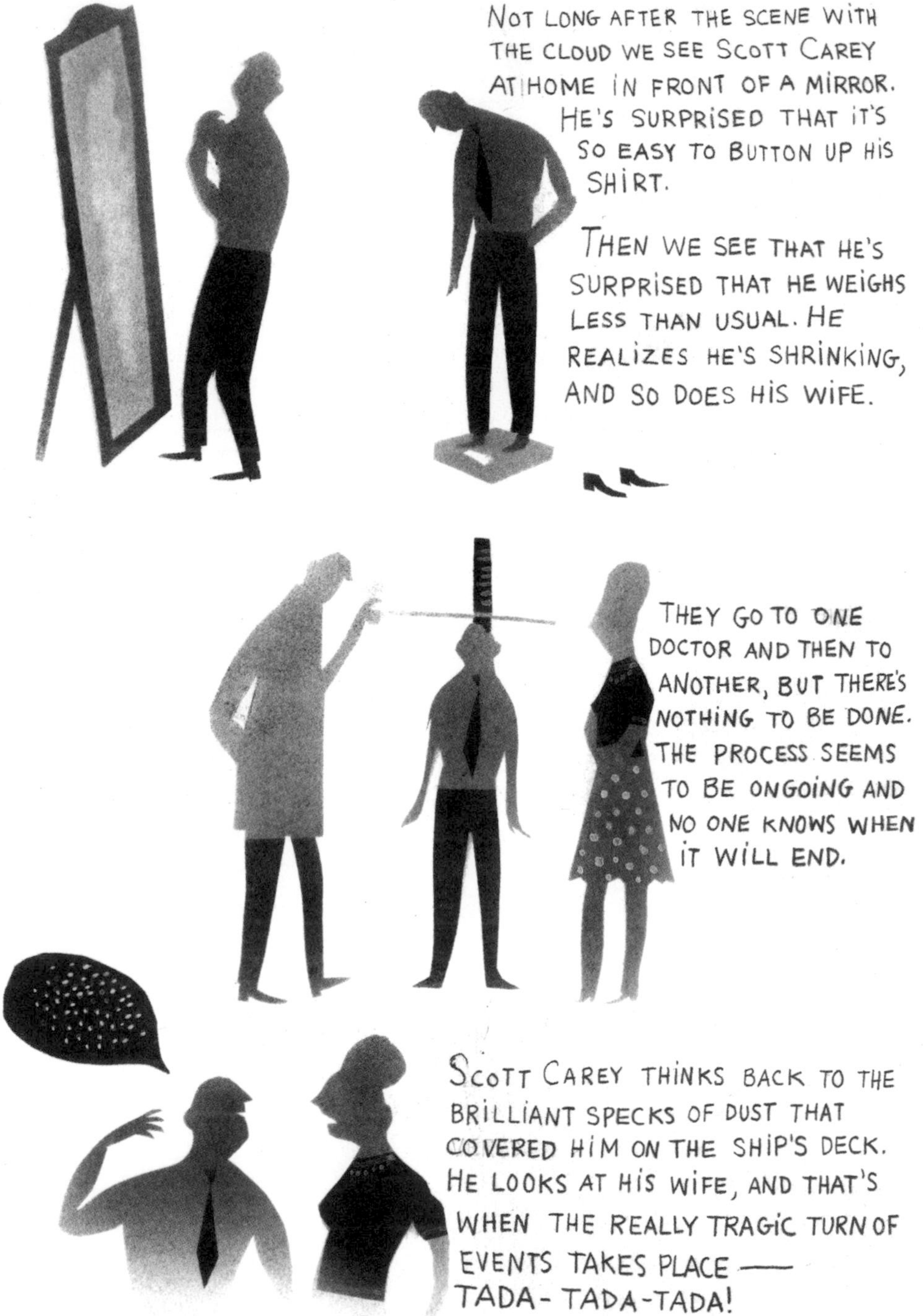
NOT LONG AFTER THE SCENE WITH THE CLOUD WE SEE SCOTT CAREY AT HOME IN FRONT OF A MIRROR. HE'S SURPRISED THAT IT'S SO EASY TO BUTTON UP HIS SHIRT.
THEN WE SEE THAT HE'S SURPRISED THAT HE WEIGHS LESS THAN USUAL. HE REALIZES HE'S SHRINKING, AND SO DOES HIS WIFE.
THEY GO TO ONE DOCTOR AND THEN TO ANOTHER, BUT THERE'S NOTHING TO BE DONE. THE PROCESS SEEMS TO BE ONGOING AND NO ONE KNOWS WHEN IT WILL END.
SCOTT CAREY THINKS BACK TO THE BRILLIANT SPECKS OF DUST THAT COVERED HIM ON THE SHIP'S DECK. HE LOOKS AT HIS WIFE, AND THAT'S WHEN THE REALLY TRAGIC TURN OF EVENTS TAKES PLACE — TADA-TADA-TADA!

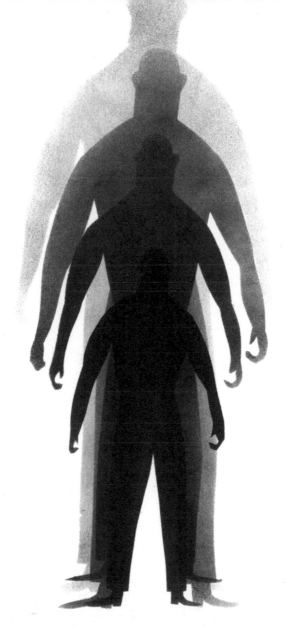

AT THAT VERY MOMENT WHEN SCOTT CAREY FULLY REALIZES WHAT'S HAPPENING (THOUGH NOT EXACTLY WHAT WILL HAPPEN), THE STORY GETS REALLY EXCITING. BECAUSE SCOTT CAREY KEEPS GETTING SMALLER AND SMALLER.

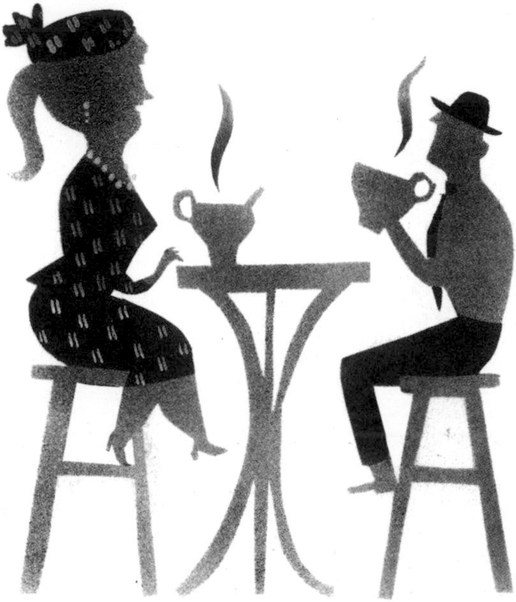

WE SEE HIM DRINKING A CUP OF COFFEE WITH A DWARF WOMAN WHO IS BIGGER THAN HE IS.

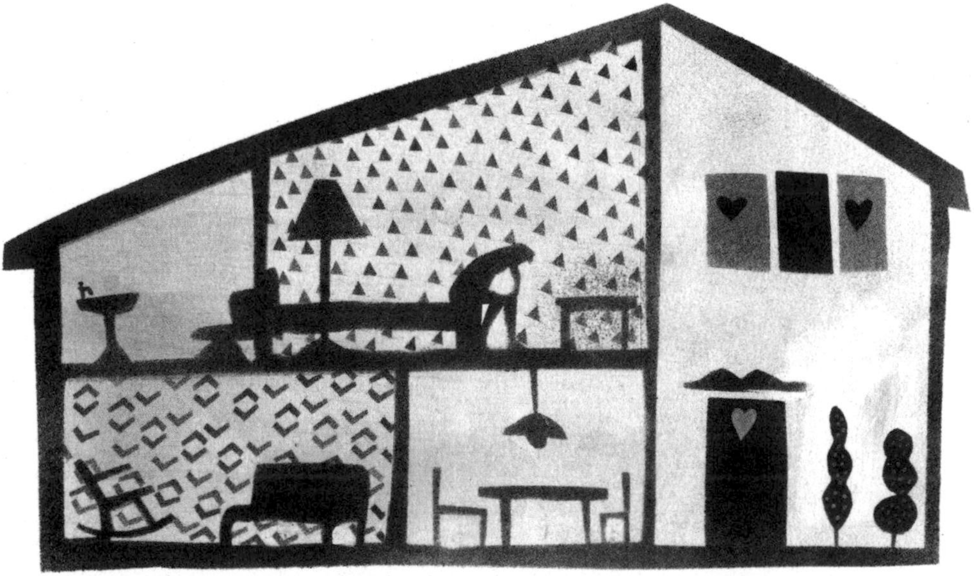

WE SEE HIM LIVING IN HIS DAUGHTER'S DOLLHOUSE.

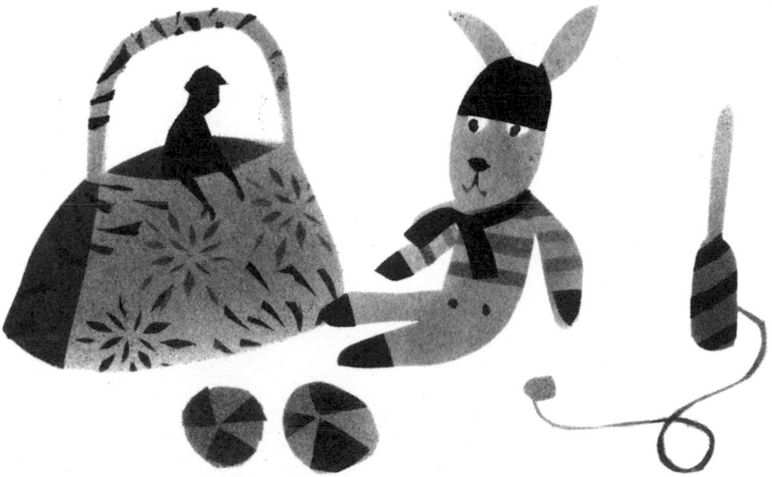

WE SEE HIM IN HIS WIFE'S HANDBAG.

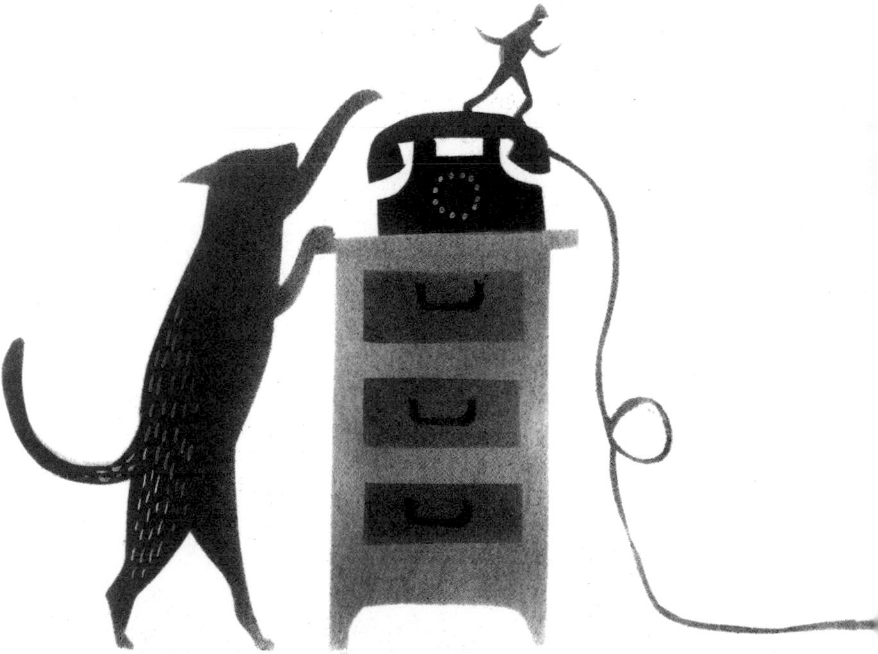

WE SEE HIM BEING CHASED BY THE CAT.

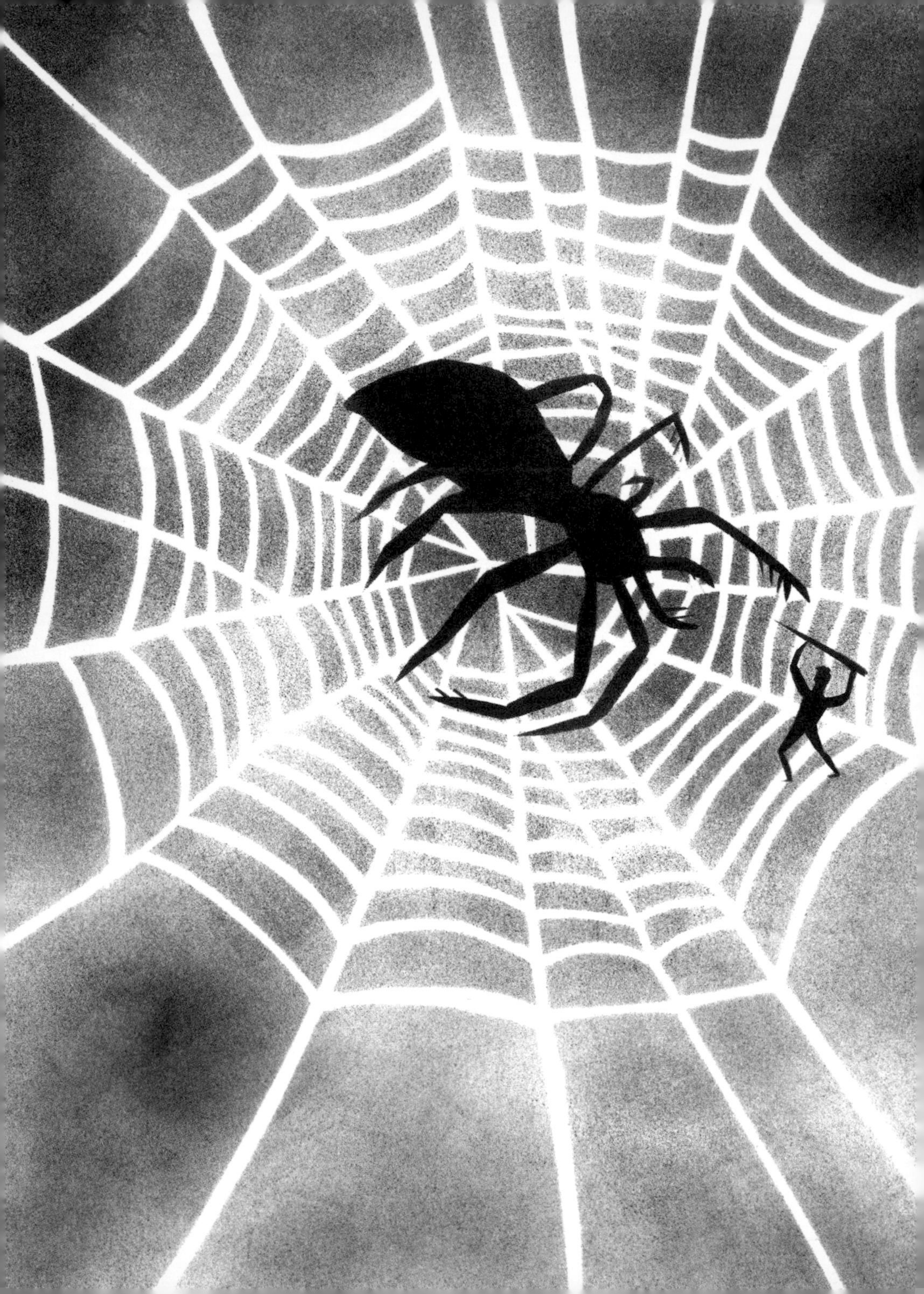

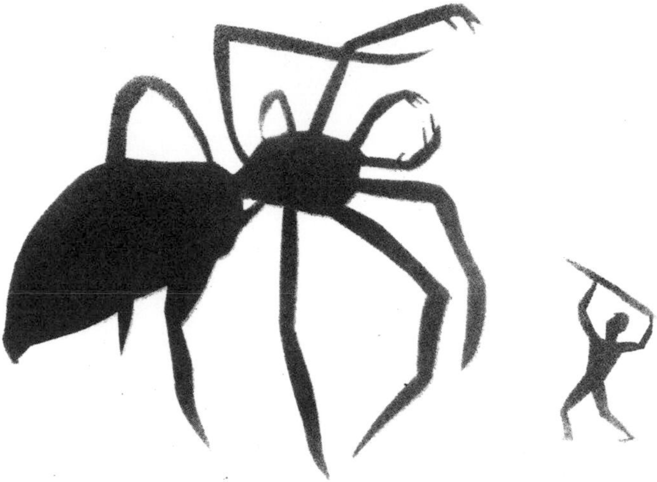

WE SEE HIM DEFEAT A SPIDER TEN TIMES HIS SIZE.

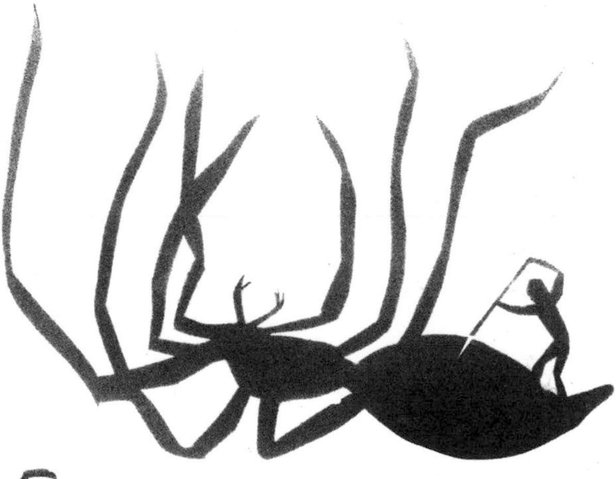

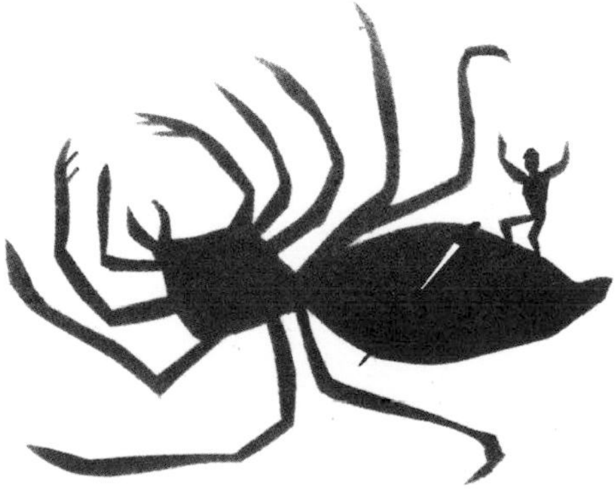

In the end no one can see him anymore. His wife has lost him. Maybe she threw out her husband when she was emptying the dustpan. She's very sad. But Scott Carey keeps on living his life. He's all alone in the night, face to face with the stars.

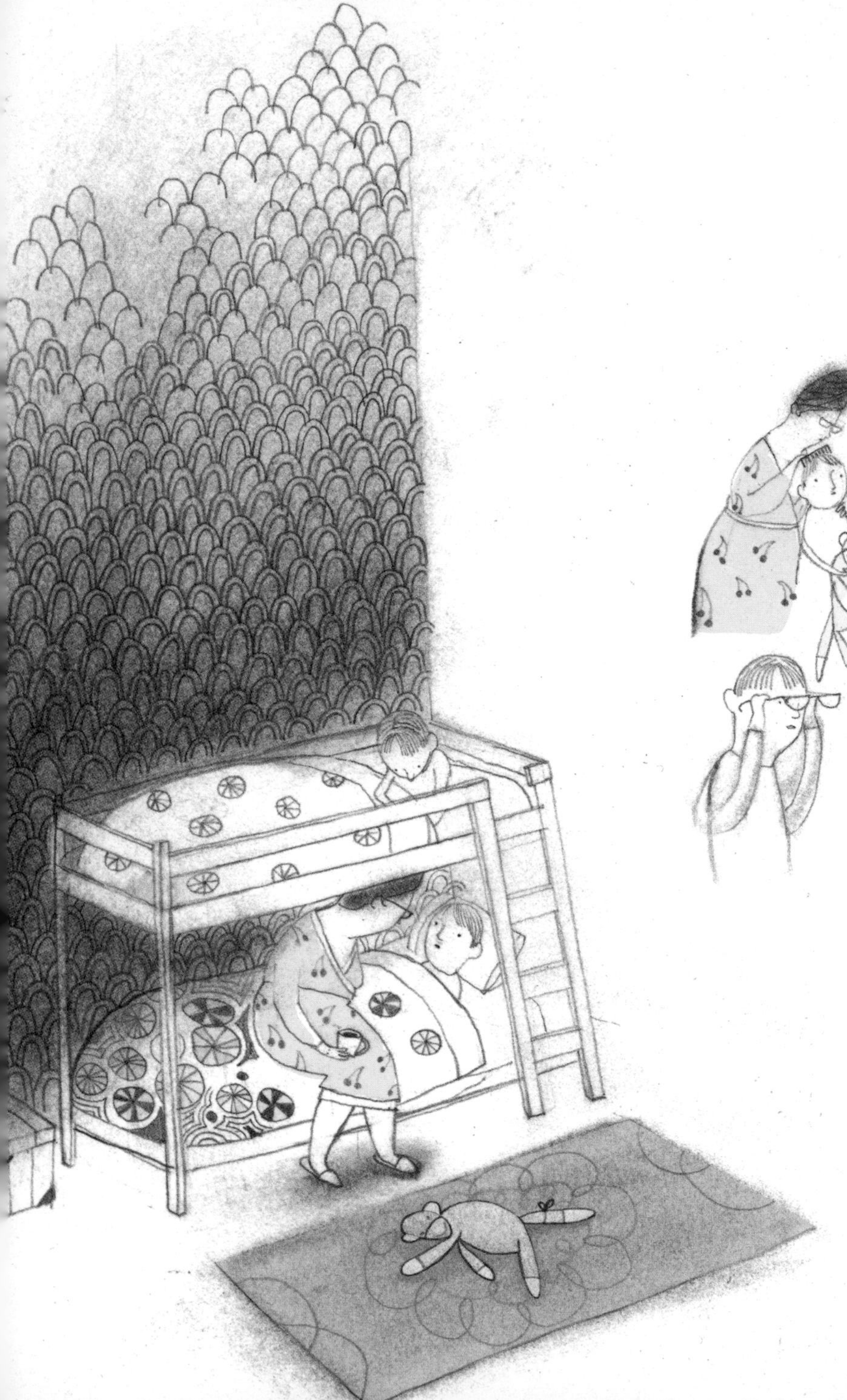

IT WAS MOTHER BOUILLON WHO WOKE US UP. WE WOULDN'T GO TO SCHOOL TODAY. WE HAD TO PUT ON OUR SUNDAY CLOTHES AND GO TO THE FUNERAL PARLOR TO SEE FATHER BOUILLON AND WE HAD TO BEHAVE OURSELVES. OKAY. WE PUT ON OUR SUNDAY CLOTHES. WE WAITED FOR AUNT MÉLINA TO COME AND PICK US UP IN HER CAR. OURS WAS SITTING THERE IN THE DRIVEWAY. IT WAS WEIRD TO SEE OUR CAR IN THE DRIVEWAY, AND TO KNOW THAT IT WOULDN'T BE GOING ANYWHERE TODAY, OR TOMORROW, OR THE DAY AFTER TOMORROW, OR THE DAY AFTER THE DAY AFTER TOMORROW, OR THE DAY AFTER THE DAY AFTER THE DAY AFTER TOMORROW, ETC. MOTHER HAD ALWAYS REFUSED TO LEARN TO DRIVE. BUT I THOUGHT THAT MAYBE NOW THAT SHE SAW OUR CAR SITTING SO STILL, SHE'D CHANGE HER MIND. BUT I DIDN'T ASK HER BECAUSE I DIDN'T WANT TO GIVE HER THE IDEA OF CHANGING HER MIND. AND I MADE A SIGN TO CANTIN THAT HE SHOULD BE QUIET ABOUT THIS IDEA, JUST IN CASE HE'D HAD IT, TOO.

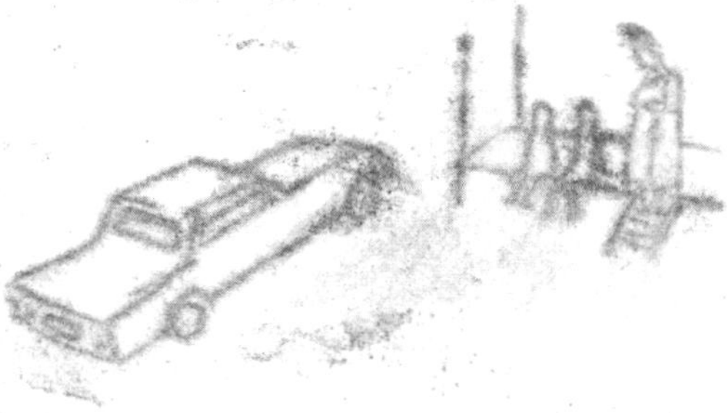

BUT IN THE END IT DIDN'T MATTER THAT I DIDN'T MENTION MY IDEA BECAUSE AS SOON AS WE HAD GOTTEN INTO AUNT MÉLINA'S CAR, HER HUSBAND, RAYMOND, ASKED MOTHER BOUILLON WHAT SHE PLANNED TO DO WITH THE CAR, THAT WAS SURELY NOT MADE TO ROT AWAY THERE IN THE DRIVEWAY.

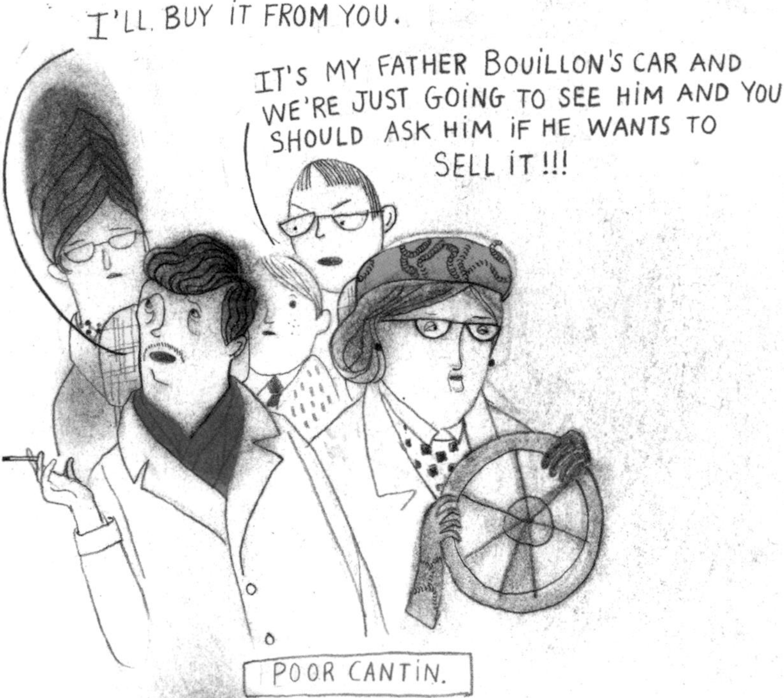
I'LL BUY IT FROM YOU.
IT'S MY FATHER BOUILLON'S CAR AND WE'RE JUST GOING TO SEE HIM AND YOU SHOULD ASK HIM IF HE WANTS TO SELL IT!!!
POOR CANTIN.

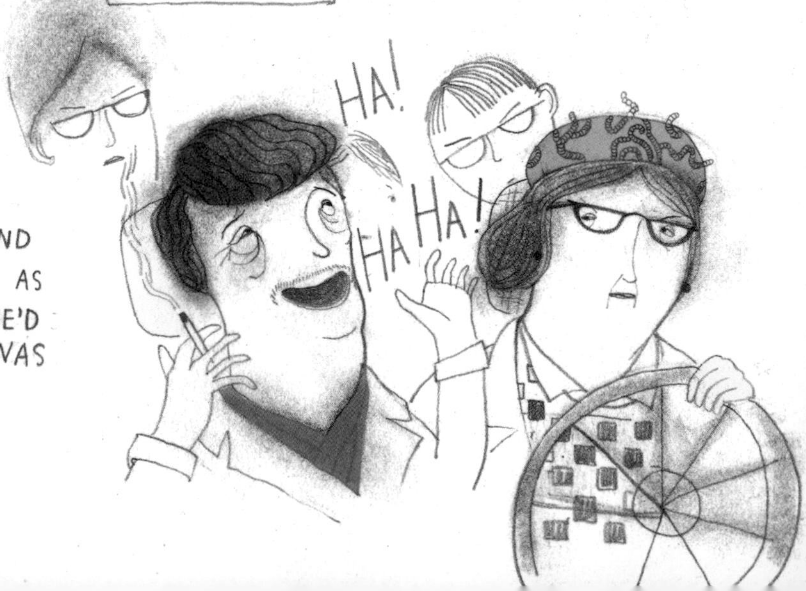
HA!
HA HA!

UNCLE RAYMOND BEGAN TO LAUGH AS THOUGH WHAT HE'D JUST HEARD WAS IDIOTIC.

BUT HE LAUGHED ALONE AND NOT FOR LONG.

MY MOTHER BOUILLON AND AUNT MÉLINA MADE HIM UNDERSTAND
THROUGH THEIR LOOKS AND THEIR SIGHS THAT HE WAS THE IDIOTIC
ONE. AND CANTIN AND I LOOKED AT EACH OTHER. HE LOOKED
VERY PLEASED THAT MOTHER AND HER SISTER HAD PUT DOWN
UNCLE RAYMOND FOR WHAT HE SAID. BUT WHAT HE SAID WAS
STILL STUPID.

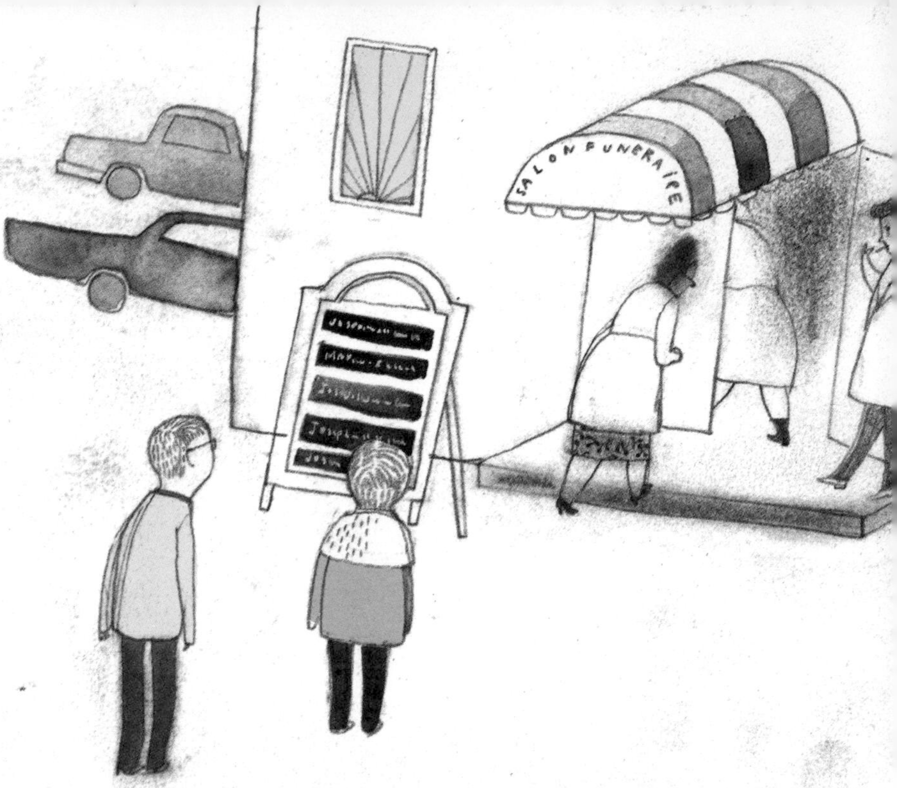
SALON FUNERAIRE

MY FATHER BOUILLON'S NAME WAS WRITTEN IN WHITE LETTERS RIGHT OUTSIDE THE DOOR OF THE FUNERAL PARLOR. IS IT REALLY HIS? I ASKED CANTIN. IS THAT REALLY FATHER'S NAME UP THERE? HE READ OUT, JOSEPH-ARMAND-ROBERT BRISSON, JOSEPH-CAROL-NOËL COUTURIER, JOSEPH-PIERRE-PAUL POULIN, MARIE-ANNIE-JEANINE VOYER NÉE BROUILLARD, JOSEPH-LAURENT-ÉTIENNE BOUILLON. THEN HE REPEATED, JOSEPH-LAURENT-ÉTIENNE BOUILLON.

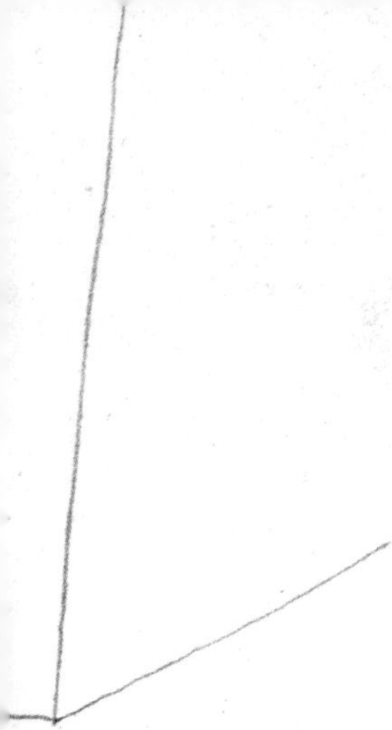

THERE WERE WALL-TO-WALL CARPETS, LAMPS ON THE WALLS, LONG ROWS OF CHAIRS. WE WENT IN TO THE FIRST OF FIVE ROOMS.

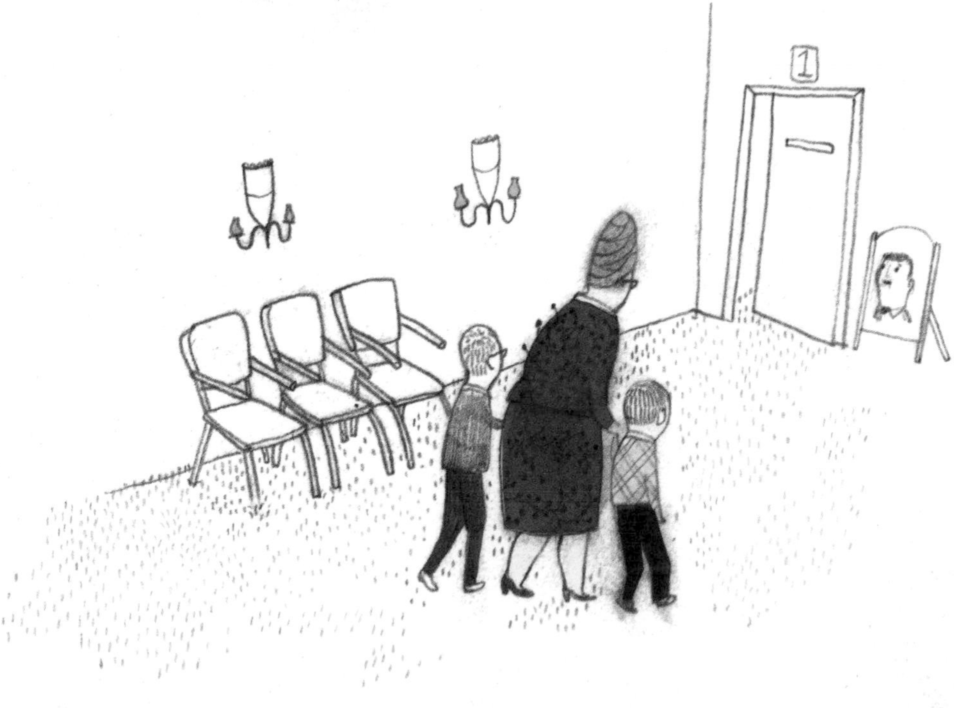
1

THE COFFIN WAS ON THE LEFT WHEN YOU CAME IN.
THERE WERE ALREADY SOME BUNCHES OF FLOWERS BY IT.
A MAN IN GRAY CAME OVER TO SHOW US WHERE TO
SIT TO RECEIVE CONDOLENCES FROM VISITORS. HE DIDN'T
EVEN SPEAK. WE WENT TO KNEEL BY FATHER.

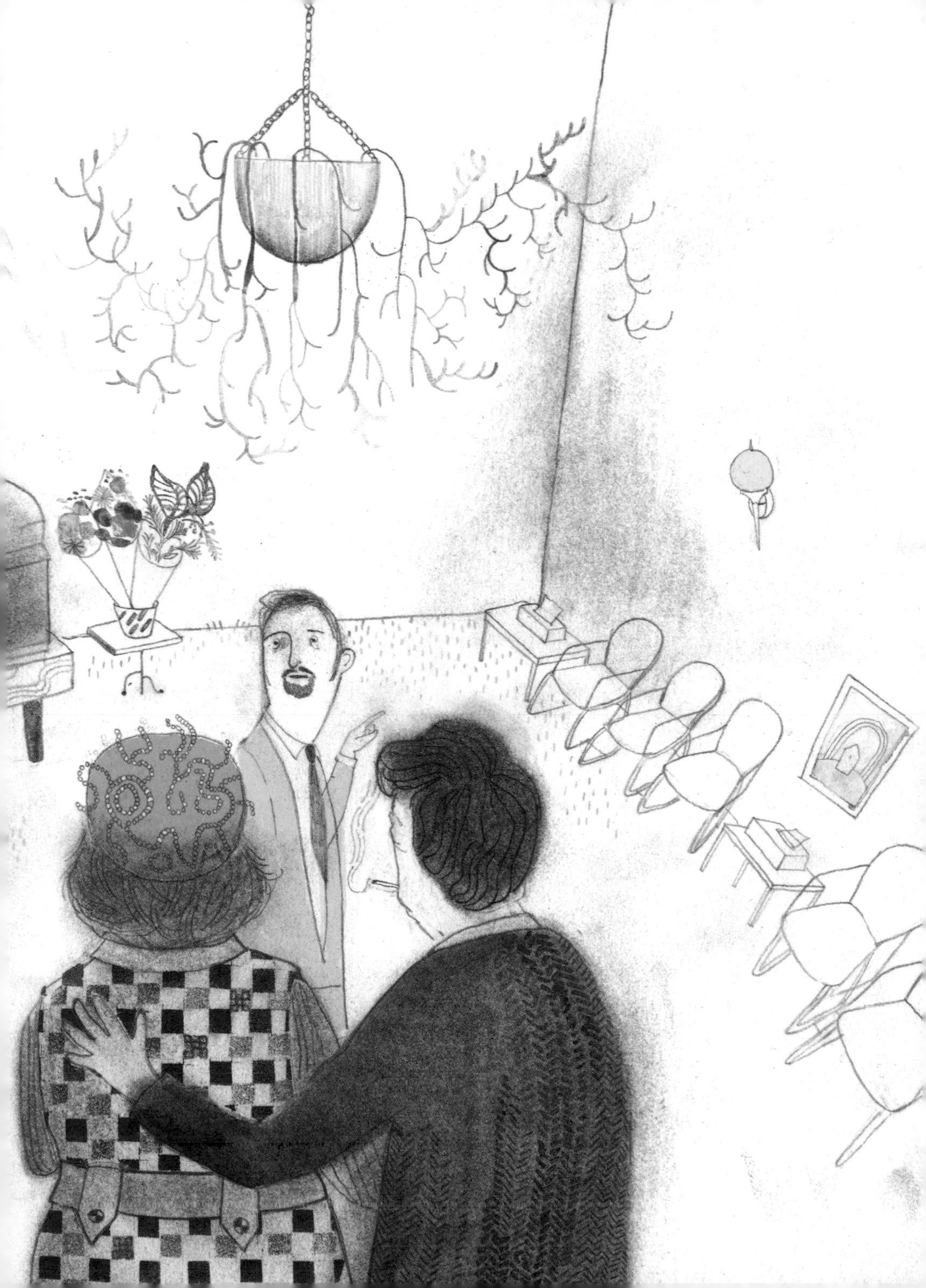

MY GOD, LAURENT, YOU'RE SO PALE.
THE SLEEVES ON HIS JACKET ARE TOO LONG. IT LOOKS LIKE IT'S NOT HIS OWN SUIT. DON'T YOU THINK, HARVEY?
NO.

DON'T YOU THINK IT'S FUNNY, HARVEY, DON'T YOU THINK IT'S FUNNY THAT HIS FOREHEAD ISN'T SHINY, AND THAT HIS MOUTH IS PULLED DOWN, AND THAT HE'S ALL THIN AND WEARING A SUIT THAT DOESN'T LOOK GOOD ON HIM?
THERE'S NOTHING FUNNY ABOUT IT.

ANYWAY I COULDN'T SEE A THING. I COULDN'T SEE MY FATHER IN HIS WOODEN COFFIN. IT WAS ON A PRETTY HIGH TABLE THAT MADE IT EVEN HIGHER. THOUGH I STOOD WITH BOTH FEET WHERE YOU WERE SUPPOSED TO PUT YOUR KNEES, I COULD HARDLY EVEN SEE THE END OF HIS NOSE. I COULD SEE THE LITTLE JESUS BALANCED ON THE LID, AND THE FRILLY SATIN, BUT THAT WASN'T WHAT I WANTED TO SEE. AND I ALSO WANTED FOR MY FATHER, EVEN IF HE WAS DEAD, TO SEE ME.

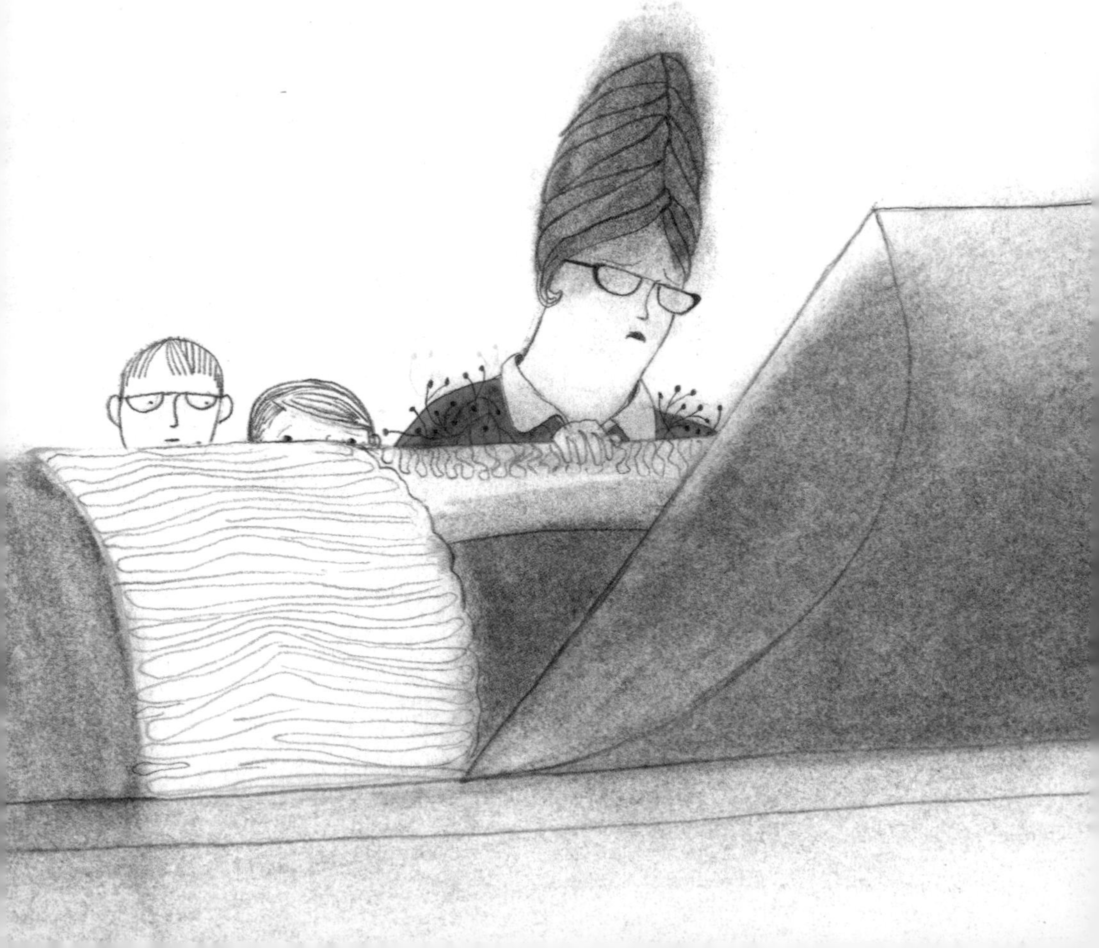

I TRIED TO PULL OVER A CHAIR SO I COULD CLIMB UP ON IT, BUT THE CHAIRS WERE ALL ATTACHED TO EACH OTHER AND I COULDN'T MOVE THEM.

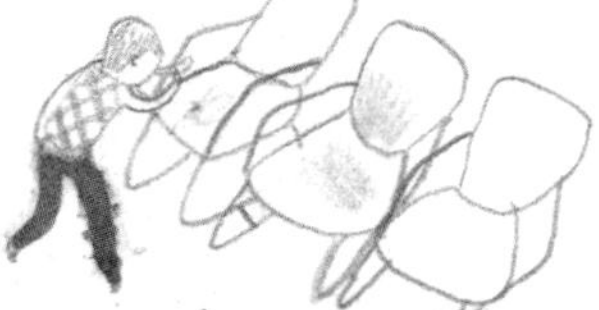

WE HAD TO GO AND SIT DOWN IN OUR ASSIGNED PLACES.

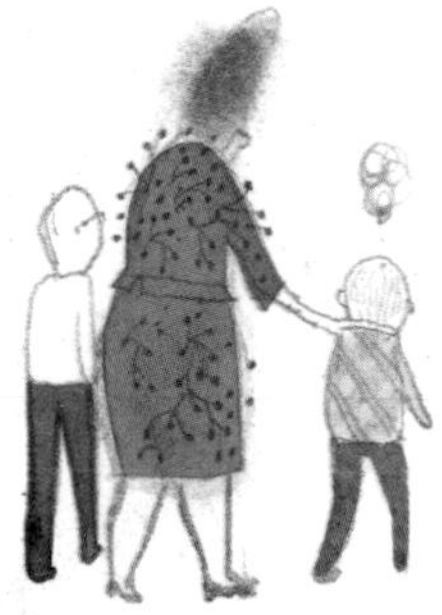

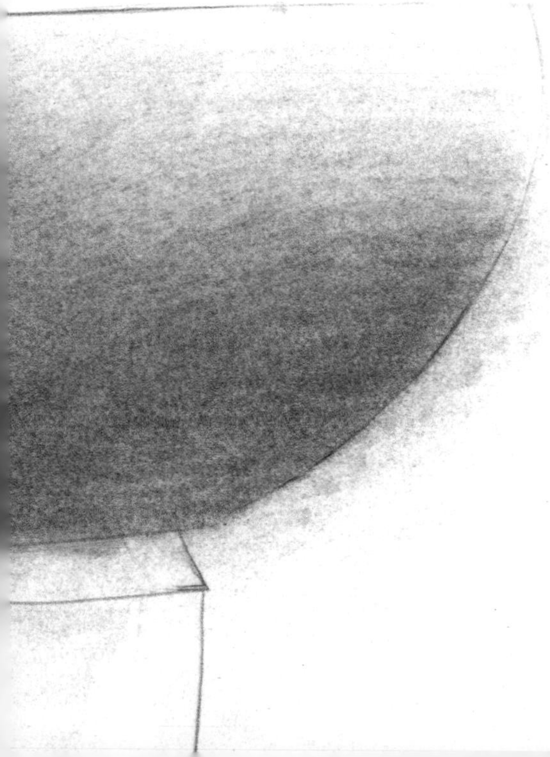

IN MY HEAD WAS A LONG STRING OF WORDS THAT YOU AREN'T SUPPOSED TO SAY.

LOTS OF PEOPLE CAME DURING THE TWO DAYS, WHICH WENT BY QUITE FAST. IN THE WORDS OF ALL THOSE PEOPLE WHO HAD COME TO SEE MY FATHER THERE WERE THINGS THAT HELPED ME TO IMAGINE HIM A BIT, BUT THEIR DESCRIPTIONS WEREN'T VERY CLEAR. THEY THOUGHT HE WAS PALE. THEY FOUND HIM KIND OF PINK. THEY SAID HE'D BEEN GIVEN A STRICT LOOK, OR THAT THEY HAD WHITENED HIS SKIN. THEY SAID IT REALLY LOOKED LIKE HIM IN THERE. OR THAT HE WAS UNRECOGNIZABLE. SOME THOUGHT HE LOOKED GOOD. LOTS OF THEM SAID, "AH!" LOTS OF OTHERS SAID, "OH!" AUNT MÉLINA THOUGHT HE'D NEVER LOOKED CLEANER. UNCLE RAYMOND FOUND HIM GRAY, AS ALWAYS. AUNT RITALINÉE SAID HIS LIPS WERE KIND OF PALE. A FAT MAN DECLARED THAT HE WAS ALONE, LIKE A MAN. UNCLE RÉGIS SAID HE WAS THIN AS A RAIL. GRAND-MOTHER BOUILLON SAID HIS FOREHEAD WAS ROUNDED. AUNT FIONALINÉE FOUND THAT HIS CHEEKS WERE SUNKEN. UNCLE MARCEL NOTICED HIS BLOCKED PORES. AUNT IONALINÉE THOUGHT HIS CHIN WAS SHARP. AUNT MA-DELINÉE FOUND HIS WINGS TO BE FOLDED. ETC. FOR TWO DAYS.

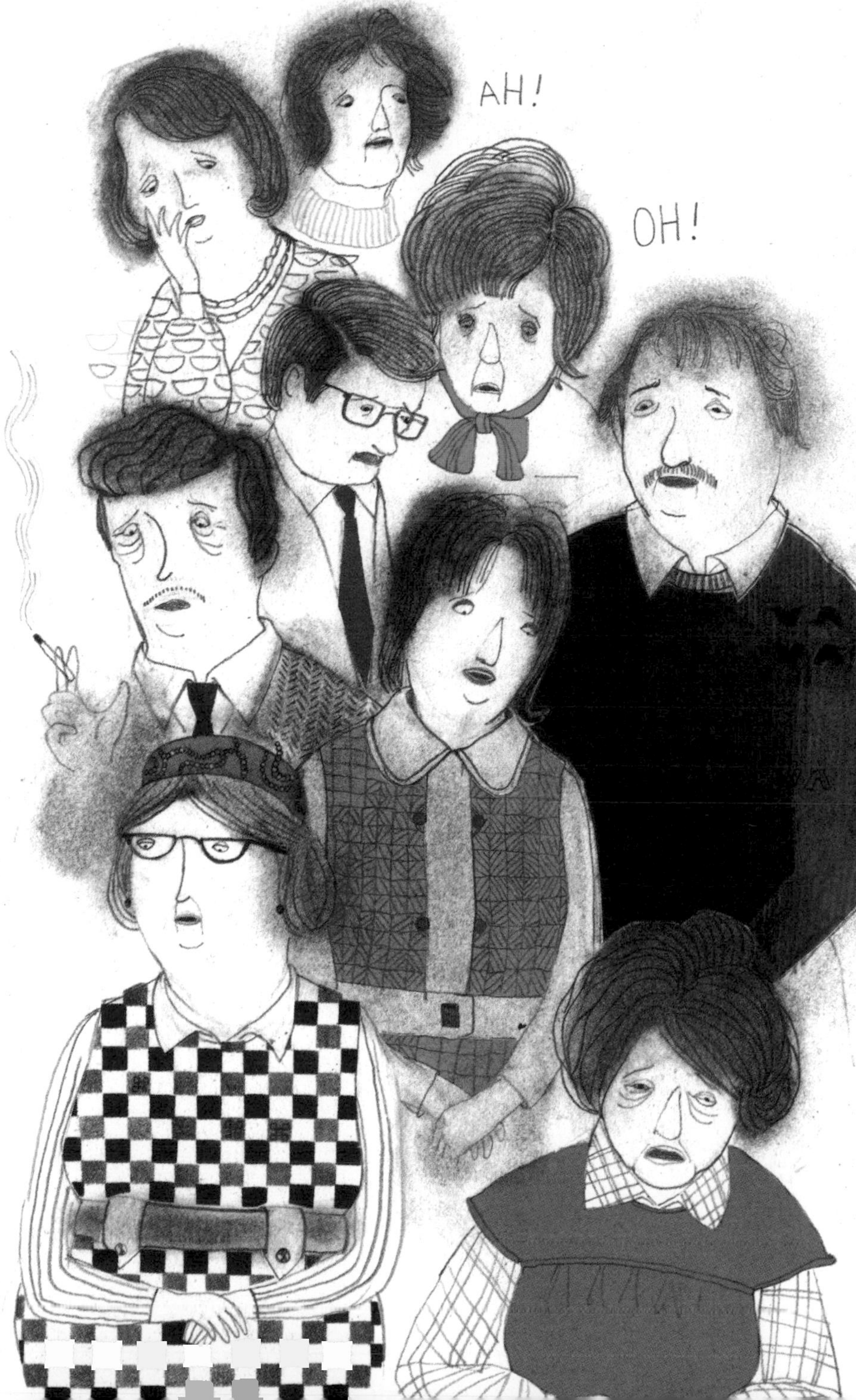
AH!
OH!

MY FATHER AND THE THINGS PEOPLE SAID ABOUT HIM:

TIGHT IN THE COLLAR

FURROW BROWED

DRAWN FEATURED

SANDY EYED

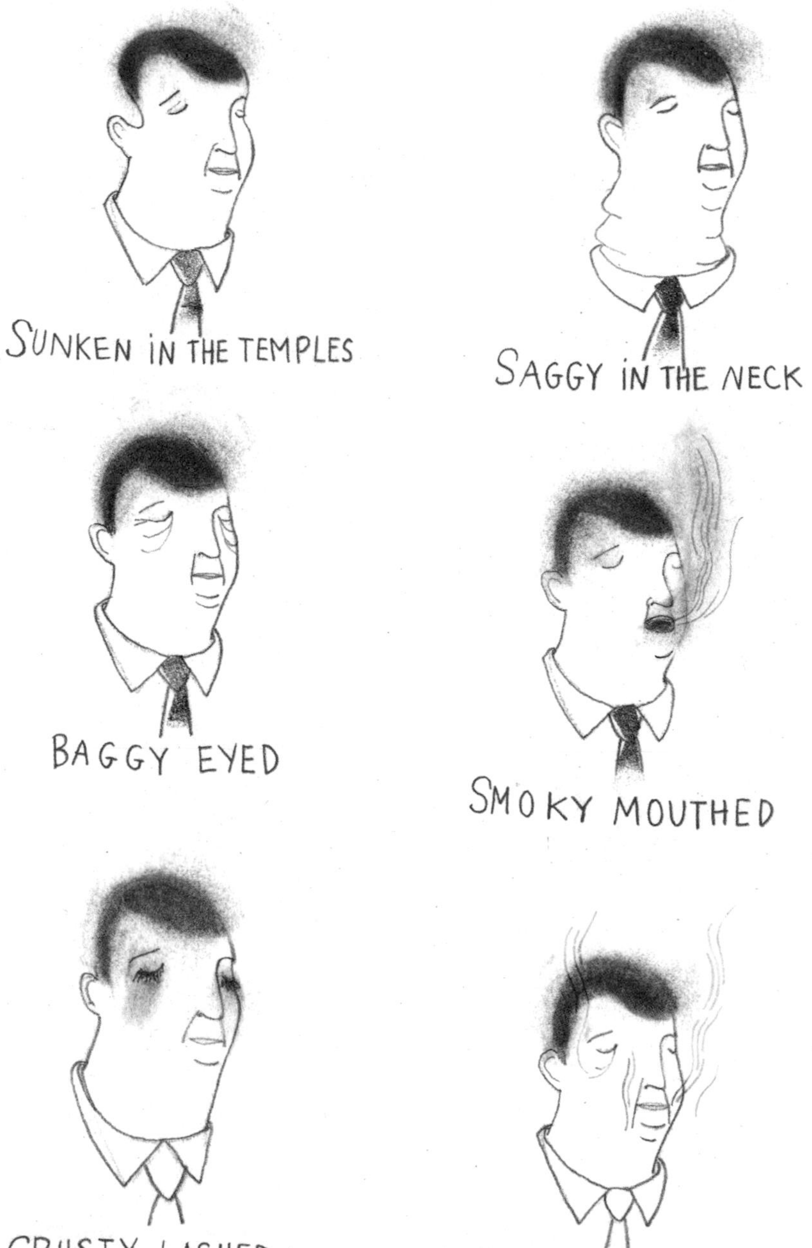
SUNKEN IN THE TEMPLES
SAGGY IN THE NECK
BAGGY EYED
SMOKY MOUTHED
CRUSTY LASHED
WRINKLY SMELLING

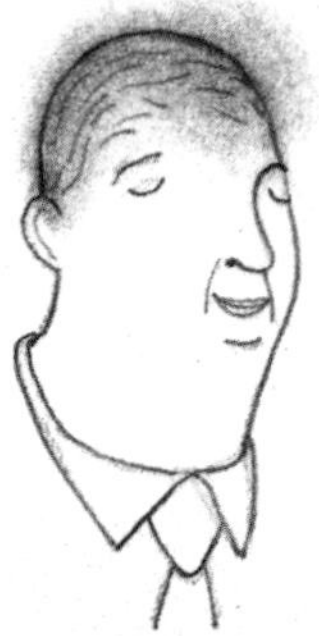

SHRIVELED UP

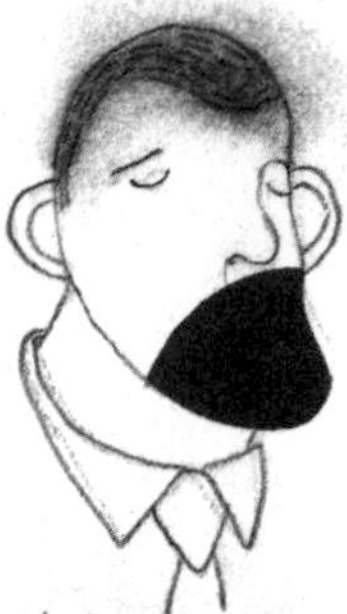

MONKEY JAWED

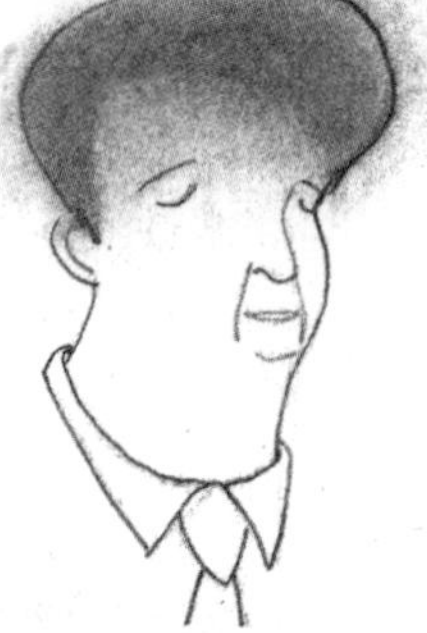

TOP HEAVY

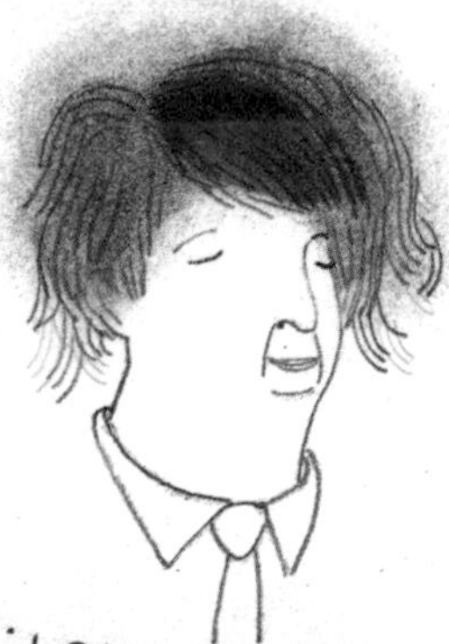

WILDLY HAIRY

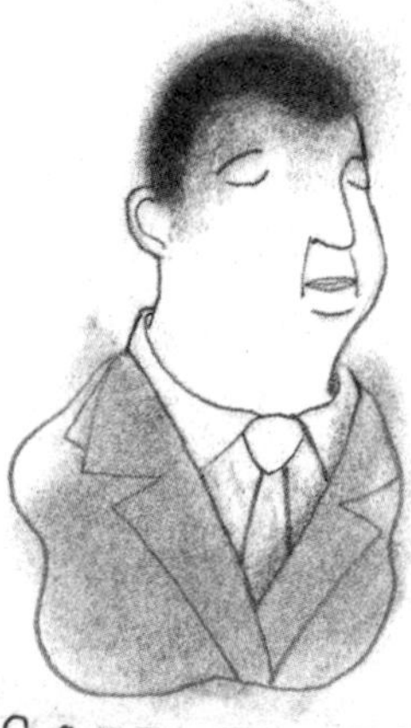

SOFT ON TOP

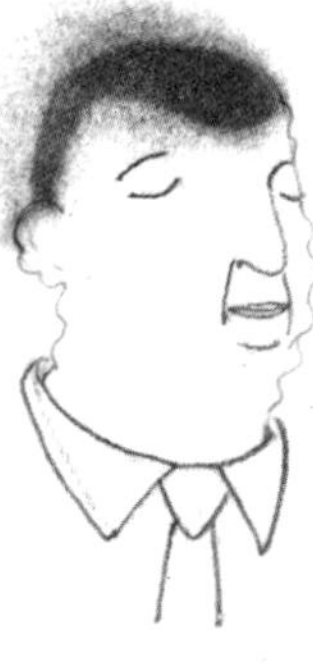

TART FACED

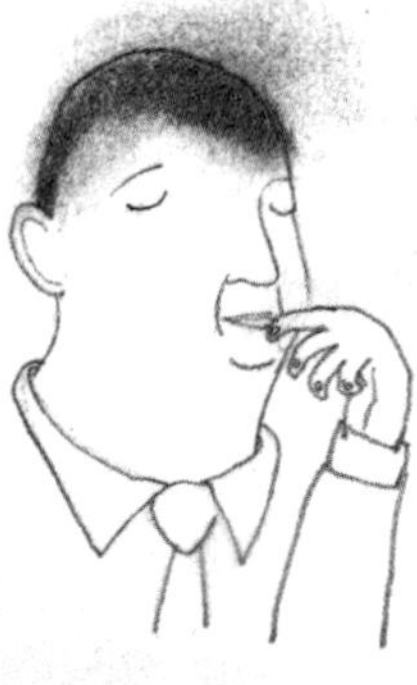

NAIL BITTEN

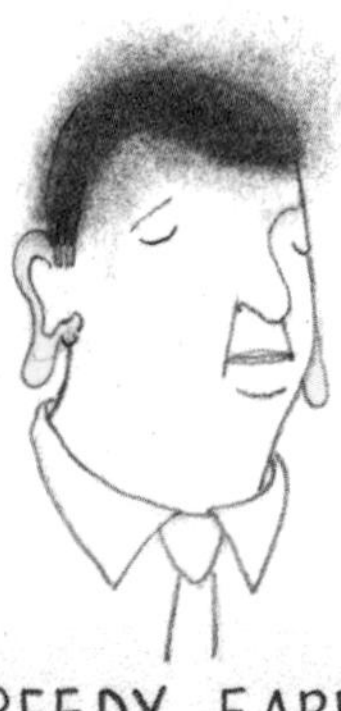

GREEDY EARED

POINTY HEADED

WAFFLE TOPPED

BLACK BROWED

BROKEN DOWN

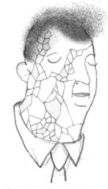

CRACKLY
COMPLEXIONED

UGLY AS A CARP

DRY AS A
DEAD MAN

DEAF TO
EVERYTHING

WHAT DOES GREEDY MEAN?

IT MEANS TO BE VERY HUNGRY.
YOUR FATHER BOUILLON USED TO NIBBLE
MY EARS WHEN HE FELT GREEDY.

I LOOKED AT HER EARS. THEY WERE STILL
THERE.

I DIDN'T UNDERSTAND VERY MUCH.

FATHER TOOK UP ALL MY THOUGHTS AND I
FOUND THAT HE, ALL BY HIMSELF, MADE
FOR A LOT OF PEOPLE IN MY HEAD.

THEN CAME THE MOMENT TO CLOSE THE COFFIN. IT WAS AN IMPORTANT MOMENT. IT WAS THE TIME FOR THE BIG SEPARATION. BECAUSE AFTERWARD YOU WOULD NEVER SEE THE PERSON INSIDE AGAIN.

I TOLD CANTIN NOT TO GO AND SEE THE CLOSING OF THE COFFIN. INSTEAD I WOULD SHOW HIM ALL THE DIFFERENT WAYS THAT OUR FATHER BOUILLON COULD BE USING WORDS AND DRAWINGS AND COLORS AND EXPRESSIONS.

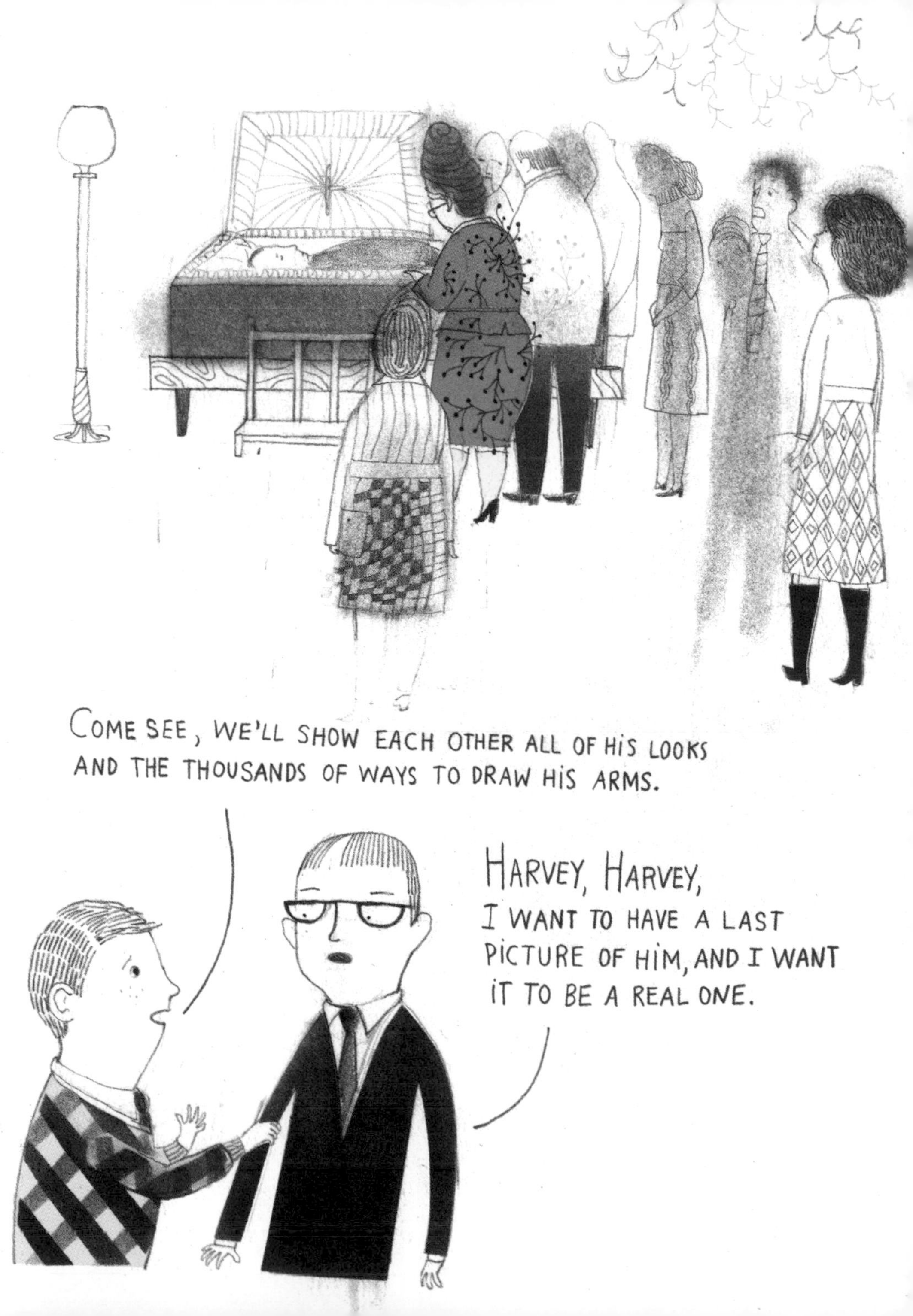
COME SEE, WE'LL SHOW EACH OTHER ALL OF HIS LOOKS AND THE THOUSANDS OF WAYS TO DRAW HIS ARMS.
HARVEY, HARVEY, I WANT TO HAVE A LAST PICTURE OF HIM, AND I WANT IT TO BE A REAL ONE.

BUT IF SO MANY PEOPLE HERE ARE SEEING THE SAME MAN, AND IF EACH OF THEM HAS A DIFFERENT PICTURE, CANTIN, THAT MEANS NO ONE IS GETTING AT THE TRUTH ALL BY HIMSELF. AND MAYBE THE WAY TO SEE FOR REAL IS TO LISTEN TO ALL OF THEM, BECAUSE MAYBE EACH OF THEM IS SEEING LESS THAN THEY THINK.

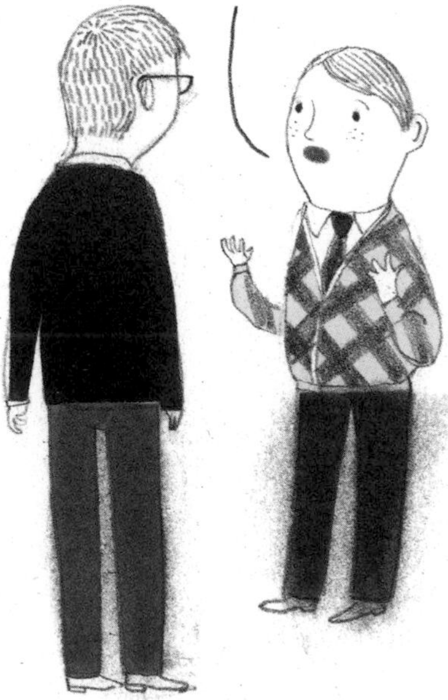

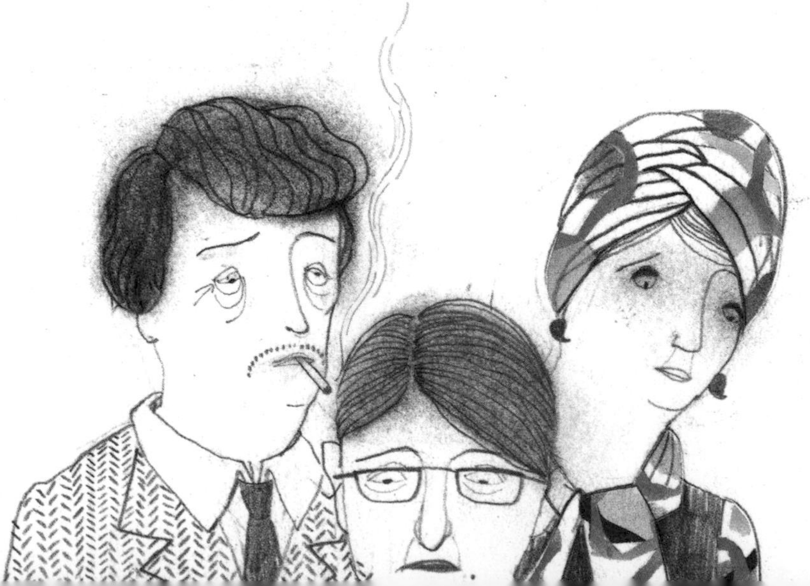

BUT HE JUST LOOKED DOWN AT ME
AND WENT TO JOIN THE OTHERS.

YES, BUT, CANTIN!

HE DIDN'T TURN BACK.

I SAW UNCLE RAYMOND HOLDING OUT
HIS ARMS TO ME.

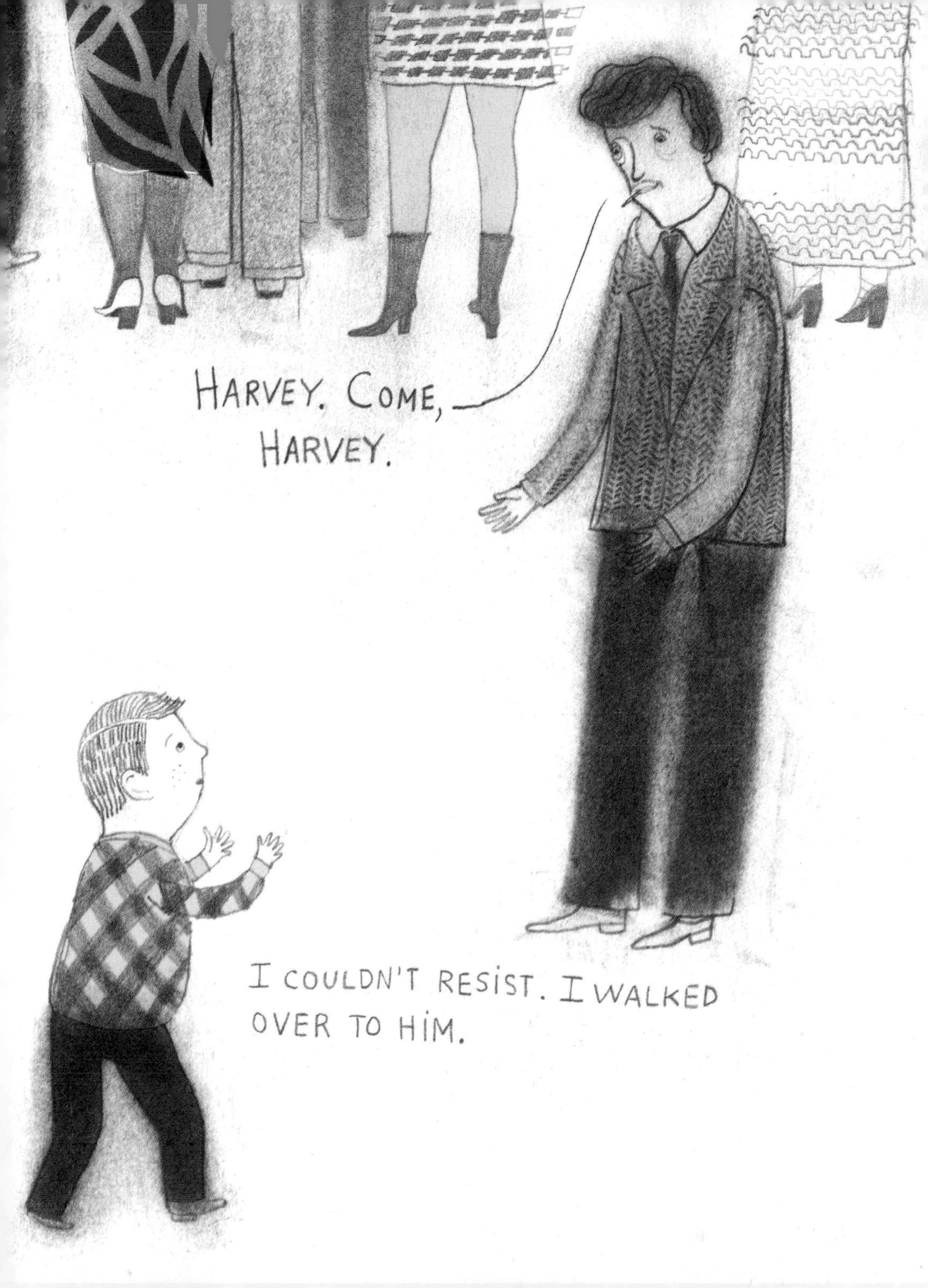
HARVEY. COME, HARVEY.
I COULDN'T RESIST. I WALKED OVER TO HIM.

HE LIFTED ME UP SO I WAS HIGHER THAN EVERYONE.

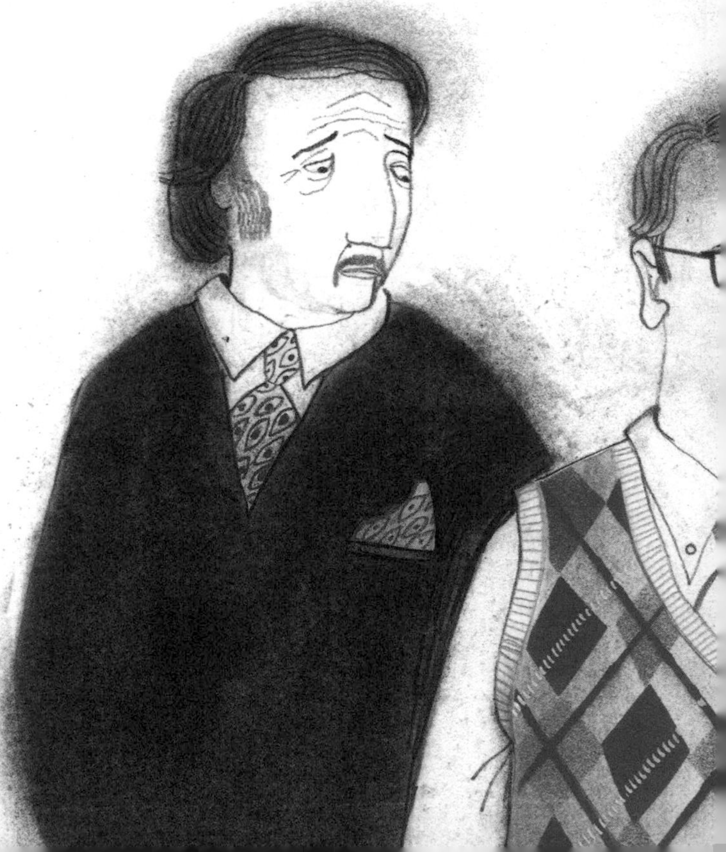

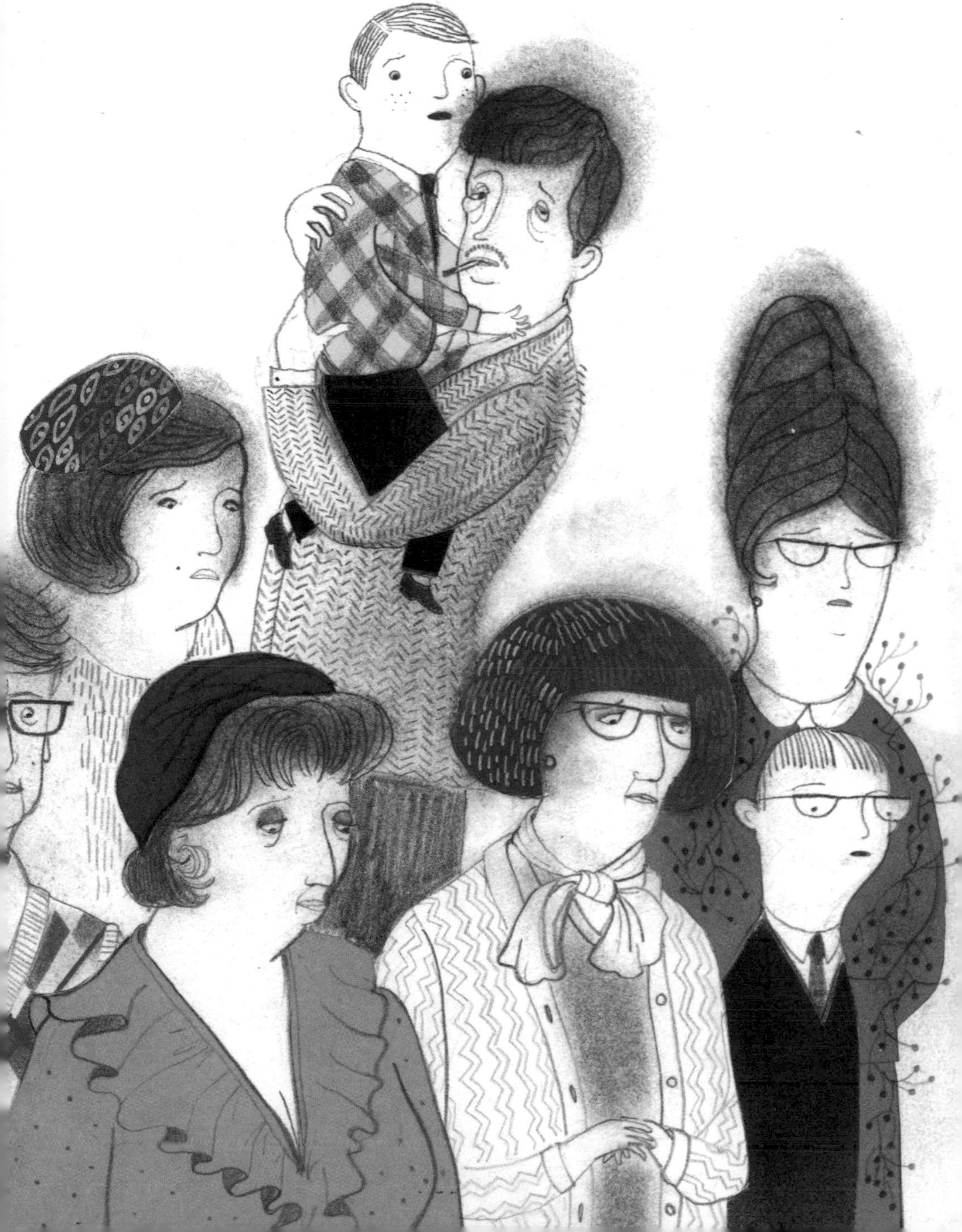

AND THAT'S HOW I BECAME INVISIBLE.

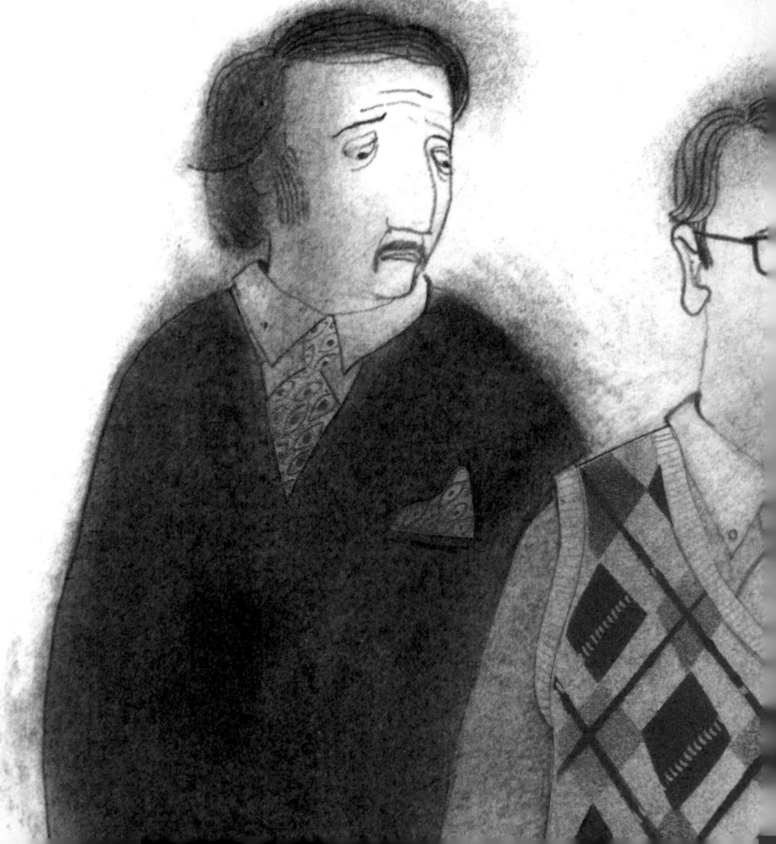

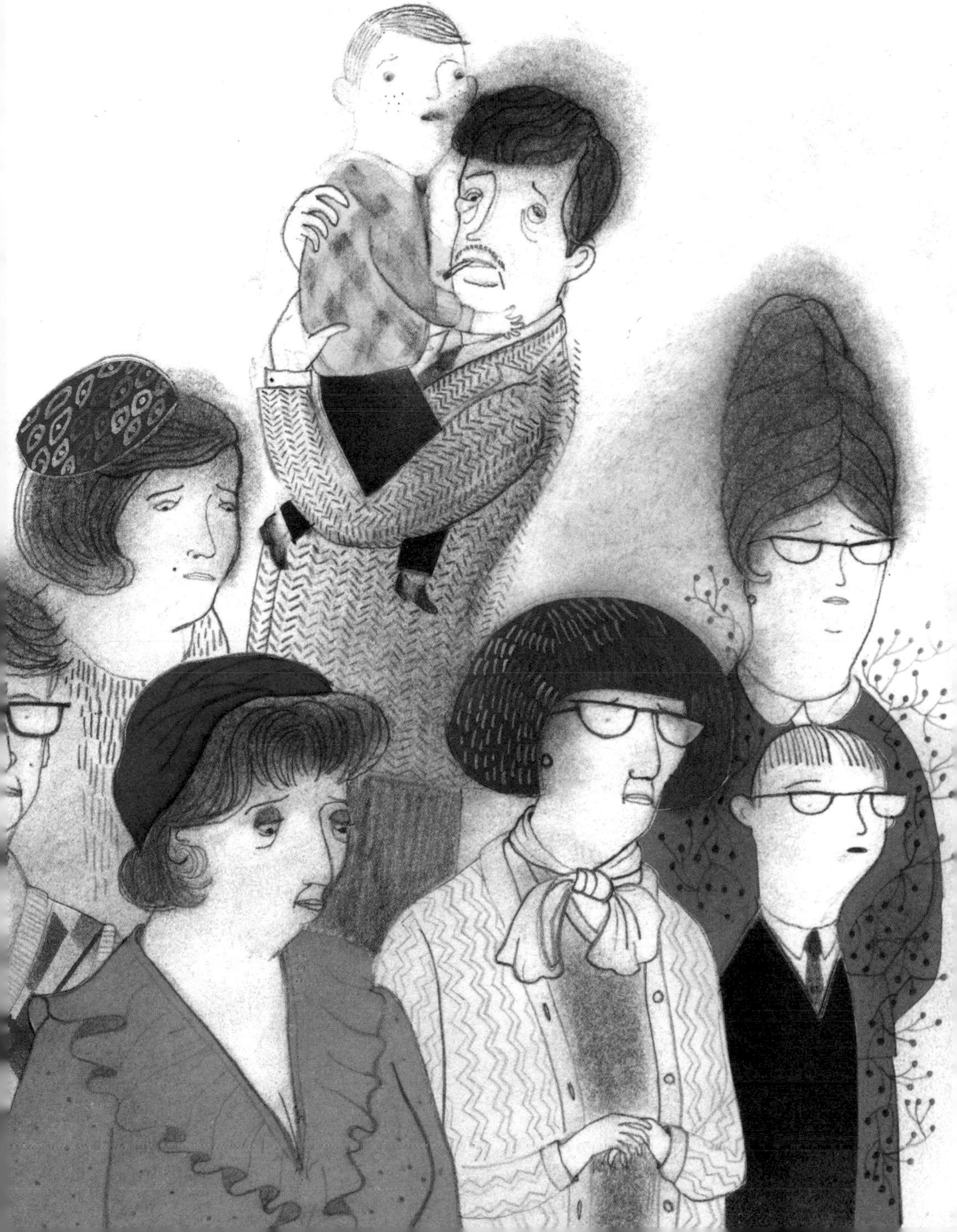

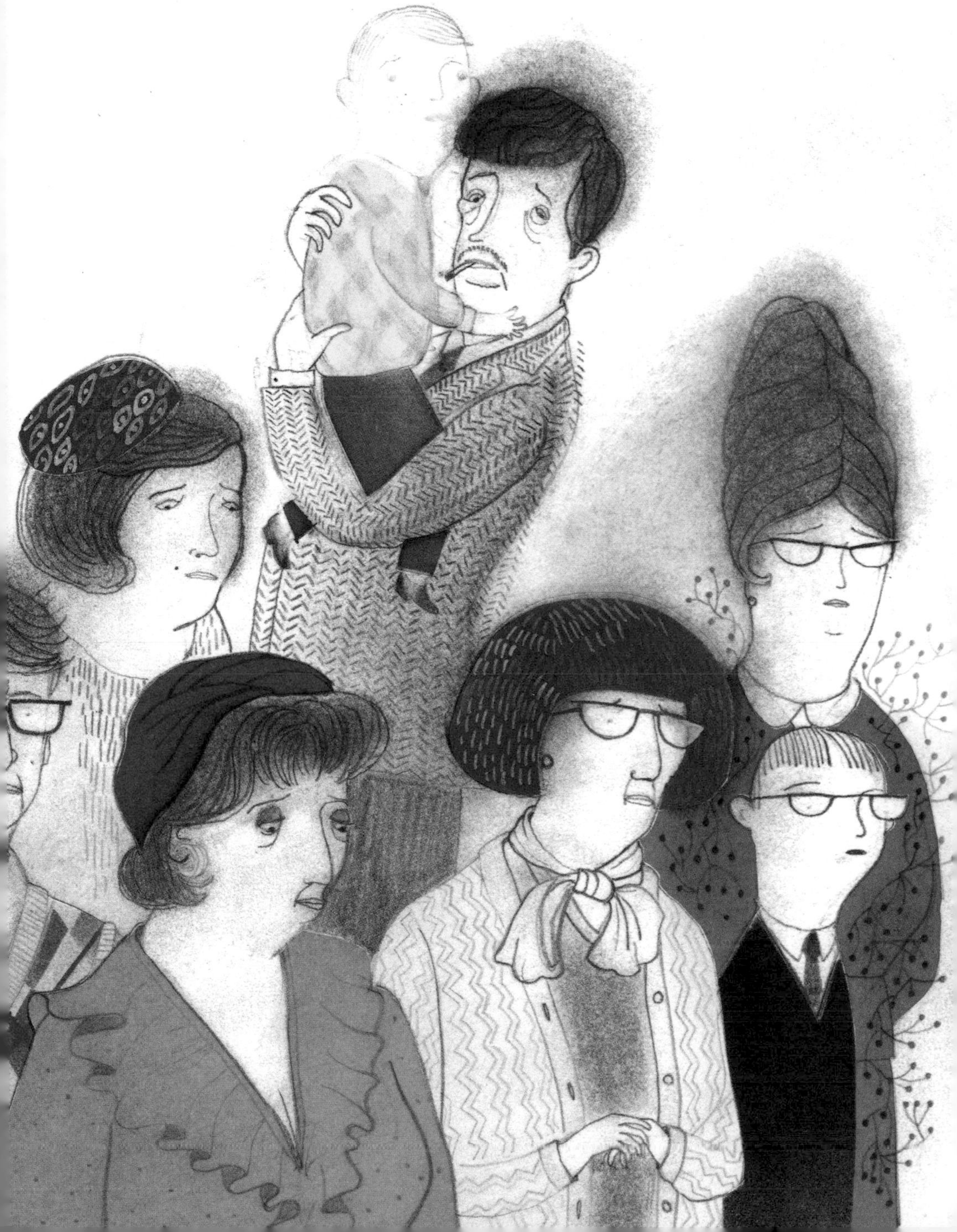

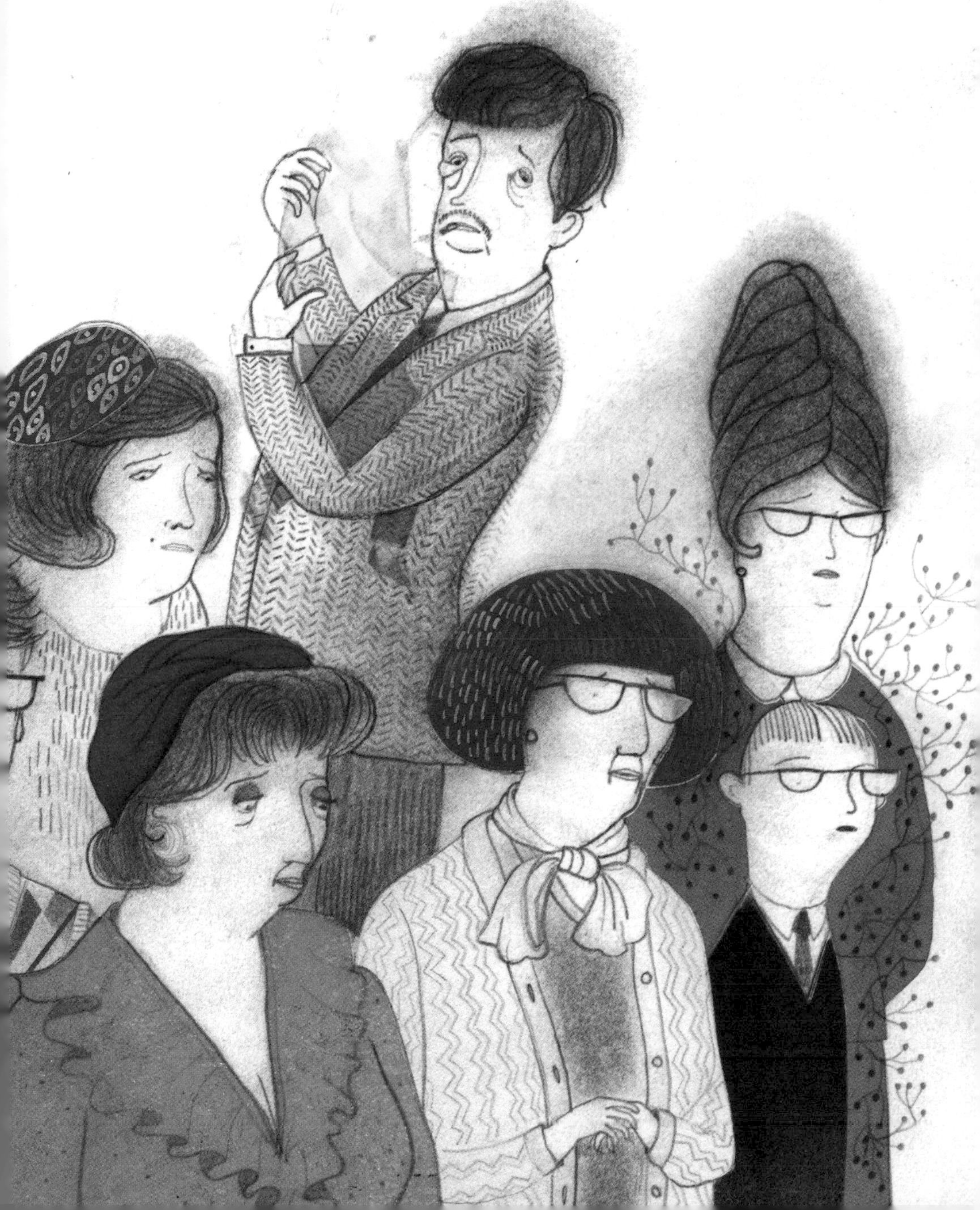